HOT NEWS

Recent Titles by Elisabeth McNeill from Severn House

A BOMBAY AFFAIR
THE SEND-OFF
THE GOLDEN DAYS
UNFORGETTABLE
THE LAST COCKTAIL PARTY

DUSTY LETTERS
MONEY TROUBLES
TURN BACK TIME

HOT NEWS

Elisabeth McNeill

This first world edition published in Great Britain 2003 by
SEVERN HOUSE PUBLISHERS LTD of
9–15 High Street, Sutton, Surrey SM1 1DF.
This first world edition published in the USA 2003 by
SEVERN HOUSE PUBLISHERS INC of
595 Madison Avenue, New York, N.Y. 10022.

British Library Cataloguing in Publication Data

McNeill, Elisabeth
    Hot news
    1. Woman journalists - Scotland - Edinburgh - Fiction
    2. Investigative reporting - Scotland - Edinburgh - Fiction
    I. Title
    823.9'14 [F]

    ISBN 0-7278-5939-0

Typeset by Palimpsest Book Production Ltd.,
Polmont, Stirlingshire, Scotland.
Printed and bound in Great Britain by
MPG Books Ltd., Bodmin, Cornwall.

Prologue

It was Saturday December 31st 1955 – New Year's Eve.

A telephone shrilled in one of the newsroom booths but nobody made a move to answer it. None of them wanted to hustle out into the rain to investigate a chip-pan fire or a minor car accident on a wet Edinburgh morning, so they all waited to see whose nerve snapped first.

Rosa's did because she was the most recently recruited, and therefore the most eager, member of the staff of the *Evening Dispatch*. She said self-importantly into the black receiver that smelled of stale cigarette smoke, 'News room here.' She still found it hard to believe her luck in actually being a *newspaper reporter*.

An excited voice shouted back, 'This is Graham McLagan from Portobello. Tell Jack I've a big story. A woman's body's been found on the beach at Aberlady. It's a murder! And make sure I get my tip-off money.'

It didn't strike her as shameful that her first emotion on hearing about someone being murdered was excited delight.

One

When she was small, Rosa Makepeace was told by her grandmother to make a wish on New Year's Eve, but to be very careful what she wished for because it might come true.

Before the phone rang she'd been sitting in front of her typewriter, looking through a rain-streaked newsroom window towards the North British Hotel at the end of Princes Street, and worrying about her wish for 1956.

Should she ask for a raise? Or a wedding ring? A job in Fleet Street, or a pledge of everlasting love? Since none of these things were likely to be granted in the near future, there didn't seem much point in wasting a wish on them. She sighed and looked around for inspiration.

The newsroom was in its usual state of chaos. It was a long nicotine-coloured cavern with a dozen sub-editors occupying one end, and two parallel lines of desks for the reporters at the other. The Chief Reporter's desk was placed crossways between the two sections. Though the Editor's office was a glass-walled box built against the back wall, his work-table, where he set up the pages, was mid-room, alongside one of the windows that gave on to a panoramic view of Edinburgh's famous main street.

The desktops were littered with piles of old newspapers; dirty teacups growing penicillin-rich cultures of green mould; battered portable typewriters; full ashtrays; half-eaten sandwiches; sheaves of typing paper sticking on fearsome-looking spikes; broken pencils; and dog-eared books. A silver miasma

2

of cigar and cigarette smoke hovered overhead. Merely breathing in the air was enough to give any delicate member of the staff a case of galloping bronchitis.

The reporters – twelve of them from a staff of twenty – lounged aimlessly at their desks, trying to avoid the eye of Jack, the Editor, a man with the face of a dissolute cherub. He was making changes to the noon edition's front page with a thick black pencil.

Jack was Jewish and a Londoner, imported from Fleet Street to transform Edinburgh's pedestrian evening newspaper. He was a big man, built like a boxer, and always dressed in smartly cut, dark-blue city suits made of a material woven with such widely separated white stripes that they looked like something even the most brash spiv would hesitate to wear. This morning his curly black hair was sticking to his head with sweat, and his shirt collar was open with his red silk tie swinging loose.

When he stabbed hard at the paper, puffing out his cheeks as if he was blowing a gale across an old map, his pencil broke in half. He threw it on the floor and shouted, 'Fuck!'

One of his favourite hobby horses was the superiority of Anglo-Saxon based words to those derived from Latin or French, so, in the interests of purity, he said, he confined his cursing to short, four-letter expletives, which he considered expressive of real rage. They were certainly more startling than any swear words Rosa knew before she joined the paper six months ago.

When Jack started shouting, some of the men who were thinking of sneaking off to the pub, went hurriedly back to in their typewriters and began clacking away, looking busy.

Big, black-haired Mike, the most junior member of the reporting staff before Rosa joined, began sharpening pencils and sticking them in his top pocket. His ambition was to be a 'toe in the door man' for the *Daily Mirror*, and he dressed to fit the part in double-breasted suits with enormous shoulder pads and shoes with thick, crêpe rubber soles that made him pad along like a menacing panther. His hair was teased into a front curl with Brylcreem and combed over at the back in the style known as 'duck's arse'. He fancied himself hugely and patronized Rosa mercilessly, much to her annoyance.

At the desk next to Mike's, Alan Cleland, the Australian theatre critic, who also wrote obscure poetry, sat up when Jack swore and stared blearily around, trying to remember where he was. He'd been asleep for the past hour with his blond head lying in a painful-looking position on his typewriter keys. As always, however, even when waking up, he looked very lordly, though thoroughly dishevelled after spending the previous night in the office, sleeping off a hangover.

When Jack took over the *Dispatch*'s editorship a year ago, he brought Alan up from London with him to do theatre reviews and inject a note of culture into the previously pedestrian copy.

Where Jack's style was pared down and simple, Alan's was florid, erudite, and liberally sprinkled with Latinisms. In his copy, people were never fat, they were 'rotund'; nor were they ever confused, they were 'discombobulated'. Jack tolerated these lapses, which he considered forgivable from a word-spinning genius who could prick pretensions with one sentence, and also because he admired Alan's immense capacity for alcohol.

'He's descended from some well-born remittance man who went out in the 1880s. These guys could really hold their drink,' Jack frequently said in admiration when contemplating the collapsed figure of his drama critic.

The rest of the staff were confused about what to make of Alan. Though pleasant enough, he was a compulsive loner. His drinking, which verged on the immoderate, was not done with them in the neighbourhood pubs they patronized. He seemed to have no friends, and, unique among the men on the staff, neither did he appear to lust after any other colleague, male or female. None of them even know where he lived.

4

Alan's alter ego as a poet was discovered when a poem by him was published in Edinburgh's highbrow *Blackwood's Magazine*, where it was found by one of the subs who passed it round the office. All the reporters pored over it with puzzled brows. 'What the fuck is the golden empyrean of eternity?' asked Mike when he'd read it three times.

When Jack's 'Fuck!' rang out, Lawrie Gorman, the racing tipster, jumped from his chair and dashed into one of the phone booths, deliberately leaving the door open so he could be heard making a call. He was nervous about holding on to his job because he had not tipped a winner for three weeks. Lawrie was such a bad tipster that none of his colleagues ever risked money on a horse he recommended. In fact they felt sorry for the poor punters who bought the paper to read what he said. He drew most of his naps out of a hat or recommended them because he liked the animal's name.

'Can you tell me if Handsome Hawk is trying tomorrow, sir? It is? Should I have a flutter then? At twenty to one? It's good of you to tell me that,' he was heard to say.

Patricia, the only other woman news reporter on the staff, whose desk was next to Rosa's, lifted her eyes from the Lewis Grassick Gibbon novel she was surreptitiously reading and said sarcastically, 'He must be talking to another horse. No owner in their right mind would tell *him* anything.'

Patricia, possessed of an adder-sharp tongue and lightning-quick wit, was, in Rosa's awed opinion, Scotland's answer to Dorothy Parker. She looked like her too, being thin and sexy, with smooth dark hair in a chignon, perfect make-up and impeccable dress sense.

Though Patricia was twenty-two, the same age as Rosa, she made her colleague feel as if she was still in kindergarten because Patricia had been working on newspapers since she was fifteen. Like the men, she scorned Rosa's university degree, saying that she educated herself out of books, and the claim was not easy to dismiss because she was remarkably well-read. It was always Patricia who knew what was the most up-to-date or significant novel.

Looking across at her, Rosa wondered if her New Year wish should be to become like Patricia, but decided against it because honesty forced her to realize that it would entail a considerable amount of surgery.

They had one thing in common though. They were both hopelessly in love with the wrong man.

Rosa's affections were concentrated on a faithless car salesman called Iain who collected women like teenagers gather acne spots. Patricia's choice was Hugh Maling, a supercilious intellectual snob who wrote disdaining reviews for literary magazines. He never had a good word to say for anybody's literary efforts but his own, and even his semi-enthusiastic commendations were laced with poison. Nobody in the newspaper set except Patricia liked Hugh, and it was a favourite Saturday night pursuit for more down-to-earth male journalists in the Press Club bar to try to fill him in at closing time.

'He's a wanker. Pat only goes for him because she's an emotional masochist,' Mike told Rosa. She suspected that he secretly longed for Patricia and was burning up with jealousy.

Suddenly, when he sensed that everyone was relaxing once more, Jack started to curse again, frantically hopping about in front of his work-table and shouting, 'What a shit of a front page! Nothing ever happens in this fucking city. There's no *news* up here.'

Because it was hogmanay, the last day of the year, an open bottle of Gordon's gin stood by his hand and every now and again he had been pouring himself a slug into a white china cup, swigging it down straight, grimacing every time as if he hated the taste.

When Jack was at the height of his transport of fury, Bob Langton, the Chief Reporter, edged up to the table and removed the typewriter standing there because, in a manic mood, Jack was capable of lifting his machine up and dashing it to the ground. The explosion of metal keys and bits of carriage that ensued was a sight worth seeing and the effect on his staff was always electrifying.

Gil, Jack's friend and Deputy Editor who had come up to Scotland with him, shook his head when the gin bottle was temptingly waved in his direction. He too was a natty dresser, but much shorter than Jack, and he looked like Jack Payne, a 1940s bandleader, with neatly combed hair that stuck to his head like a black swimming cap.

Gil was certainly not averse to gin but cautious about drinking in the middle of the day. The last time he yielded to temptation, he handed in his resignation to the Managing Director and had to go crawling back next day to be reinstated on the staff. There was also a story that once, in London, when he got drunk in the morning, he ran away to Paris to join the Foreign Legion and Jack had to travel to Corsica to buy him out.

Thwarted in his efforts to persuade Gil to join him in getting drunk, Jack turned his attention to his staff, and regarded them with undisguised scorn. 'Look at you. What a useless fucking shower. Good reporters go out and *find* stories. They make things *happen*. They don't sit on their arses and wait for stories to find them!' he yelled.

They stared back apprehensively because there was no way of knowing where his mood – and the gin – would take him. He might fire them all or, on the other hand, he was capable of changing tack in an instant and taking everybody out to the pub. Everybody that is except old Bob, the Chief Reporter, whom Jack did not like, but couldn't get rid of. If they went to the pub, Bob, whom Jack suspected of being a spy for the management that tried without success to cut back on his prodigality with money, would be left to man the phones.

Every time the Editor glanced in Rosa's direction she quailed because she was sure that he was planning to fire her. She had not yet turned in a decent story and was afraid that the next time Jack threw a temperamental fit, he would single her out for dismissal, *pour encourager les autres.*

He'd done that already to an inoffensive young man who expressed qualms about some article he'd been ordered to write. It went against his principles to exploit people, he said. Jack grinned wolfishly as he told him to take his principles where the sun didn't shine and clear his desk.

Rosa was prepared to sacrifice her idealistic principles to survive in the office because it was where she'd always wanted to work. During her schooldays and through university, she dreamed about becoming a newspaper reporter. It had not been easy to find a job because places for girls in reporters' rooms were few and, originally, Jack only took her on trial. Since then she'd limped along, avoiding his eye, from week to week, wondering if he'd forgotten about her, and praying for a chance to impress him with her keenness and capacity.

Suddenly she decided what her New Year wish ought to be.

Let me be Jack's sort of reporter, the kind who makes things happen. Please give me a scoop, she whispered to her guardian angel.

Then the phone rang . . .

Two

'There's been a murder!' she shouted into the office, opening the booth door with one hand. She was so excited that her voice came out as a hysterical squeak. When she heard herself, she wished she could replay the scene and sound like Lauren Bacall . . .

'Hold the front page. It's a mur-der,' she should have drawled, tossing back a curtain of hair.

Squeak or not, her colleagues reacted as if she'd lobbed a bomb among them.

'Where?' Jack snapped, tearing the old rough draft front page off the table in front of him and quickly pinning on a clean sheet.

'Aberlady.'

'Where the hell's that?' Jack, like many metropolitan types, had only a sketchy idea of the geography of Scotland.

'Just down the coast, not far, half an hour away,' she told him.

'Great! Who's on the line?'

'Graham McLagan. He says he wants his tip-off money.'

Gil said quietly, 'That's all right. McLagan's an ex-cop. His information's usually good.'

Jack shouted to Rosa, 'Get the details from him and ask if anyone else's on to it.' Then he turned round to scan the faces of his reporters. All the young ones, except Alan and Lawrie, were looking eager. A murder guaranteed a by-line, with the reporter's name in capital letters, and by-lines were

9

important to people who saved up their cuttings so they could apply for jobs in Fleet Street. Some, like Mike, saved other people's cuttings as well.

'You go, Tom,' said Jack, pointing his broken pencil at a middle-aged man with a drooping moustache.

Tom Mavor shambled to his feet. He was the oldest and shabbiest reporter in the office, past bothering about by-lines, because he was an ex-*Daily Express* star on his way down. His word-spinning talent had almost dissipated though he could still produce first-class copy when sober, but that wasn't often nowadays.

He was always trying to borrow money from the juniors because his bitter wife appropriated his salary direct from the office every week and allowed him nothing in his pocket except what he could squeeze out of the company account-ants for 'expenses'.

Tom cleared his throat and said, 'Er . . . sorry,' as he looked at Jack.

'What the hell's the matter? Get on your way. It's a big story and I want the copy for the last edition. I'll give you the front page.' Jack was clearly excited.

'It's just that Aberlady isn't on a bus route, old boy,' Tom said in his gentlemanly voice.

Jack screamed in disbelief, 'A bloody bus route! This is a newspaper for Christ's sake! Take a car.'

'They won't give me the office car – I had a slight acci-dent last time. Not my fault you understand . . .' Tom's state-ments always tailed off in a dying fall.

'Ask for a driver then. This is a *murder*!'

'I'll drive him,' Rosa piped up from the phone booth. Her nerve at taking the initiative surprised everybody, including herself.

Bob Langton laughed. 'Will you really, Miss Makepeace?' he said sarcastically and, turning away from her, asked Jack, 'Which of the boys will I send with Tom?'

'None of them can drive, and my car's parked in Cockburn

Street,' Rosa went on defiantly. She didn't know how she found the nerve.

'I'll ring for one of the drivers,' said Bob, ignoring her and lifting the phone on his desk but Jack shook his head. 'Hold on, getting a driver'll take too long. Let the girl go.' He never called her by her first name, and she was not even sure if he knew it.

Langton looked at her with undisguised loathing. He'd started his journalistic career as a copy boy in the *Dispatch* office forty-five years ago when the only women allowed inside it were the cleaners. As far as he was concerned, there was still no place for females in a well-run reporters' room.

He'd been vehemently against Jack's decision to employ first Patricia, then Rosa. If it was up to him, all they'd get to write about would be Women's Institute AGMs and flower shows, but Jack took pleasure in challenging these prejudices, and Bob was afraid of his Editor's formidable temper.

'You're sure you can drive?' Jack asked Rosa. There was a funny expression on his face.

'I've been able to drive since I was eighteen. I'll show you my licence if you like,' she replied with a boldness she did not feel.

'Trust you, miss smarty pants,' muttered non-driver Mike bitterly as he saw the coveted by-line swimming out of his grasp.

'OK. Take Tom to Aberlady. Anyway it'll do you good to see how a real professional works. And if you mess up don't bother coming back,' said Jack as if he was delivering an ultimatum.

Three

Rosa's car was a grey Morris Minor, not new nor smart but all her own, thanks to a legacy from her grandmother, the same one who told her about New Year wishes. She left her granddaughter a legacy of three hundred pounds to be handed over when she reached the age of twenty-one – which Rosa achieved the previous year.

It was parked in Cockburn Street, opposite the top of Fleshmarket Close, so she ran up the stairs from the back door of the *Scotsman* building – the *Dispatch* was housed there too because it was the *Scotsman*'s evening newspaper – and waited by the car for Tom, who came toiling slowly up the steep flight of stone steps to the street. Edinburgh is a punishing city, for everything is built on hills. The inhabitants either die young from the effort of getting about, or live to be ancient and crotchety because, though their legs are exhausted, their hearts are in first-class condition from all the climbing they have to do.

Wheezing, Tom climbed into the passenger seat after she swept a pile of newspapers and magazines onto the floor to make room for him.

'I see you read *Vogue*,' he said. 'Would you like to work for it?'

Another patronizing man, she thought.

'Not really. I'd prefer to work for the *Daily Mirror*,' she replied and he laughed because he thought she was joking, which she was not. She would much rather be a hard news reporter than a feature writer but nobody seemed to think women could tackle news. Even Patricia, who was even more ambitious and able than Rosa, only dreamt of subbing on *Woman* or *Woman's Own*.

She swung the car around in the road and headed down the High Street towards the Canongate, Holyrood Palace, and the Queen's Park. Tom, thrown back in his seat by this manoeuvre, regarded her with alarm. 'Steady on!' he said, and it was obvious he had the same feelings about women drivers as he had about women news reporters.

'It's all right,' she reassured him, 'but we must get there as quickly as possible. The *Daily Express*'ll be on to it by now.'

'We'll be first. McLagan's an old policeman. His mates tell him things and he tells us,' said Tom.

'And then he tells the *Express*, before telling the *Mail* and the *Telegraph* and the *Herald* and the *Evening News*,' Rosa said sceptically, 'They all pay for information, don't they?'

Tom sighed. 'You're probably right. The only one he won't tell is the *Scotsman* because they wouldn't cover anything as vulgar as a murder.'

Reporters on the *Dispatch* jeered at their parent newspaper for being more interested in aesthetics than news. There was a popular story about a *Scotsman* drama critic who wrote a long piece about the significance of circuses, and only mentioned in the last paragraph that the lion tamer was eaten by a lion during the performance he reviewed.

When they were tearing down Willowbrae Road, Tom tentatively asked, 'There *is* a speed limit here, isn't there?'

Cautioned, she slowed down for a bit and he asked again, 'You know where you're going, don't you?'

'Of course. McLagan said the body was found on Aberlady beach. A woman walking her dog found it this morning.' Rosa's foot was itching to hit the accelerator because she couldn't get there fast enough. Speed limits were made to be broken in such circumstances, so she let the speedometer creep up again to fifty and hoped her passenger didn't notice.

'You know this part of the world well?' he asked, as they rushed through Musselburgh.

'Yes, I often drive down the coast on Sundays. There are some good pubs there,' she told him.

He brightened at the mention of pubs. 'So there are. I say, you couldn't lend me a pound till pay day, could you?'

She'd been conned by him too often before so she shook her head. 'Sorry. I'm broke.'

He looked around the car and said, 'How could you afford to buy this then?'

'My granny left me some money and I've spent it all.'

'Make it ten bob,' said Tom.

'Sorry.'

'Five bob?'

'Half a crown. That's all I can afford.' She knew only too well that she'd never see a penny of it back.

He put her half crown piece in one of those leather purses with fold-over flaps that open like crocodiles' mouths, and was so mollified by her generosity that he stopped protesting about her driving.

Aberlady beach was a sinister place. The strip of coast between the railway line and the water always struck Rosa as grubby, doom-laden and unpleasant, even on sunny days, which this certainly was not. The sky above their heads was dark grey like beaten metal, and a bitter wind, howling in from the North Sea, whipped the dirty-looking sand into little whirlwinds, sending screwed-up fish-and-chip papers up into the air, where they stuck in the branches of low, scrubby trees bent almost horizontal by the onslaught of centuries of gales. These trees grew together so tightly that it seemed impossible to cut a way through them.

They drove slowly along a strip of road beside a high stone wall with another impenetrable thicket of trees behind it, till they spotted a trio of police incident vans drawn up on the sea verge. Some men in plain clothes were standing with their arms crossed over their chests in an ineffectual effort to keep warm, for the wind was as fierce and cutting as butchers' knives.

They turned and stared unsmiling as Tom got out of the car and hurried over to them. He was recognized by one of the men who said, 'Oh, it's you, Mavor. They've taken her away. How did you get on to this so quickly?'

'Contacts, contacts,' Tom said, suddenly looking more authoritative and impressive as he went into enquiry mode. 'Who is she?'

'A kid on the game, we think. But she picked the wrong client last night.' The speaker was a tall, lean man in a pale-coloured mackintosh coat belted tightly around his waist. He spoke without compassion and had a strangely impassive, expressionless face dominated by bright-blue eyes.

Pointing at Rosa, he said to Tom, 'Who's she?'

'Only my driver,' replied Tom grandly, pulling out his note-book. 'Now let me have something on this, lads.'

They took him into their little circle and turned their backs on her. Seething with resentment, she walked past them towards a young uniformed policeman who was standing by a cordoned-off section of the beach. Inside the coloured ropes there was a semi-circle of well-trodden sand and a huddle of scrubby bushes.

The young policeman was visibly shuddering with cold. When she said, 'Freezing, isn't it?' he nodded and replied, 'You can say that again.'

'Is this where the poor girl was found?' she asked in an innocent voice, pointing at the enclosed space.

'Yeah, under that bush. She was just a wee thing, not strong enough to fight off a flea.' Rosa warmed to him because he seemed to be the only person around with any pity for the dead girl.

'What was she doing here? Or was her body dumped?' she asked.

He was eager to talk and did not suspect a naïve-looking girl of belonging to the press.

'They think she was on the game,' he told her.

'That's awful. Did you see her before they took her away?' she asked. Already in her short journalistic career she'd learned that a limpid blue gaze brought out a good response from male interviewees.

'Aye, she was just an ordinary lassie wi' yellow hair, awful skinny – and stark naked . . .' He shuddered again at the memory of what he'd seen as well as the cold and they stood side by side staring bleakly at the sinister patch of fenced-off earth and prickly bushes.

'How was it done, do you think?' Rosa asked after a pause.

'She was strangled with her stockings.'

'Ugh,' she said with a convulsive shiver that made him feel protective and chivalrous, so he looked pitying at her as he said, '*Strangulation*, that's the usual way.'

All of a sudden, the wind became even stronger and whipped around their legs, chilling Rosa's blood with the realization of the wickedness that had been done there. An overwhelming sense of evil, so close, so recent, made her feel nauseous.

When there was a shout from behind, she turned to see Tom waving. 'Bye,' she said to the friendly constable and ran back. In the car she asked, 'Did you find out who the dead girl is?'

'They're not sure yet, but even if they knew, we couldn't use the name until her next of kin have been informed and that'll take time,' he told her.

She thought with horror about the reaction of some unsuspecting family, then, after a pause, she said, 'The policeman guarding the place she was found told me she was strangled and was only a little thing, not strong enough to fight back. God, isn't this is a desolate hole? It's exactly the sort of place where foul deeds are done, like something from a Shakespeare tragedy.' She was overcome by the feeling of tragedy and evil.

Tom was more hardened and impervious to weakness.

'They're pretty certain she was on the game. They think she's one of Flora's girls,' he told her as if that was some sort of explanation for murder.

Flora Black was Edinburgh's best-known madam, the owner of the city's most famous brothel, who made occasional appearances at the High Street Burgh Court, charged with keeping her 'disorderly house' in Danube Street.

Rosa first saw her a few weeks before when she was reporting that court and was deeply impressed by Mrs Black's aplomb and magnificent grooming. A woman of late middle age, she was beautifully made-up and sported a luxuriant silver-fox fur slung over one shoulder of her black suit. On her white hair perched a chic hat with a plume of glistening black-cock feathers falling down over her ear.

When the magistrate fined her £100, she took a thick fold of notes out of her crocodile handbag and disdainfully handed them across to the court clerk. *What style*, Rosa thought.

The girl the policeman described to her did not sound in the same class as Mrs Black however.

Tom interrupted her thoughts by saying, 'Let's find a phone box. Jack'll be waiting for his story.'

They drove on for about a mile till he spotted a red phone box standing outside a welcoming-looking hotel. Shouting 'Stop!', he consulted his watch and said, 'Good, they're still open. There's time for me to have a drink. I'll nip into this bar and write out a few pars. You wait here and when I'm finished you can phone the story over for me.'

At that moment a big car full of *Daily Express* men drove up from the opposite direction and the sight of them galvanized him into action. Moving faster than she had ever seen him move before, he dashed into the hotel, shouting over his shoulder, 'Get into the phone box and reserve the line so they can't use it. Don't let the *Express* get at the phone whatever you do.'

For thirty minutes she stood shivering in the phone box with the receiver in her hand, pretending to talk into it, and fending off shouting reporters from rival newspapers. At last Tom emerged from the hotel and shoved some sheets of paper torn from a spiral notebook into her hand. 'Send that over and then come into the bar,' he told her. He'd obviously been drinking because his eyes were even more bloodshot than usual.

The copy-taker who answered the office phone was Marie, a girl Rosa liked and with whom she sometimes drank coffee in the canteen. Marie was nicer and more tolerant than the other copy-takers who were apt to say things like, 'Is there much more of this?' or take exception when a reporter tried to spell a name or long words for them.

'I'm quite capable of spelling *that*,' they'd say huffily. Yet when they got it wrong, which they sometimes did, it was the reporter who shouldered the blame.

Marie never sighed with impatience if a phoned-over piece extended to more than two paragraphs, or told the caller, 'He won't use all this, you know.' She was more likely to say encouragingly, 'That's very good. He'll like it.' *He*, of course, was Jack, who ruled all their lives.

'Hello, Marie, it's Rosa, I'm in Aberlady on the murder.' Saying that made her feel important and Marie reacted most gratifyingly: 'Imagine! You'll get the front page tonight.'

'It's Tom Mavor's story unfortunately. I'm only driving him,' Rosa had to admit.

'Never mind, your turn will come,' consoled Marie, 'Just read it over to me. He's waiting for it.'

Rosa unfolded Tom's copy and started to dictate . . . '*A thin wraith of a girl who was too frail to fight off her attacker died last night on a desolate strip of windswept beach at Aberlady, which is exactly the sort of place where the foulest deeds are done, as Shakespeare would have said . . .*' it began. When she read out the words, fury almost choked her.

He's nicked my comments, and he's used the quote I got from the policeman! So that's how a real professional works. I wish I'd never lent him that half crown, she thought.

In the pub, when she eventually went in, the atmosphere was convivial and Tom was sitting in a corner with the *Express* contingent, who were lavishly supplied with expenses, and ordered up doubles for everybody in sight, including Rosa. She asked for a brandy because even her bones felt frozen.

One of the *Express* men slipped out to use the phone box and the others sat around talking about everything except the murdered girl. It took more than an hour before she could persuade Tom to leave and when he did, he was too drunk to complain about her driving and slept, snoring noisily, all the way back to the office.

Fortunately Jack was in a good mood when they returned. A murder on the front page in the last edition of the last day of the year cheered him immensely. When the paper was brought up from the throbbing presses in the basement at half past four, all the staff rushed to read it and Rosa was gratified to see that beneath the huge black headline –

GIRL'S BODY FOUND IN ABERLADY

was printed:

By Reporters T. C. Mavor and Rosa Makepeace.

So Jack knew her first name after all.

She looked across at him, wondering if she should thank him for the by-line, but he was shaking the dregs of the gin bottle into his cup and ignoring everybody.

Four

R osa loved the view from the newsroom windows when darkness was falling because Princes Street became magically transformed into a long ribbon of light, and smutty, smoky Waverley Station disappeared. The huge *Scotsman* building soared like a battlemented fairy castle above the dark valley that used to be the Nor' Loch but was now the station and Princes Street Gardens.

After the evening edition appeared on the last day of the year, the atmosphere in the office became festive because the staff were buoyed up by two realizations: first that hogmanay parties and celebrations would soon be starting, and, second, that they had scored a major scoop. Their chief rival, the other city evening paper, the *Edinburgh Evening News,* only carried a short mention of the Aberlady murder in their Stop Press column. Streams of office workers hurrying home would definitely buy the *Dispatch* tonight rather than the *News*.

At half-past five, when the last edition was safely out on the street, Jack and Gil took themselves off to their favourite pub, Jinglin' Geordie's, a few steps down Fleshmarket Close. The younger staff members drifted over to their preferred gathering place in the Cockburn Hotel where the first-floor cocktail bar was presided over by a red-haired midget called Etta. Her lack of inches was not relevant because she was muscled like an all-in wrestler and capable of single-handedly throwing out men twice her size. All the regulars were terrified of Etta.

20

She took a keen interest in the newspaper world and read every edition of every paper, which, hot off the presses, were delivered to her for nothing by the printers among her patrons. Her bar was an unofficial office for reporters too. If one of her regulars was not at their desk when summoned by their Editor, the first place to check for them was at the Cockburn where Etta covered up for her favourites and passed messages on.

When Rosa walked into the bar, the barmaid's bleak stare did not intimidate her because she knew that Etta rarely smiled.

'I see you and Tom Mavor got by-lines for that murder tonight. It was a good story. Good atmosphere,' said Etta, in unusually fulsome congratulation.

'Thank you,' Rosa replied, suddenly sobered when she remembered her resentment about Tom's blatant theft of her description of the crime scene. It was a lesson not to blab about her good ideas, she realized.

'You're coming on fine. I had Sylvia in this afternoon and she thinks she might know the poor lassie that was killed,' continued Etta, energetically polishing pint glasses because she never wasted time in only talking.

'The police at Aberlady said she was on the game. They thought she worked with Flora Black. Does Sylvia know her name?' Rosa asked hopefully for she knew that Sylvia, a regular at the Cockburn, was also on the game.

'She isn't sure but she thinks it's wee Sadie Jamieson. She said she'd ring me later if she finds out for sure. If it is Sadie, Sylvia'll be cut up because she liked the lassie,' said Etta.

Though Sylvia was a tart, she was a high-class one who didn't belong to Flora Black's stable but operated on her own as a call girl. She looked more like a society lady than a prostitute and could pass for a model because she always wore expensive clothes bought at Princes Street's most fashionable clothes shops, Jenners or Greensmith Downes. Her long blonde hair flopped down in a Veronica Lake one-eye-covering fall; she had scarlet fingernails, and her stilt-like legs were exaggerated by the three-and-a-half-inch heels of her fine Italian shoes.

In spite of the way she earned her living, she demanded respect because she was always incredibly dignified, and spoke with a posh English accent. In fact it was rumoured that she was a renegade member of a titled family. Like Camille, her glamour was even more enhanced by the fact that she suffered from ill health of a romantic but unspecified cause, and sometimes went off to Switzerland or exotic foreign health spas in search of a cure.

Etta, a great supporter of hers, once told Rosa in a portentous tone, 'Sylvia won't make old bones and she knows it. That's why she lives the way she does and I don't blame her.' Rosa, dazzled by Sylvia, agreed.

While she and Etta talked about her scoop, the bar filled up with other journalists, men who were unmarried – or very loosely married – and had no homes calling urgently for them. In fact they were planning a night of roistering. Seven reporters, including Rosa, squeezed round a round table and started to debate which of the several parties on offer they should attend to see the New Year in.

One of the advantages of being a woman in a predominantly male office was that she was paid the same wage as the men. But there were disadvantages too and a minor one was the inaccessibility of the women's lavatories from the newsroom. Even in extremis, Rosa and Patricia had to rush up a steep flight of stairs to a cloakroom two floors above their office. This was the previously unchallenged domain of a clique of bitchy females from the accounts department who wouldn't talk to women reporters, who they suspected were too big for their boots.

A bigger disadvantage was the fact that because they earned the same money as the men, Rosa and Patricia were expected to take their turns buying rounds in the pub. Not only were they expected to stand their hand like the men but they should drink like them too.

When she started working in the *Dispatch*, Rosa was warned by Patricia that she must at least appear to down drink for drink with the boys. The girls looked out for each other, with one or the other often ending up an evening by holding her friend's head over a sink or calling for a taxi.

On many mornings, after a night in the Cockburn, the only thing either of them could stomach was an Alka Seltzer, but often the noise the tablet made fizzing in the water only made their heads throb in agony.

By eight o'clock on the last night of the year, there was no sign of Patricia and several untouched glasses of gin stood on the table in front of Rosa.

She viewed them with disquiet and wondered how she was going to down them all, for leaving them undrunk would earn her scorn from her male colleagues.

In spite of the drawbacks however, Rosa could not imagine any other job that appealed to her more than the one she was so perilously holding on to. If she lost it, she knew that her father would insist that she went to training college and become a schoolteacher. The tedium would kill her. She'd sooner die happily of alcoholic poisoning.

The din in the Cockburn was building up to a crescendo and people crowded round Etta's bar, eager to get in their orders before closing time.

'Where's Patricia? Surely she's coming. She can't let me down tonight,' Rosa wondered, but though people came in and out of the bar, there was no sign of her friend. Then at last, when Rosa's perceptions were becoming very blurred, Patricia turned up, but didn't sit down with them. Leaning over Rosa's shoulder she whispered, 'Sorry darling, no partying for me tonight. I'm going home. My family all get together at hogmanay and they expect me to be there.'

Patricia lived with her parents, two brothers and two sisters in a council house in Musselburgh where she had grown up.

The oldest child in a working-class family, she shouldered the burden of contributing to the family's living expenses when she was fifteen. To the grief of her teachers, who spotted her intelligence and wanted her to go on to higher education, she left school to take a job in the local newspaper office as a filing clerk.

Within a year she'd become a reporter; within two she was Deputy Editor; within three she was on her way to Edinburgh, where she became one of the stars on the staff of the *Dispatch*. Her parents and siblings were dazzled by her success, for she earned far more than her father, more than the rest of them put together in fact.

Patricia with her glossy brown hair and attractively gap-toothed smile cut a glamorous figure because she always dressed in the height of fashion, turning herself out like a model from the glossy pages of *Vogue*. What most people did not know was that her glamorous wardrobe was home-made, churned out in the early hours of the morning on her mother's old treadle sewing machine.

Patricia could have made a top-class career at anything she touched and had a wonderful flair for dressmaking, copying her clothes from fashion photographs. She could turn C & A's stock into Christian Dior, and knew how to pin an artificial flower on to a lapel and transform a dowdy jacket into something special. On her, even Christmas-cracker jewellery looked impressive.

An admiring Rosa tentatively tried to imitate Patricia's style but as soon as she saw her reflection in a mirror, she knew she wasn't the type – she didn't have the necessary clothes-horse thin frame or the ineffable look of mystery. In Patricia's sort of clothes, Rosa felt ridiculous, and reconciled herself to wearing more casual things like trousers, thick sweaters and camel-hair coats.

Patricia, who was dressed tonight in a navy grosgrain suit with a pencil-thin skirt, patted the top of her friend's head, pointed at the undrunk glasses of gin and whispered, 'Dump those. If I'm not there, you'll have to look after yourself. Don't drink too much. Where will you go tonight?'

Rosa's heart suddenly sank as she remembered that, until the adrenalin rush of scoops and celebration wiped all other thoughts out of her mind, she'd been hoping to see Iain, the unsatisfactory love of her life.

Though he'd phoned and promised to meet her in the Cockburn at eight o'clock, by a quarter to ten, there was still no sign of him. It wasn't the first time he'd stood her up and she didn't want to ask Etta if he'd left a message because she knew that the answer would be a pitying 'No'. Etta's sceptical expression and pursed mouth whenever Iain was around made it obvious what she thought about his cavalier treatment of Rosa.

Pretending gaiety, she looked up at her friend with a bright grin and said, 'I'll be all right. I'll stay here with the gang and go on to one of the parties or maybe see the New Year in at the Tron.' She knew that the boys wouldn't desert her because none of them were going anywhere special either. They were just having a good time, sitting around laughing, drinking and boasting about their latest stories. The next stage in their descent into incapability would be rambling discourses about the novels they planned to write one day. Journalists all seemed to think they had a best-selling novel in them – what they lacked was the time to write it.

Patricia's warning about the gin however made her realize that she ought to retain some sobriety if she was to see the New Year in without passing out, and she could not trust the men to look after her then. She sat back in her chair and surreptitiously poured a double gin into a potted fern on the window ledge. Then she leaned forward again, determined to enjoy herself and not think about Iain, but her gaiety was forced and she felt sad again.

What saddened her most was that, unlike her friend, she had no home to go back to, no admiring family party waiting for her. She lived alone in a rented bed-sitting room in Northumberland Street with a landlady called Mrs Ross, who watched her comings and goings with a puritanical eye.

The reason Rosa lived in lodgings was because her mother died when she was twelve years old, and her father, who never really recovered from the grief of his wife's death, retreated to a remote cottage high in the hills above Selkirk. He had been a school teacher in Glasgow but gave up his job and scraped a perilous living by inventing things that he was confident would one day make his fortune. So far, ten years later, his inventions had not lived up to his expectations but both he and his daughter lived in hope.

Though she wished she had a real home, Rosa knew she was lucky to be in Northumberland Street because the room at Mrs Ross's was far better than the average 'digs'. In fact, it was quite a cosy little nest, comfortably furnished and warm, with a bathroom next door and enough hot water for a bath twice a week. Rosa was the only lodger but after she closed her bedroom door at night she often felt very lonely.

Mrs Ross laid down a lot of rules, but underneath she was kind and pretended not to know that Rosa boiled kettles on a little paraffin heater in her room and often carried in food – something that was strictly forbidden for fear of attracting mice.

When Rosa took the room, Mrs Ross also warned her that if she was not home by midnight, the door would be bolted against her unless she phoned in advance. She quickly worked out that when she wanted to stay out late, all she had to do was say she was out 'on a story'. Mrs Ross was so impressed by the glamour of her lodger's job that she made no protests.

If Rosa had ever been so daring as to try to smuggle a man into her room however, there would be no forgiveness and Mrs Ross would have her out on the pavement in half an hour. 'There's no immorality or loose living in this house,' she was warned when she moved in.

Fear of Mrs Ross was as big a defender of Rosa's virtue as her terror of getting pregnant. The techniques of contraception were unknown to her, or even to the more sophisticated Patricia, though both pretended to be very worldly and knowledgeable when teased by the men in the office, particularly by racing tipster Lawrie, who made it his purpose in life to find out if they were virgins.

They pretended sophistication and would sooner have died than admit to him that they were still *virgo intacta,* because they were ashamed of their innocence, but too scared of the consequences to test the water. The mysteries of sex fascinated and terrified them in equal measure.

Patricia, who was close to her mother and had helped her through four pregnancies by the time she left school, was Rosa's chief source of information. She had a fund of knowledge about childbirth and labour but little about the art of seduction, though she talked as if she knew it all.

Rosa had no one else whom she could ask about the forbidden subject. Her family was very small; for she had only one aunt called Chrissie, her father's sister, a fat, comfortable person who lived with her husband and three children in Peebles. On the few occasions when Rosa went to visit her, Chrissie provided her with a sumptuous tea but as she bustled about in her flowered pinafore, it was impossible to imagine her succumbing to a tide of passion.

Rosa's only other female relative was even less help. That was her mother's aunt Frances, known as Fanny, a prim spinster and retired schoolteacher in her seventies who thoroughly disapproved of Rosa's father and never missed an opportunity of pouring scorn on him.

'What's your father inventing *now*? Is it perpetual motion again this month? What a pity none of his ideas ever work!' she always said when Rosa visited her spartanly furnished bungalow in Corstorphine.

When Rosa got her job on the newspaper after graduating from university, Fanny suggested that her great-niece should live with her but was obviously relieved when the offer was turned down. Rosa explained it was too far to travel from Corstorphine to the North Bridge every morning and was glad when Fanny accepted that excuse, because living with her would have been more convent-like than living with Mrs Ross.

After Patricia left, the group in the bar began to shrink and the fern which Rosa continued to refresh with gin was looking distinctly unwell. By ten twenty-five only the hard core of revellers was left – Rosa, Mike, the dedicated news man with his duck's arse haircut; Tony, a minister's son who was trying very hard to live a life of dissipation; sharp-faced Peter, who would have no scruples about betraying his own mother in pursuit of a story; big bumbling Patrick, who kept falling over his own feet; and a photographer called McGillivray Thomson, an example of the strange habit of Scottish parents of giving male children their mother's maiden name as a Christian name.

Just before Etta was due to ring the bell for closing time at ten thirty, she called across the bar to the journalists' table, 'Hey, Rosa, Sylvia's been in touch.'

As Rosa crossed the floor, she was horrified to realize that her head was swimming and she was finding it difficult to stand upright without swaying.

I have to pull myself together. God knows what I'd be like if I'd drunk all those gins, she thought, fixing her eyes on the mirror behind the bar and heading firmly towards it.

Etta looked grim as she leaned over the counter and whispered, 'Sylvia was right about that dead girl. It was wee Sadie Jamieson.'

Immediately Rosa's head cleared as if it had been plunged into a tub of icy water. 'Sadie Jamieson?' she queried.

'Yes, you heard me, didn't you? That's what Sylvia said. She was greetin' when she told me,' said Etta looking around to make sure no one else could overhear.

Again, to her later shame, Rosa felt no thrill of pity or

sorrow. Instead a wild exhilaration seized her when she realized that the identity of the dead girl had just been revealed to her and her alone.

She had a scoop! No newspapers would be published the next day, for, not only was it a Sunday which was a non-publishing day for the *Dispatch*, but it was also New Year's Day, the only day in the year when no newspapers appeared anywhere in Scotland.

So she would have to hang on to her scoop till Monday but there was no way she was going to share this information with anyone. After what happened with Tom, she didn't trust one of her colleagues not to claim her information as his own if she was so indiscreet as to talk.

What'll I do? she thought, as the gin rapidly cleared away from her brain. *I know. I'll leave a note on Jack's desk so he can publish the dead girl's identity in our first edition of the year on Monday. I must do it now. There's no time to lose.*

'We're going to George's café in Tollcross for spaghetti bolognaise. Are you coming?' said a voice behind her, interrupting her thoughts. It was Mike, and she was terrified in case he'd overheard the exchange between her and Etta. He wasn't above selling the dead girl's name to one of the morning papers that would appear early on Monday morning before the *Dispatch*'s first edition hit the street.

Pretending coquettishness, she gently pushed him away from the bar, out of earshot of Etta, and said, 'I'd love to have some spaghetti, but you go on and I'll join you later. There's something I have to do in the office first.'

He stared suspiciously at her. 'You're going back to the office? What for?' he asked.

'I've forgotten something . . . Something personal – you know . . . but I'll see you at George's in half an hour. Don't eat all the spaghetti,' she told him playfully and this time he fell for it. He put his arm round her and gave her a playful squeeze. 'I won't,' he promised, full of alcoholic goodwill.

She watched him weaving his way through the crowd to

the door and realized that he too was acting a part, just like Patricia and herself. Underneath his slick suits and affected bravado, Mike was also an innocent, yearning for sophistication and experience.

Five

A lone on bleak, deserted Cockburn Street, where sinister shadows clustered in corners and loomed in the mouths of the sinister closes that led off to the left and right like the ribs of a fish, Rosa began visualizing what the girl on Aberlady beach must have gone through.

To reach her office she had to descend the unappealingly named Fleshmarket Close, a steep flight of steps running northwards down the side of the Cockburn Hotel to Market Street and Waverley Station. Even on a bright summer day, it was not a pleasant place but that night it was transformed into an entrance to Hades. One dim street lamp glimmered halfway down the stairs and the slumped figures of drunken tramps, surrounded by puddles of pee, were huddled in corners with their backs against the high enclosing walls. There was a nauseating smell of urine mixed with beer and vomit. The closes of Edinburgh's Old Town must have smelt like that for centuries, especially on hogmanay, thought Rosa, as she leaped from step to step, two at a time.

Her heart was thudding in her ears when she hurried past the first drunken body, cringing away from it because she was afraid that a hand would reach out from the bundle of rags and grab her ankle. Stifling growing terror, she headed for the shaft of light coming from the office back door, hoping that, though the office was closed, the nightwatchman would still be on duty. She had nearly reached the sanctuary of his lighted cubby hole when someone ran down the steps behind her and put a hand on her shoulder.

She screamed. Stopping dead in her tracks, she opened her throat and screamed again, louder this time, letting the noise rip through the night like a buzz saw. It did not matter because none of the comatose tramps even twitched. The man at her back said, 'For God's sake, shut up! You'll get me arrested. It's only me. Your pals in the Cockburn told me you'd gone back to the office.'

Her knees sagged and she felt her breath go out in a huge exhalation of relief. Her pursuer was Iain. She turned round to look at him, and, as always, her annoyance was swept away by the physical thrill of him, tall and broad shouldered, the image of Burt Lancaster the film star. They had the same dark brown hair, bold face and casual grace. She knew nothing about Lancaster's character but Iain was a rotter and she wished with all her heart that he didn't have such a devastating effect on her.

Her heart began beating double time but not from fright. All she wanted to do was to lean her head against his chest and feel his arms around her.

Yet she must appear indifferent.

'Oh, hello. I didn't expect to see you tonight,' she said, managing to sound cool in spite of her confusion. Though he was usually casually dressed when they went out together, tonight he was formally got up in a smart grey flannel suit, a white shirt and a striped silk tie.

'I'm a bit late,' he admitted.

'You said you'd phone if you weren't coming. What stopped you?' she asked, angry at herself for betraying disappointment.

'I forgot.' He was lying of course. In fact, she rarely believed a word he said because he was notorious for keeping two or three women on a string at one time but, as usual, whenever they were together, she had to steel herself against him. He was so *beautiful*, and so sexy.

Her fixation with him was purely sexual of course, but she excused herself by thinking that she had no choice. She was a victim of human biology, a fecund female picking out the best-looking stud to father her children. *But not tonight,* said her inward voice, and she fought to hold her raging hormones at bay.

'What exactly do you want?' she asked him stiffly.

He grinned. 'You know what I want!'

'Well you're out of luck,' she snapped.

'OK, I can wait. Tonight I thought we could go up to St Giles for the midnight service,' he said, suddenly acting penitent.

She stared at him in disbelief and asked, 'St Giles?' He'd never shown any interest in churches or religion before. 'You did say St Giles?' she repeated stupidly, eyeing him up and down, taking in his formal get-up.

'Yes, St Giles. It's a big church up there. Where all the best people go to get married.' He was grinning again as he pointed up the steps behind them towards the High Street.

'It's a cathedral actually,' she said pedantically. The bit about getting married was only a carrot he was dangling in front of her and she knew better than think there was any significance to it.

'OK. So it's a cathedral. Do you want to go to the service there with me?' he asked. She felt dazed. Surely he meant something serious by asking her to the midnight service? What was he up to? Could she trust him after all? Thoughts ran chaotically through her head, but she brushed them aside. *Pull yourself together*, she thought.

'Not yet. I've something to do first,' she told him. Even the lure of going to St Giles with him couldn't be allowed to divert her from her scoop.

Bert, the disabled man who guarded the office's back door, was still on duty because he loved his job and obsessively relished being part of the bustling world of the press. It didn't matter to him that no papers would be published next day, he'd even turn out to man an unpunched time clock. Besides he'd nowhere better to go because he spent all day in the newspaper building, and slept every night in a squalid hostel in the Grassmarket.

'Where are you going at this time of night?' he asked Rosa as she shoved her face against the wire grille of his little office.

'Let me into the newsroom, Bert. I've a story.'

Like Mrs Ross, the words 'a story' worked magic with him and he unlocked the door to let them in. Their footsteps make weird, hollow, echoing noises as they clattered down the iron stairs to the *Dispatch* office, which occupied a floor below the rooms of the prestigious *Scotsman*.

The big daily newspaper's rooms and front offices were very grand and imposing with intricate plasterwork, beautiful Victorian wood panelling, wrought-iron stair balustrades and veined marble pillars and fireplaces; but the *Dispatch* offices were much more bleak and industrial. Down at the very bottom of the building the presses were housed, lurking in the darkness like leviathans.

Everywhere beneath street level reeked with the strong, pungent smell of printers' ink, which Rosa loved, but tonight, as she ran downstairs, she felt strangely ill at ease. Something was wrong, something was missing.

It took a moment before she realized that what unsettled her was the stillness. The building's floors and immensely thick stone walls normally quivered like the heaving flanks of a panting animal with the clatter and thudding of the immense printing machinery in its bowels, but tonight, because the presses were idle, the cavernous place seemed to be holding its breath.

Only one overhead light was shining in the *Dispatch* newsroom, which Rosa thought was deserted until she saw the slumped figure of Alan, still asleep at his desk with a half-empty bottle of whisky and a curling ham sandwich by his elbow. The sight of him quickened her suspicions that he actually lived in the office. Perhaps, like Bert, he had nowhere better to go.

He didn't move a muscle when she pushed past him and sat down at her typewriter to type out the name Etta had given her.

SADIE JAMIESON, she wrote and sat back to look at the letters. She could have written it by hand of course but wanted to make it look as official as possible so it had to be typed in capital letters.

Then, beneath the name, she wrote in smaller letters: *The identity of the girl found murdered on Aberlady beach on New Year's Eve has been revealed (to* Dispatch *reporter Rosa Makepeace) as Sadie Jamieson.*

It didn't seem much when she read it and she imagined Jack's voice saying, 'So? Do you call this a story? How old is this Sadie Jamieson? Where does she live? Didn't you get a quote from her family?'

If it hadn't been so late, she'd have gone looking for Sylvia to provide her with more details. 'I'll find her tomorrow and add more to my piece before Jack gets in,' she decided as she began rolling the sheet of paper out of the typewriter carriage.

Iain was standing behind her with one hand on her shoulder and leaned down to read what she had written. 'Not much information in that,' he said dismissively.

'I know. I'll get more tomorrow. I have to find Sylvia first though,' she protested, flustered and defensive because he'd pinpointed the insufficiency of her information.

'Sylvia who?' he asked.

'I don't know her surname but she's a tall blonde who comes into the Cockburn sometimes. I've seen her in the Doric and the Beehive as well. She's a very good-looking English girl and Etta says she knew the victim.'

'The victim! You're starting to talk like a robot,' he scoffed.

'Well she was a victim, poor thing,' Rosa protested.

'By "Sylvia" do you mean the high-class tart?' he asked.

Rosa bristled. It didn't seem right to call Sylvia a tart because she was far too impressive for that.

'What makes you think she's a tart, as you call it?' she asked.

'I've seen her about,' he said airily, too airily. She looked beadily at him, too interested to feel any jealousy. 'Do you know where she lives?' she asked.

'Yes, a pal of mine knows her. She has a flat in Queen Street, near a house with two statues at the doorway. It's the Society of Physicians or something and she lives close by – on a top floor.'

She was so pleased to get this piece of information that she didn't care how he came by it. She took her sheet of copy paper across to Jack's worktable and placed it right in the centre, held down by dirty teacups so that it would be the first thing he saw on Monday morning. He couldn't miss it.

Then she went into one of the phone booths and rang up Mrs Ross to warn her she would be late getting home.

'But it's New Year's Eve. Surely you're not working tonight, are you?' Mrs Ross asked when Rosa announced her intention of being late

'No. I'm not working, but I've decided to go to the midnight service at St Giles,' Rosa said piously and could tell by the way her landlady said, 'St Giles. Fency that!' that she was impressed. The door would not be bolted against her.

Six

Agnosticism and puberty seemed to hit Rosa Makepeace at the same time, and since deciding that religion was not for her she'd hardly given a thought to matters spiritual. It was different with matters sexual though. She thought about that a lot, especially when she was with Iain.

In spite of her entrenched religious scepticism however, she found the atmosphere of the ancient church of St Giles in the High Street unexpectedly awe-inspiring. It was the first time she'd ever been inside it, and when Iain found them places in one of the box-like, green-painted pews near the back, she was overwhelmed by the thought that thousands of long-dead people had prayed within these stone walls and under the arches that loomed above her.

They prayed because they believed, so who was she to presume that they were wrong? She felt the presence of their ghosts all around her, crammed into the pews, and listening to the soaring notes of the organ.

Behind where she sat, rose a life-size statue of John Knox, an unlikeable man according to anything she'd read about him. In his sculpted cap and gown, he looked scaringly life-like in the shadowy void, as if he was about to burst out with one of his harsh denunciations of Mary, Queen of Scots, and all womankind.

Fading flags swung from massive stone pillars; ancient oaken beams arched far above her head; dim figures sitting with bent heads all around could be from any period, or any age. Her skin prickled involuntarily as if Knox's harsh eyes were really watching her.

When the choir began an anthem, she was surprised to find that her eyes filled with tears, and she found she was thinking about the murdered girl, Sadie Jamieson.

Till that moment she hadn't thought much about the dead girl as a person. Yet she must have been someone like herself, a girl with the same concerns, trivial hopes and fears. Did anyone love her? Did she have ambitions and hidden terrors, secrets and little vices? When she died, all her life lay in front of her. What would she have made of it? Rosa realized that her interest in the girl as a front-page story had hardened her and made her insensitive to a genuine tragedy.

Now in the shadowy church, she was filled with remorse for being so insensitive. Was it necessary to become tough and unfeeling in order to do her job?

Beside her, with his shoulder disturbingly brushing hers, Iain sat staring straight ahead, and she wished she could share her thoughts with him. How would he react if she said, 'I feel rotten about that dead girl Sadie Jamieson. Till now she's only been a great scoop as far as I'm concerned and I never thought of her as a human being. Does that mean there's something wrong with me?'

He'd probably turn it into a joke. 'Yes, you're as tough as old boots,' he'd say.

With the overwhelming atmosphere of reverence and spirituality all around, she found she wanted to pray for Sadie and when Iain saw her lowering her head, he surprised her by suddenly taking her hand.

Her heart turned over. Tenderness, and, in a rush, a feeling of closeness with him, filled her as she stared down at their entwined hands. There was something terribly trusting about giving another person your hand, especially in a church.

She was melting with love as well as being overawed by the immense seriousness of the place and the occasion while the words of the clergyman's address rang sonorously through the church without her really hearing them because she was overwhelmed by the solemnity of history and the nearness of Iain. Her hand lay in his and she closed her eyes while the only thought in her head was: *I love him, I love him* . . .

It was as if she could feel his blood flowing through her own veins and his heart beating in time with hers through their clasped hands.

Only when the bells in the tower above their heads began to ring out at midnight was the spell broken, and the congregation stood up to watch the dignitaries of Edinburgh making their way in solemn procession down the central aisle towards the main door.

The most important man in the line was solemn-faced Sir Gordon Gideon, the Lord Provost, his black suit emblazoned by an immense gold chain of office. He was preceded by his mace bearer and followed by a procession of the great and the good of the city, soberly dressed, self-important men, accompanied by ultra-smart women in frothy hats from Jenner's or Forsyth's, clutching kid gloves and glossy handbags.

These were the local MPs, bailies, town councillors, and judges, most of them identifiable to Rosa because they appeared frequently in newspaper photographs.

She spotted the prosecutor from the Burgh Court, where she was often sent to report on minor cases. He was followed by the advocate who ineffectually defended the city's ne'er do wells; and, Boyle, the brutal-looking, but somehow disturbingly attractive, blond police sergeant who was in charge of the cells beneath the court. They walked solemnly past her, faces impassive and staring straight ahead.

Near the end of the procession walked a portly, red-faced middle-aged man in a well-cut grey suit accompanied by a very pretty dark-haired girl in a pale-green coat with a mink collar and a tiny green hat. This was a town councillor and magistrate called Derek Hamilton-Prentice, and the girl with him was his daughter, Brenda, who often accompanied him to official functions because he was a widower.

Iain and Rosa stood side by side in their pew watching while organ music swelled, and the swinging lights flickered. It was an effort for Rosa to bring herself back to reality for she felt as if she had been in a trance and she was still feeling slightly bemused when Brenda Hamilton-Prentice reached the end of their pew. As she walked past, she turned her head, looked straight into Iain's face and her eyes opened wide.

It was obvious she knew him and was surprised to see him there. At the same time her father turned to look too and the glare he directed at Iain could only be described as malevolent. Iain stared back balefully and it was obvious that he was also surprised and discomfited by their reactions.

'Do you know these people?' Rosa whispered.

He shrugged. 'Yeah. He came to buy a car from me last month and nearly got me fired,' he said. The cars Iain sold for a living were not battered old Morris Minors like Rosa's, but upmarket models ranging from Armstrong Siddeleys to Humber Hawks, Jaguars and Rovers.

'Why? What did you do to annoy him?' Rosa asked.

Iain's answer sounded defensive. 'Nothing! He said I was insolent. Because he's on the Town Council he thinks he can throw his weight around. He was lucky I didn't pop him one.'

'You probably were insolent,' Rosa said, but she wondered if the bailie's hostility could have been because Iain made a play for his daughter. The soft and contemplative mood that had soothed her for the past hour was gone and reality took over again. The magic spell of the ancient church was broken and she felt sad that it had gone.

Once again Iain had aroused a trait that she loathed in herself, but she could not stop thinking about Brenda Hamilton-Prentice, and kicking herself for feeling jealous. The bailie's daughter, in that immaculate ensemble, resembled a Victorian china doll, the kind that were dressed up in silks and laces and kept well away from children in glass-fronted display cabinets. She was everything Rosa was not – curvaceous, well-groomed and elegant, with the sort of smooth expressionless face that often indicated a lack of liveliness or intelligence.

That wouldn't matter to Iain though because she was very pretty and he certainly preferred his women to be undemanding.

As the procession disappeared through the main door, he and she edged into the aisle and followed the people into the open square outside where the din was deafening because every bell in the Old Town seemed to be tolling at once and the pavements were crowded. Some of the crowd began shaking hands, and exchanging kisses but the more sober revellers were already drifting away as if, like Cinderella, their time for celebration ran out at midnight.

Iain and Rosa did not kiss each other. He tried but she turned her head away.

1956, the New Year, had begun. It crept in without her noticing and she was filled with her old, pagan dread of the unknown future. A terrible feeling of depression always seized her at the turn of a year. It scared the hell out of her.

With Iain following, she started to walk down the High Street towards the tall spire of the Tron Church, which stood out because of its illuminated clock. The hands were standing at twenty minutes past twelve, and people were massed round the foot of the church steps because the Tron was the traditional place for Edinburgh people to see the old year out and the new one in.

This was a more disreputable crowd than the congregation at St Giles and people were singing, 'Should auld acquaintance be forgot . . .', grabbing each other and shouting, toasting each other with whisky or throwing up on the pavement – normal behaviour at this time of the year. Before Rosa and Iain could join in however, there was a staccato noise of someone running down the pavement behind them in high-heeled shoes. Gasping, Brenda Hamilton-Prentice ran up, and grabbed Iain's arm, pushing Rosa aside as if she did not exist.

'What were you doing at the service?' she accused him.

He stopped dead and replied angrily, 'You told me you and your father weren't going there tonight.'

'He changed his mind,' she snapped and it looked as if she was on the verge of bursting into tears. Then she held Iain back and, without bothering to lower her voice, said, 'Don't go. There's something important I must tell you . . . It's awful.'

The look of hatred she cast at her made Rosa's gut clench because she realized that there was a lot more between this couple than a flirtation over the sale of a car. She didn't want to hear any more of their exchange because she feared that things were about to be said that could devastate her. In an effort to get away, she leapt forward in a half run, and almost collided with a line of giggling girls who were dancing arm in arm up the pavement.

Their line split at her intrusion like a wave breaking on the beach, but a hand reached out to grab her and a voice she recognized carolled, 'Steady on! Oh, Rosa, it's you. Come on, join in.'

It was Marie from the typing pool. Her blonde hair was tousled and she was transformed into a hoyden, laughing and animated, as she whooped, 'Come on. We're going down to the Gardens to dance. Come with us.'

Rosa linked arms in the line and started doing a hop, skip, kick like the rest of them. They passed Iain and the girl in green, still talking together, as they headed for the Mound and Princes Street Gardens. Rosa didn't look back and he didn't look after her either.

An hour later, she and Marie walked up Cockburn Street from Waverley Station in stocking feet, carrying their shoes in their hands. They were laughing and cheerfully groaning about the pain in their calves from all the frenzied high kicking they'd done dancing up and down the paths in Princes

Street Gardens. Rosa had no idea where Iain was and told herself she didn't care. Her New Year resolution was to dump him, to harden her heart against him. She hoped she had enough will to stick to it.

'Thank God, there's no work tomorrow,' said Marie, tossing back her curly yellow hair as they drew near to Rosa's parked car.

Rosa put the key in the door lock and said, 'Yes, thank God. We can have a long lie-in! I'll drive you home. Where do you live, Marie?'

'Sighthill,' was the reply. Rosa's heart sank because Sighthill was miles away, out on the western side of the city. The late-night buses had stopped running and she was dog-tired but she would have to stand by her rash offer of a lift.

'Get in. I'll drive you home,' she said again but Marie shook her head, and said, 'It's a long way to Sighthill. Where do you live?'

'Northumberland Street,' said Rosa, gesturing northwards in the direction of the New Town.

Marie laughed. 'Then don't be daft. It's miles from there to my house. I'll get a taxi.'

What a relief, thought Rosa because she was exhausted and the round trip to Sighthill would take another hour.

'Are you sure?' she asked Marie, who fortunately nodded.

'Of course. I often take a taxi home because it's a long walk from the bus stop to home. I'll pick up one in the High Street . . .'

Rosa frowned. 'They'll all be busy tonight. At least let me take you to a rank. We could go to the station but there's usually a queue there. What about going to the North British Hotel? The doorman will whistle a cab up for you and it'll be quicker than waiting at the station.'

'OK, good idea,' said Marie, climbing into the passenger seat and struggling to put her shoes back onto her swollen feet.

When Rosa pulled the Morris Minor away from the kerb,

she noticed that a car that had been parked behind them began pulling away too. As she switched on her lights, the other driver did the same and she saw in her mirror that only one of the headlights was working. For a moment she wondered if the car had been waiting for them.

If that's Iain, I've a bloody good mind to lead him on a wild goose chase and take Marie to Sighthill after all, she thought but she was so horribly tired that she could hardly keep her eyes open. The misery she felt about the encounter between him and Brenda Hamilton-Prentice came back and almost overwhelmed her.

Marie noticed her change in mood. 'Are you all right, Rosa?' she asked anxiously.

'Yes, I'm tired, that's all. Such a lot has happened today. It started with that murder in Aberlady this morning and it's gone on ever since . . .' Rosa yawned as she spoke.

Marie nodded. 'Of course. I'd forgotten about the murder. Poor girl . . . what a terrible thing to happen to her. Let's hope they get the brute who did it.'

Her first reaction to a murder is pity – so different to my own, thought Rosa with a pang of remorse. To her, Sadie Jamieson was a story again and already she was planning to find out more about her next morning.

Two minutes later she pulled her car up at the brightly lit front door of the huge North British Hotel. There were no taxis waiting outside but a tall doorman, wearing a smartly cut buff uniform and black top hat, was standing on top of the carpeted steps. He came down to open the door for Marie. 'Good evening, miss,' he said gravely.

'I'll wait with you till a taxi comes,' Rosa offered, but Marie got out and shook her head.

'No. Go home. You look exhausted. I'll be fine. This chap will get me a taxi. Won't you?' The last question was directed at the doorman, who nodded in agreement.

When Rosa drove off, her friend was standing beside him at the top of the hotel steps, waving cheerfully.

She looked in her mirror and saw the single-headlighted car, which had followed them from Cockburn Street, suddenly appear behind her again, but when she turned down into Leith Walk, it went on straight ahead and disappeared into the blackness of Waterloo Place. She was almost disappointed that it wasn't Iain after all, for a row with him would finish off the night perfectly as far as she was concerned.

'He's a bastard. You're well rid of him,' she said aloud to herself, but in spite of sounding so positive, she was hurting like hell and, now that Marie was not there to see, tears began cascading down her cheeks. From the very first day she met him she knew he was bad news but that was part of his attraction. Going out with him was like risking her life in a tiger's cage.

It hurt to realize that she had only been one of a string of gullible girls as far as he was concerned, but why had he taken her to St Giles, why had he sat in the dark church holding her hand so tenderly? Was he only softening her up?

Yet when Brenda Hamilton-Prentice accosted him outside St Giles he was obviously taken aback and disconcerted, caught on the hop. What was going on between them? Iain was ambitious; he wanted to live like the men who bought cars from his employer – but he had no money and nothing much to offer except his physical attraction, so perhaps he thought that marrying a rich man's daughter would be the easiest way of achieving his dream. It was all right to play around with girls like Rosa but he would marry someone like Brenda; he'd sell himself to the highest bidder.

He's a bastard and I've been a fool, Rosa told herself but that didn't help much because her pride, as well as her heart, was wounded.

What a way to start a New Year, she thought as she wiped her eyes and turned the key in Mrs Ross's front door.

Seven

It was nearly ten o'clock next morning before Rosa woke and for a moment she did not remember anything of the previous night. Then, in a rush, the misery of loving and losing Iain swept over her. It even overwhelmed the pleasant memory of dancing in the Gardens with Marie and her friends.

But she had a lot to do and must not give in to self-pity. Leaping from bed, she put on her warmest clothes – red tartan trousers, a black sweater, and a navy-blue pea jacket with brass buttons that her father bought for her at Jaeger's last year when he sold the patent for a left-handed can opener. For breakfast she grabbed a glass of milk and an apple before dashing downstairs to her car, trying not to make a lot of noise or annoy Mrs Ross, though she had almost certainly been up and about since her normal time of 7 a.m. – New Year's Day was just another day as far as she was concerned.

Reassuring herself that girls like Sylvia were unlikely to be early risers, Rosa drove fast to Queen Street. Unsure of where her quarry lived, she stopped at the edge of the pavement opposite the headquarters of the Royal College of Physicians, which was the only building in the street with an entrance adorned by two large statues. She should have asked Iain to be more specific about Sylvia's address, which he almost certainly knew.

From where she was parked she could watch the comings and goings at properties on both sides of the Physicians' building but there was not a soul to be seen, and curtains in the upper windows were drawn. There was always something to read in her car, so she groped around on the littered floor among the magazines till she found a Penguin paperback, which turned out to be Stella Gibbons' *Cold Comfort Farm*, an old favourite. Propping it on the steering wheel, she settled down happily to wait.

Stella's wit kept her amused for an hour till her feet began feeling very cold, the toes tingled when she moved them, so she hopped out of the car and jumped up and down on the pavement a few times to make her circulation flow again.

Then she went back to her book for another half hour but the cold became excruciating and she was on the point of giving up and going home when a woman came out of the main door of the second house along from the Physicians' College.

She was wearing a black astrakhan coat and her long hair glittered like beaten gold. It was Sylvia all right. That peroxide hair was her trademark.

She hurried down the steps and headed towards the Leith Walk end of Queen Street at a brisk pace. Quickly Rosa started the car's engine, swinging it around in the road to catch up with her quarry, who paused at a junction before crossing the road.

Rosa screeched to a halt beside her, leaned over to open the passenger door, and said, 'Hello, Sylvia, can I offer you a lift?' Where did she get the nerve? It seemed that when she was on a journalistic assignment, she was able to do things that she would never dream of doing under normal circumstances. It was like being on stage.

Sylvia did not seem surprised. She only raised her plucked eyebrows a little and said, 'It depends on where you're going.'

'Oh, nowhere in particular,' said Rosa.

Sylvia leaned down and looked quizzically into the half-open door. 'What exactly are you up to, my dear?' she asked in her cut-glass voice.

Rosa came clean. 'I'm a journalist and I want to ask you

some questions about a story I'm doing,' she said.

'Thank heavens you're not trying to hire me. I don't do women,' was Sylvia's reply. Rosa felt her face flushing crimson. The idea of propositioning Sylvia had never crossed her mind and she was appalled at being suspected of it. Damn, I shouldn't have worn the sailor's jacket – or the tartan trousers, she thought. It was so difficult trying to keep up with sophisticated people.

Sylvia saw Rosa's reaction and, laughing, climbed into the car, settling the skirts of her luxurious coat round her legs as she turned to look at the driver. 'Don't worry, I recognized you. You're the reporter that Etta likes. She told me your name but I've forgotten it. Isn't it something funny?'

'It's Rosa Makepeace if that's funny. Does Etta really like me? I'd never have guessed from the way she treats me.'

'You should be glad. She's only polite to people she can't stand. Yes, she says you're terribly green but there's a chance you'll toughen up,' said Sylvia, still laughing.

'Great!' said Rosa stiffly and turned to stare through her side window for oncoming traffic as she prepared to drive off but the road was totally empty as if everyone else in the world had disappeared.

Sylvia watched this manoeuvre with a sceptical expression before she asked, 'Get on with the questions then, unless you're running a car hire service in your spare time. If you are, I'll go to the High Street.'

'I want to find out about Sadie Jamieson,' Rosa replied.

Sylvia's smile disappeared and her face hardened. Underneath her make-up she suddenly looked drawn and ill and Rosa wondered how old she was. Normally, in artificial light, she didn't look more than twenty-five, little more than Rosa herself, but today in the cold glare of winter sun, she could have been forty.

'What do you want to know about poor little Sadie?' she asked in a bleak voice, staring straight ahead through the windscreen.

'Anything – everything. How old was she? Where did she live?'

'She was just a kid, like you.'

'I'm twenty-three,' Rosa said defensively, exaggerating her age by several months.

'You're twenty-three coming on sixteen,' replied Sylvia opening her handbag and bringing out a gold-embossed pack of Passing Cloud cigarettes, which she waved in Rosa's direction and asked, 'Want one?'

In fact Rosa didn't enjoy smoking much and only lit up in company but she nodded because she couldn't bear the thought of appearing unsophisticated. Sylvia lit one and passed it over to her. There was a lipstick mark on its end and she didn't really like putting it in her mouth, perhaps because of Sylvia thinking she was being propositioned. She overcame her qualms though and drew on it defiantly, wishing she could blow smoke rings like a vamp in the movies. Instead it made her cough.

'I was sent down to Aberlady when Sadie's body was discovered and I'm trying to find out about her,' she explained as they drove along.

Sylvia was drawing deeply on her own cigarette, seeming to swallow the smoke and Rosa wondered if it would come out of her ears. 'You're going to write about Sadie?' she asked.

'Yes. I want to.'

'Funny job you do,' mused Sylvia. Rosa stared at her, thinking her comment a bit rich considering the way she earned her own money, but forbore from making any comment, and Sylvia went on, 'Why ask me? Won't the police give you all the facts?'

'Eventually they will, but they give the same information to every paper and they never include anything personal. I'd like to write something fuller and more sympathetic than a police incident report. She was very young . . .' Rosa explained.

'She was only seventeen. I wish I could get my hands on

the bastard who killed her,' Sylvia replied bitterly.

'You're sure it's Sadie Jamieson who died? The police hadn't announced the name by last night,' Rosa asked.

Sylvia sighed and viciously stubbed her cigarette out in the car ashtray though it was only a quarter smoked. 'Oh, it was Sadie all right. I went with Flora to identify her. She lived in Flora's house you see.'

'You knew her well?'

'Quite well, because I know Flora, and Sadie went to live there about a year ago. Flora took care about the people she introduced to her because she was a timid wee thing. She didn't go out on the street, so none of us can understand what she was doing at Aberlady. She'd never allow herself to be picked up by a casual punter . . . I don't think she was taking customers on her own and pocketing the money either, she wasn't that sort. I don't suppose she'd have lasted long in the business really, her heart wasn't in it.'

Sylvia obviously thought of her trade as a sort of a vocation, which surprised Rosa. 'What did Sadie look like?' she asked.

'Childish, even younger than her age, pale-blonde hair, and very thin. As I said, just a kid. Some of them like that sort.'

Rosa shivered. She didn't want to explore that angle. 'What was she like as a person?' was her next question.

'She was far too soft-hearted, and religious. Not very bright really. She read those mushy books you buy in a newsagent's all about true love – imagine! She adored things like teddy bears, puppies and kittens – in fact she reminded me of what I was like at that age.' Rosa shot a glance at the high-nosed, imperious profile beside her and found the last comment hard to believe.

'Where did she come from?' she persisted.

'The High Street of course. That's why I'm going there now.' Sylvia glared at her as if she was being deliberately obtuse.

Hurriedly Rosa asked, 'Are you going to see her family?'

'If you can call that mother of hers family. The police will have told her what's happened to her daughter by this time, I expect. They couldn't find her last night. God knows where she was, so Flora had to identify the girl.'

'What a rotten job,' Rosa said.

'Being Flora or being a policeman?' Sylvia asked sarcastically.

'No, of course not. I mean it's a rotten job for you having to go to see her mother.'

'I'm doing it for Flora. She was pretty cut up about the girl and she's never liked the mother, so she asked me to go to see her. She thought I'd do it better than she could.' Sylvia's face hardened even more as she spoke.

'Whereabouts exactly in the High Street does she live?' Rosa asked.

'Roxburgh Close. Do you know it?'

'Yes, I do.' It was almost directly opposite St Giles and the Burgh Court where Rosa spent much of her time because reporting that court was the job usually given to junior reporters. They cut their teeth on the cases there, and most of the people who came up on charges were old lags who only committed trivial offences.

So far Rosa had written stories about women fighting in the street and an old man being drunk in charge of a pony and cart. She'd listened to tales of petty thieving, shoplifting and minor housebreakings, but was never bored. In fact she enjoyed covering the Burgh Court because funny things often happened there.

The quest she was on now wasn't funny, however, and she was solemn faced as she drove up the Bridges, turning off into the cobbled stretch of the High Street that led to George IV Bridge and the Mound. Roxburgh Close was near the top on the right-hand side and it looked like a dark rabbit hole diving into the ground floor of a tall tenement beside the City Chambers.

Sylvia leaned forward and pointed. 'That's it. Down there. She lives in Flat Seventeen B, Roxburgh Close.'

Rosa pulled up on the street and Sylvia got out of the car. There was no traffic and nobody walking on the street. It seemed that last night's revelry had been a dream. Standing on the pavement, Sylvia looked at her driver and said, 'Coming?'

Rosa did not have to be asked twice. She was out of the car in an instant and running behind Sylvia along the close, which was too narrow for them to walk side by side. The pathway was dark and slippery and sloped vertiginously down to Market Street far below at an angle so steep that it felt as if they were descending Ben Nevis.

Rosa didn't like heights, so she kept her eyes on her feet and did not allow them to stray towards the horizon, which showed a distant vista of the coast of Fife. About halfway down, her guide stopped suddenly and Rosa almost collided with her fur-clad back.

'Seventeen. This is it,' she said, indicating an ancient wooden door.

'I'll wait for you if you like,' Rosa said as the door was pushed open.

'Aren't you coming in too? You're not much of a newshound if you don't,' Sylvia replied.

Seventeen B was the first door off the second landing of a twisting spiral staircase with stone steps deeply worn in the middle by the passage of people climbing up and down for centuries. Sadie's mother's flat was next door to a communal lavatory that smelt so foul it made both women gag and Sylvia put a lace-edged handkerchief up to her nose.

No one answered her knock but she tried the handle and the door was unlocked. When she pushed it open, they found themselves staring into a cheerless room where two women huddled, one on each side of a smoking coal fire. Glasses stood on the floor by their chairs. The room was carpetless, sparsely furnished, very dirty and smelt of cat pee.

The women were toasting their bare legs in front of the fire and the heat had mottled the dead white flesh with deep purple veins like marble. Both were raddled, with smeared make-up on their faces, and tousled hair. Later it was a shock for Rosa to realize that they were actually quite young, probably still only in their early thirties, but at first sight they looked like aged crones.

One woman, whose hair was dyed jet black, looked up at the intruders with a blank-eyed, incurious expression which indicated she was very drunk.

'Whae're you?' she mumbled.

'I'm Sylvia Playfair, a friend of Flora Black,' said Sylvia.

The second slumped woman, a blonde with a skeletal face, raised her head and flashed bloodshot eyes at the strangers. 'Flora's a fuckin' bitch. It's her fault my bairn's deed,' she muttered.

Sylvia kept her cool. 'You can't blame Flora, Mrs Jamieson. She was good to Sadie, and, anyway, you were the one who asked her to take in the girl. She's sent you some money but you don't have to take it if it goes against your sensibilities.'

She brought a wad of notes out of her handbag, waved it around and was about to put it back again when the blonde woman jumped to her feet and reached for it.

'I'll take her dirty money. She owes it to me onywey,' she said.

Sylvia handed it over with the crisp words, 'There's a hundred pounds there, to give Sadie a decent funeral. Don't drink it.' The dead girl's mother folded the money and stuck it into the front of her blouse, watched blearily by her friend.

With an expression of disgust, Sylvia turned on her heel and was about to leave, but Rosa put a hand on her arm to hold her back, and said to Sadie's mother, 'I'm very sorry about your daughter, Mrs Jamieson.' She was determined not to leave the squalid room till she got a good quote from the mother for Jack.

'What is it to you?' the woman shot back.

'I was at Aberlady where she was found. When did you hear what happened?' Rosa asked.

Mrs Jamieson's companion chimed in on behalf of her friend, 'Twae bobbies cam' ower from the station to tell her. Puir sowl. It's nae wonder she's havin' a few drinks.' The High Street police station was next to St Giles and the Burgh Court, directly across the road from Roxburgh Close. Rosa was impressed by the close proximity of everything in the High Street, for life there was closely interconnected like a honeycomb in a beehive. It was an enclosed world within the city of Edinburgh.

The authorities had started trying to move families out of the warrens of little flats in the tall, ancient tenements and rehouse them in modern council houses in the suburbs. It offered a better life for them, said the do-gooders, but Rosa thought it would be a tragedy if the transfers succeeded because there were families in the High Street whose ancestors had lived in the same tenements for centuries. They were the custodians of the street's history. Even if they did get drunk, fought and caused mayhem every now and again, their uninhibited way of life was a refreshing contrast to the hidebound conformity of people in the better-off areas of the city.

With Flora's money safe in her breast, Sadie's mother sat down again and began rocking back and forward in her seat, keening, 'Oh, my bairn! Aw my God! Aw my God!' Then she looked at her friend and said, 'Gie me another wee nip, Nelly.'

Her glass was refilled but nothing was offered to Sylvia or Rosa, which was a relief to them both because it would have been difficult, and probably dangerous, to drink or eat anything in that filthy room.

'When did you last see Sadie?' Rosa persisted, ignoring the wailing.

'Wha'd ye mean?' asked Mrs Jamieson, abruptly breaking off her tears.

'Was she living here with you when she went missing?'

'I'd nae idea she was missing. She lived at Flora's, didn't she? This place wasnae good enough for her.'

'So when did you last see her?'

'Maybe a month ago. I cannae mind.' So Sadie hadn't been home for Christmas though Flora's house was only a short bus ride away. Rosa didn't blame her.

'Do the rest of your family know that she's dead?' she asked.

'Family? There's naebody else but me. Naebody else gies a tuppenny damn.'

'So there's only you and her?' said Rosa and the friend, sensing her interest, suddenly became suspicious and glared aggressively as she asked, 'Whit are ye after exactly? Whae are ye? Are you frae the police or the social?'

Rosa shook her head. 'No, I'm nothing like that. I'm a reporter with the *Dispatch* . . .'

'She's frae the papers, Betty,' the friend said to Sadie's mother and they both perked up, hoping for another source of money.

'How much are you payin'?' was Betty's next question.

'Nothing,' said Rosa.

'Then you can get the hell oot o' here,' shouted Sadie's mother and lifted the poker with murderous intent.

Sylvia and Rosa stepped back in unison and left, with Rosa saying, 'I'm sorry. I only came to give you my sympathy at this terrible time . . .'

Sadie's mother burst into tears again. 'Aw ma poor bairn. Whae did it? That's what I'd like to know. She's gone and left her mither all alane. There's naebody left for me noo. I hope the bastard that killed her burns in hell!'

The last glimpse Rosa had of them was of the friend leaning forward to console the mother and saying, 'Ye're no on your ain, ye've got me, Betty. Come on, gie me some o' that money and I'll buy anither carry-oot frae the pub.'

Betty glared at her departing guests and yelled, 'Are ye

still here? If you're no' going to pay me anything more, get the hell oot.'

They fled, ran up the close and drove off quickly. Back in Queen Street, Rosa stopped the car and stared at her companion.

'What a pair of harpies!' she gasped.

'You got what you wanted though, didn't you? You got the grieving mother's quote. Very sharp of you,' said Sylvia.

'Don't make it sound so calculated,' Rosa said, but she was only slightly ashamed, and already regretting that she hadn't asked Sadie's mother for a photograph of the dead girl. Jack liked photographs.

'But it was calculated, wasn't it?' persisted Sylvia.

'I won't lay it on thick when I write the story,' Rosa promised.

Sylvia nodded as she said, 'Good. Don't make her sound pitiful because she doesn't deserve any sympathy. She ill-treated and neglected her daughter when she was little so the authorities took her away and put her in an orphanage at Balerno when she was nine. But at sixteen she was out in the big cruel world again and the only place she could go was back to her mother who didn't want her. So she gave her to Flora.'

'Couldn't she have got a job or worked in a shop or something?' Rosa asked.

Sylvia's eyes flashed. 'Instead of going on the game, you mean?'

'She was just a kid, she couldn't know what she was doing,' Rosa protested.

'That's right, she was a kid and in spite of everything she loved her mother but the only thing that woman up there loves is her bottle. She'll squeeze as much as possible out of this murder and that makes me furious. Sadie was not a bad kid. The orphanage did a good job on her and she could have made a good life, but she had her mother breathing down her neck. Betty only looked on her as a source of money. She sent her to Flora, and spun her a yarn about it being only for a little while, till she got on her feet. Sadie was so innocent! She really thought that some knight in shining armour would come into Flora's house and fall in love with her!' Sylvia's voice throbbed with anger and for a moment Rosa thought she was about to weep, but her expression closed down and she didn't. Instead she turned into a woman of ice and immense hauteur.

As she was getting out of the car however, she changed again, turning to Rosa and saying in a tone of reconciliation, 'Fancy a drink? I think we might both need one after that.'

'Good idea. But everywhere is closed today. There's nowhere to go,' said Rosa.

'There's my flat. I've a bottle of wine in the fridge.'

She lived on the second floor of a very discreet-looking Georgian building with a beautiful arched fanlight above the front door. Her drawing room would have been a master bedroom at one time and had two bay windows that looked over the tops of the trees in Queen Street Gardens to the river Forth and distant Fife. The weather had cleared, so it was possible to see for miles, a cold sun was shining and the sky was a pale shade of blue. The world looked incredibly beautiful but somehow cruel.

'Take off your coat and sit down,' said Sylvia, leading the way into an opulently furnished room with long cream curtains of slub silk, deep armchairs and two sofas piled high with blue, green and turquoise silk cushions. In a corner there was a real rarity, a television set masquerading as a walnut cabinet with slatted doors. Over the black marble fireplace hung a brilliantly coloured painting of a vase of pink roses and a couple of apples on a tabletop.

'That's a super picture,' Rosa said impulsively because it immediately attracted her.

'You've got taste. It is good. It's a Peploe,' laughed Sylvia. 'It's new. I bought it at Christmas from Aiken Dott's as a present to myself because I thought I needed cheering up.

One day it'll be worth a lot of money, I hope.'

As she spoke, she was rummaging behind a cocktail bar in the corner and came out with a bottle of champagne, which she deftly opened and poured the bubbling golden liquid into two flutes.

'Happy New Year, Miss Makepeace!' she said, raising her glass in a toast.

'Gosh, I'd forgotten about New Year,' Rosa said. For the past few hours it had been a relief to put it out of her mind and not grieve about her loneliness and her fear of being alone all her life.

'I wonder if I'll see another,' said Sylvia suddenly. She had taken off her fur coat to reveal a tightly fitting scarlet wool dress that was elegantly draped over the hips. It emphasized her extreme thinness.

'What do you mean?' asked Rosa in surprise.

'I wonder if I'll see another New Year. I'm not very well right now,' was the sombre response.

It was difficult to know what to reply because Rosa had heard the rumours about Sylvia being ill but didn't want to sound pessimistic. 'People get better from all sorts of things nowadays,' she said lamely.

'I've got leukaemia,' Sylvia said bleakly, turning back to look at her guest.

Rosa knew little or nothing about leukaemia except that it was to be dreaded. 'Are you having treatment?' she asked, floundering even more.

'Yes, I am. The doctors in the Royal Infirmary are quite cheerful when they talk to me but I suspect they're just trying to keep my spirits up. I'm only twenty-eight, you see.' Sylvia poured more wine into her glass as she spoke.

'The doctors up there are the best in the world. And you don't look ill. Does it make you feel very bad?' It was difficult for Rosa to know the right thing to say in reply to Sylvia's frankness. Most people she knew avoided talking about illness. Her parents never even told her when her mother was ill, far less warn her that she might be dying.

Sylvia seemed to need to talk, however. 'I might not look too bad to you, but without make-up I look awful, and I feel like hell a lot of the time. Champagne helps and when it gets too bad they give me blood transfusions. Then I'm fine for a bit. I've just had one, so I should be on good form till mid-January with any luck.' She sounded very matter-of-fact as she refilled the glass. Rosa sipped from hers again, letting the bubbles explode inside her head. She'd never tasted champagne before and was pleasantly surprised by the invigorating effect it had on her.

'Sylvia,' she said with absolute, alcohol-fuelled conviction, 'I'm sure you're going to be fine. I'll make a wish for you to get better. Everybody gets one wish when a new year begins, you know.'

'Haven't you made this year's wish already, and don't you want it for yourself?' Sylvia asked with a smile.

'I've been saving it up because I don't want to waste a good wish. Besides, I don't want anything in particular for myself that I can't get by a bit of luck and hard work,' Rosa replied. Except for Iain, what she said was true.

The rest of the champagne was divided between them, then Sylvia said, 'Make your wish and drink up, because you'll have to go. I'm expecting a visitor.'

Gulping it down, Rosa closed her eyes and wished, wondering if the visitor was business but didn't presume to ask. As she ran down the stairs on her way out she reflected that Sylvia's immaculate flat must be expensive to keep up because everything in it was of superb quality. There were two huge vases of fresh flowers in the drawing room, and that Peploe couldn't have been cheap.

Back in Northumberland Street she lay on her bed and read more Stella Gibbons which made her laugh, but her jollity dissipated when she closed the book and remembered Iain.

It was almost four o'clock when she realized that there was nothing in her room to eat except a cup of milk and a packet of digestive biscuits. She'd had no lunch except two appetite-sharpening glasses of champagne, and all the local cafés were closed for the holiday.

She was getting out the biscuits when Mrs Ross called up the stairs, 'There's a gentleman here to see you, dear.' She sounded cordial, though she didn't usually approve of Rosa having callers, especially if they were male.

Downstairs in the sitting room, Dr Roddy Barton was tolerantly listening while Rosa's landlady described a wheezing in her chest, which had recently been giving her trouble.

He smiled at Rosa, stood up and said to Mrs Ross, 'The best thing for you to take is a small hot toddy and an aspirin before you go to bed every night.'

'Oooh, I never touch alcohol! I signed the pledge when I was ten,' she exclaimed in horror.

'A little whisky will do you no harm, no harm at all,' he said in a solemn professional tone. Roddy will have a great bedside manner one day, Rosa thought with hidden amusement.

Mrs Ross was very impressed and gathered herself as if making a huge decision before she said, 'Then if that's what you think, Dr Barton, that's what I'll take. Thank you very much!'

In the hall the two young people looked at each other and laughed. They met at university and had been friends ever since. Though Rosa always told Roddy there was no chance of romance between them, he kept turning up in her life with such dogged persistence that she was afraid one day she'd give in and marry him.

She couldn't put him off. He was impervious to rejection. Tonight she was beaming at him because she was genuinely pleased to see him.

'What are you doing here? I thought you'd been posted to Catterick,' she asked when they went outside and stood on the pavement to talk because Mrs Ross wouldn't let her entertain even him in her room. He was doing his National

Service but seemed to be able to organize it so that he was never very far away. Catterick was the farthest he'd gone so far.

'I've a few days leave, so I thought I'd come up to see my mother and look in on you too. How are you doing?' he said with a smile. She smiled back because he was a pleasant-looking fellow, but not a patch on Burt Lancaster.

'I'm fine. I was sent on a murder story yesterday,' she told him, and then, to her astonishment, heard herself pouring out her fears about becoming hard-boiled, and having no feelings for other people.

His eyes never left her face while she was speaking and when she stopped he said, 'I suppose you have to be tough to be a reporter or else the things you hear might get you down. It's a bit like being a doctor.'

'But we don't try to make people better like you do. We just exploit them.'

'If it worries you, change your job,' he replied.

'But I love it! *That's* what worries me. The first thing I felt when I answered the phone and heard about the murder was pure adrenalin-powered excitement. Isn't that shameful?'

He shook his head. 'It's your job. It's like being an actor. You should play the reporter when you're working, and luxuriate in your guilt feelings in private.'

She looked at him narrowly, not sure if he was being sarcastic, but he smiled blandly back and said, 'I came to invite you to supper with my mother.'

She clapped her hands. 'Great! I'm starving and there's nothing to eat in my room.' Then she had a moment of doubt, having met his mother before when he took them both to tea last summer in the café above the Edinburgh Bookshop in George Street. Mrs Barton terrified her because she was so genteel and really did stick out her little finger when she was drinking tea.

'Does she know you're asking me?' she enquired cautiously.

'Of course. She lent me her car to fetch you and she'll be very hurt if you don't come.'

Rosa ran back upstairs to fetch her coat, debating whether or not she should change out of the tartan trousers, but decided against it. If Roddy's mother didn't like her style, she might persuade her son to give her up, and that would solve the problem of what to do about him. Somehow she seemed unable to give him up. *She'd* have to be dropped.

Mrs Barton turned out to be a formidable cook and the table in the dining room of her Morningside flat was loaded with food. They ate honey-baked ham with Waldorf salad, brown bread and butter, scones with home-made strawberry jam and a delicious sponge filled with whipped cream. Rosa knew that her thanks sounded over-effusive, but was genuinely grateful because she hadn't eaten such a good meal for ages.

'Can you cook, dear?' asked Roddy's mother, who bore a strong resemblance to the actress Margaret Rutherford.

'I'm afraid not,' Rosa told her.

She looked concerned. 'That's a pity but I suppose you're too busy with your job. What is it you do exactly?'

'I'm a reporter. I write stories for the *Dispatch* newspaper.'

'How nice! I do enjoy the Woman's Page in the *Dispatch*. There's often good recipes in it.' She was obviously trying to find some common ground between them, but Rosa bridled because she and Patricia scorned the Woman's Page, which was put together by a morose woman called Harriet Holliday, who filled it almost entirely with syndicated material. If the other girls were asked to contribute 'little woman'-type material when she ran out of cosmetic tips, they protested violently.

'I don't write that kind of thing,' Rosa told Mrs Barton.

'What *do* you write?' came back from a woman with a steely look in her eye.

'Well, yesterday I was on the story about the girl who was found strangled on Aberlady beach and today I interviewed her mother,' Rosa told her and she visibly reeled before exclaiming, 'How awful for you! Maybe they'll move you to the Woman's Page soon.'

As they were driving back to the New Town, she and Roddy did not discuss his mother. When they passed Queen Street, Rosa remembered Sylvia and decided to commit the cardinal sin of people who meet doctors socially. She'd pick his brains on a medical question.

'How bad is it if someone of my age is diagnosed with leukaemia?' she suddenly asked and he nearly drove off the road, before he replied, 'You haven't been diagnosed, have you?'

'No, of course not. It's a friend of mine.'

'How old is she?'

Rosa said, 'Twenty-eight. She's getting blood transfusions.'

'How often?'

'About every month I think . . . She says she gets very tired between transfusions. She looks quite thin and pale actually.'

'I'm afraid that if she's being transfused so frequently there can't be much hope. Is she a close friend of yours?'

'I met her recently and like her a lot.'

'Is she married?' he asked and Rosa shook her head as she said, 'No.'

'Then tell her to enjoy herself as much as possible, do all the things she wants to do.'

She understood what he was telling her. 'Oh God, isn't life cruel?' she said and tears rose in her eyes. All her sorrows seemed to descend on her at once – Iain's lack of fidelity, her foolish infatuation with him, Sadie's tragic death and awful life with that dreadful mother, the cruelty of human existence. *Maybe I'm not totally hard yet*, she thought.

Eight

A cruel frost had the city in its grip when Rosa drew back her bedroom curtains at half past six on Monday morning. Because it was not yet light the street lights glittered on frozen puddles at the side of the road, and the cold made her breath hang like a mist around her as she hurried about, lighting the little stove to make a cup of tea. After breakfasting on tea and a digestive biscuit, she was out of the house and heading for the Old Town before Mrs Ross was awake.

No one else had arrived in the office when she got there. Her note for Jack still lay on his table, and she sat down to add to the story with a description of her meeting with Sadie's mother. Other reporters drifted in eventually, some, especially Mike, looking very hung-over. Then Jack appeared, wearing a black plush fedora and wrapped up in a huge camel-hair coat that made him look like a giant teddy bear.

He ignored his staff and went into his glass-walled private office alongside the newsroom, where his Australian secretary, Big Stella, was languidly varnishing her fingernails. Rosa sat at her desk with her heart hammering until he reappeared and began looking at the papers on his worktable.

First of all he lifted her note about Sadie, read it, stared across at her and said, 'This is a bit late. The *Express* and the *Mail* both carried her name this morning – and a photo. The police put out a press notice on her yesterday.'

'But I've done an interview with her mother too. I've got it here,' she said brandishing a sheet of copy paper.

He raised one eyebrow and said, 'Let's see it.'

She handed it over, standing beside him as he read: *A weeping mother cursed the person responsible for her daughter's brutal murder yesterday. 'I hope he burns in hell,' said Mrs Elizabeth Jamieson (33), whose daughter Sadie (17) was found strangled at Aberlady Beach on New Year's Eve. The grieving Mrs Jamieson, who lives alone in Edinburgh's Roxburgh Close, High Street, was told of her only child's death by two policemen . . .*

He nodded. 'It's not bad. But miss out the hell bit, our strait-laced readers won't stand for that. What's she like?'

'She's awful, a drunken tart.'

'Of course she isn't. She's a grief-stricken widow mourning her beloved child. Write it again and lay it on thick. She's not going to complain so long as we make her sound good.'

So she laid it on as thick as she could force herself, depicting Sadie's mother as a tragic figure and watering down her phraseology. Because the *Dispatch* always put people's ages in brackets beside their names even if they were only witnesses to an accident, it was necessary to make a guess at Betty's age but on reflection Rosa changed her original estimate to thirty-eight because readers who did their maths would realize what sort of mourning martyr they were dealing with if she made her too young. Adding on a few years might give her credibility.

Jack was pleased with her story, though of course he didn't say so, but only handed the carbon to a copy boy and said, 'Tell one of the photographers to go along to Roxburgh Close and get this woman's picture.'

Rosa slunk away, trying to look inconspicuous in case he hit on the idea of sending her too because the prospect of going back to that horrible-smelling room was not enticing. The photographer who came slouching in a few minutes later was tall, skinny Bob the Basher, who had as bad a case of news fever as Mike and who certainly would not want a woman tagging along with him on a story.

He looked across at Rosa and asked, 'What's she like?'

'Difficult,' said Rosa, 'and probably drunk.' She didn't think the Basher had much of a chance of winning round Betty.

'Not your Morningside type then,' he said cheerfully. Amazingly, less than an hour later, he was back with a dramatic shot of Sadie's mother staring mournfully out of the opening of Roxburgh Close. The bleak nobility of her face and the way her hands were clasped together made her look like the epitome of tragedy. She was hardly recognizable as the woman Sylvia and Rosa met the previous day.

The picture, blown up large, was on the front page of the first edition with a photo credit for the Basher and another by-line for Rosa. When it came up from the presses, Jack permitted himself a half-smile in Rosa's direction and she was transported by delight.

In the canteen at lunchtime she and Patricia sat down beside the Basher, and Rosa said with genuine admiration, 'That girl's mother was an awful woman. How did you get her to pose for such an affecting photo?'

He grinned. 'She was hung-over, so I bought a bottle of whisky and promised her she could have it if she let me take her picture. She looks so mournful because she was worried in case I wouldn't ante up with the Scotch. Jack says I can put it on my expenses.'

'You'll go far,' she told him.

'So will you. None of the other papers knew about the mother till your story came out. I was the first photographer up there. They'd all gone down to Flora's because she identified the body but she's giving nothing away.'

When the Basher left, Lawrie joined the girls and started on his usual tack of boasting about the number of girls he'd seduced during the New Year jollifications. His sexual appetite was apparently insatiable, and they found it difficult to believe his stories and boastings of success because he was small, dark and troll-like, certainly not heart-throb material.

'How do you win all those girls over? What do you say to them?' Patricia asked in amazement.

'I make them laugh, that works every time. Then I say, "Fancy a fuck?" and it's amazing how often they say yes.'

'It wouldn't work with us,' said Rosa primly.

Lawrie scoffed, 'What makes you so sure? Anyway you're both peculiar. There's something wrong with the pair of you. Neither of you girls have had an orgasmic experience yet, have you?'

Patricia kept her cool and arched her eyebrows as she said, 'I wouldn't be so stupid as to tell *you* about it if I had.'

'Come on,' said Lawrie, 'you're still a virgin, aren't you? It's bothering you. I can tell. Get rid of it. You'll be a different woman when you've taken the plunge. Free yourself of your Church of Scotland guilt.'

'I'm a Catholic actually,' she said haughtily.

'So am I and that's worse,' Lawrie asserted. 'But it's better once you give it up. Your health will improve, you'll get rid of those spots.'

Instinctively both of the girls put their hands to their faces and chorused anxiously, 'What spots?'

He guffawed, 'Virgins! Both of you. I knew it.'

'I hate you, Lawrie,' said Patricia coldly. They turned their backs on him and began listening to an animated conversation going on at the next table.

The chief talker was Eileen, head supervisor in the copy-taking office, and she was banging on about the shortcomings of her staff. Eileen, the bitchiest of the copy-takers, was coy and flirtatious with the men reporters but nasty to the girls. Rosa dreaded calling in with a story and getting her on the other end of the line. She managed to make it seem that all the copy being dictated was rubbish. Even though she said nothing, it was the irritating way she breathed that conveyed her contempt.

Now she was complaining to her colleagues: 'No sense of responsibility, that's the trouble with those girls. They're only out for a good time, they've no commitment! When I think how dedicated I was at that age! I'd never dream of not turning up for work without a very good reason . . .' The companions all made noises of agreement and nodded their heads.

Patricia looked at Rosa and whispered, 'Would dropping dead be a good enough reason for not turning up?'

'Probably not but she should try it,' Rosa replied and they both giggled, but stopped when Eileen glared at them. She had the power to mess up their phoned-in copy or fail to deliver it at all. She could get them fired if she tried hard enough.

With a flounce of the head, she gave them the evil eye and turned back to her table. 'Two of them never came in today. That flibbertigibbet Patsy doesn't surprise me but I expected better of Marie. Not even a phone call. How am I expected to man the phones with two girls absent?'

Now Rosa was listening hard, wondering what could have happened to Marie. She was all right when last seen at the North British Hotel. Later in the afternoon, she walked along the corridor to the phone room and stuck her head round the door to enquire, 'Marie about yet?'

Eileen, wearing earphones, was sitting at a desk in the middle of the floor with a pile of paper beside her typewriter and a fretful look on her face. 'No, she isn't, though we could do with her. She's not shown up all day, and she's not had the courtesy to ring in either.'

'Have you rung her?' Rosa asked.

'Rung her? Why should I? It's only courtesy for her to ring me. Anyway I can't ring her, she hasn't got a phone at home.'

'Where in Sighthill does she live?' Rosa asked, worried because she left Marie alone in the middle of the night. *I should have driven her home*, she thought.

Eileen was very irritated. 'I've no idea where she lives. Lillian, one of the other girls, knows, but she's off sick till tomorrow. At least she's really sick – she's been off all week.

I'll give that Marie something to think about when she does come back – *if* she comes back.'

Frowning, Rosa went back to the newsroom. She'd always liked Marie and after their night of dancing in the Gardens she'd liked her even more. They were set to become real friends. Over and over again, she accused herself of failure in friendship by not driving Marie home – perhaps she caught a chill, perhaps her taxi was in an accident . . . Things go in threes, whispered a superstitious little voice in the back of her mind – Sadie Jamieson gets killed; Sylvia tells me she's dying of a terrible disease; and now Marie's absent from work. What's wrong with her?

Imagination ran riot, and she had to remind herself not to be stupid. Marie was probably ill or hung-over – there was a lot of flu about – perhaps she had simply decided to take a day off. Without a phone in her house there would be no way she could contact the office. She'd be back tomorrow.

The practical part of Rosa said, *Get a grip on yourself. Don't be silly.*

Nine

All that night she tossed and turned, drifting in and out of sleep, plagued by nightmares that made no sense because they were filled with people she was unable to recognize but ought to know. Just when she was about to see them clearly, they drifted away.

Waking exhausted at seven o'clock when it was still dark, she was relieved to remember that Tuesday was her day off. She didn't have to get up yet. The world outside seemed strangely still, so she lay dozing for a while and, when she looked at the clock again, it was half past eight, but still deathly quiet. What was wrong? There should be the noise of traffic and people hurrying past the house on their way to work, but today there was only silence.

When she pulled open the curtains, she stepped back in surprise because the glare from outside was dazzling. Snow had fallen during the night, muffling the city in a blanket of white. All tiredness was forgotten and a tremendous excitement welled up inside her because she loved snow.

She leaned on the window sill, staring down at the street, and allowed herself to be carried back in memory to the time before her mother died. She'd loved snow too and Rosa remembered being wrapped up in layer upon layer of woollen clothes and taken out by her mother into a magic world. She was pulled along on a little sledge and helped her mother to pelt her father with snowballs. Her mother's face had been bright and happy, plump, red-cheeked and smiling, not gaunt and grey as it was before she died.

The snow brought happy memories back most vividly and Rosa realized that the person she'd been seeking through her dreams during the night was her mother – perhaps subconsciously she'd known it was snowing. She was able to summon her up most vividly when it snowed.

Poor Mother, she died too young. The cancer that carried her off at thirty-three was swift and inexorable. She fell ill in the spring of the year Rosa was twelve and by November she was dead. No one warned her daughter what was about to happen and the word 'cancer' was never uttered in the house. Even the mourners at the funeral spelt it out rather than say it.

Tears blinded Rosa as she stared out at the snow, which her mother would have loved, which she was cheated out of seeing by that cruel illness.

And what about Sylvia? Leukaemia was a kind of cancer, wasn't it? *Perhaps it's because of what happened to my mother that I'm so concerned about her,* she thought and the disquiet of the previous day came flooding back – Sadie, Sylvia and Marie. Three blonde girls. Two of them figures of tragedy . . .What about Marie?

Was she back at work yet? Rosa looked at her watch and saw it was nine o'clock. The office would be in full swing. Mrs Ross did not allow the use of her private phone, though she took messages for Rosa if she approved of the callers – she never passed on messages from Iain, whom she instinctively distrusted.

If Rosa wanted to find out about Marie, she would have to go out and use a phone box. She also wanted to call her father – he must have been in last night's dream too and memories of her mother made her appreciate the depth of his loneliness and continuing grief. They hadn't been in contact since Christmas and suddenly she was desperate to hear his voice for he was the only close relative she had in the world.

Fortunately she'd bought some food the previous evening,

so cornflakes and milk provided an adequate breakfast. Then she piled on three layers of sweaters and stuck her feet into a pair of zip-up fur-lined boots before she braved the arctic conditions outside. The little Morris car looked like an igloo because it was completely covered with snow, and she didn't even try to get into it but set out to walk to the phone box at the end of the street. It was occupied, and she stood flapping her arms across her chest in an effort to make the woman inside finish her call, but she only cast a baleful eye in Rosa's direction and turned her back.

Accepting defeat eventually, she headed uphill towards Queen Street. The next phone box was occupied too, so she kept on going and suddenly was looking across at Sylvia's flat. She plodded over the snow-filled roadway, which was hardly marked because there was so little traffic, and rang the bell. There was a clicking of the lock and when she pushed at the door, it swung open.

Sylvia, standing on the top landing in a red woollen dressing gown, called down, 'What are you doing wandering about in this weather, Rosa?'

She stopped halfway up the first flight and called back, 'How did you know it was me?' Surely a girl like Sylvia would not open the main door to anyone who cared to ring the bell?

'I have a mirror fixed on my window sill. It's a good spy system. Come on up,' was the reply.

There was a lovely smell of fresh coffee in the flat and Rosa was offered a cup. They drank it in the kitchen – all pale green formica and so incredibly tidy that it did not look as if much cooking went on in it – and Sylvia leaned back against the cooker as she said with a smile, 'So what do you want apart from a coffee?'

'Can I use your phone? For a reverse-charge call . . . Every box was occupied, you see, and it's quite urgent . . .'

'Go ahead. It's in the hall.'

The *Scotsman* phone-room number was answered by Eileen.

'Is Marie in?' asked Rosa.

'No she isn't.' Eileen sounded even more bad-tempered than usual.

'Is Lillian in?'

'It's that Makepeace girl, isn't it? What exactly do you want? Do you have copy to dictate? If you haven't, get off the line. We aren't allowed to waste time in idle chatter even if *reporters* are.'

Mumbling apologies, Rosa hung up.

When she went back into the kitchen, Sylvia said, 'You didn't get far with that, did you?'

When the answer was a disconsolate shrug she added, 'Do you want to make any other calls?'

'I was going to phone my father and wish him a Happy New Year, but that can wait. I don't want to add to your phone bill,' said Rosa.

'Why? Where does he live – China?'

'Selkirk actually.'

Sylvia laughed. 'Oh, I think I can afford a call to Selkirk. Go ahead.'

It took ages before her father answered the phone and she guessed he'd probably not been able to find it because, as usual, it would be buried beneath piles of books and papers. 'He-llo?' his suspicious voice said at last.

'Hi, Dad. It's Rosa. Just calling to say Happy New Year.'

He sounded pleased. 'Thank you, dear, and the same to you. Is it snowing in Edinburgh?'

'Yes, there's been a very heavy fall overnight. It looks lovely. Have you got snow?'

'Masses of it, drifts as high as the house.' He was jubilant because he too liked snow.

'Oh dear. I hope you've enough food.'

'I'm fine, I've lots to eat, lots of logs, a couple of bottles of whisky – and I'll be able to try out my latest invention,' was his cheerful reply.

'What is it?' She sounded suspicious and cautious – some

73

of his inventions in the past had exploded, gone on fire or fallen apart when he tried them.

'It's a snowmobile and motorized skis. They'll make our fortune,' he said.

She groaned because she'd heard the invisible fortune mentioned too often in the past. 'Please take care. Don't do anything dangerous. Don't drive off into the snow without telling Eckie where you're going,' she pleaded.

Eckie was a retired shepherd who lived in the nearest cottage – fortunately within shouting distance of her father's house. He was a lovely old man in his eighties who spent his time reading poetry and was particularly fond of Milton, screeds of whose work he could recite by heart. He regarded Rosa's father as a harmless lunatic, but watched out for him. If he got struck in a snowdrift, Eckie would dig him out.

'Don't worry. I'll be fine,' he assured her before he hung up.

'What's your father doing that's causing you so much worry?' Sylvia asked when Rosa returned to the kitchen with her brows furrowed. When told the story, she giggled and looked so young and carefree that Rosa felt stupid when she remembered how worried she'd been about her last night. Perhaps she was not as ill as she feared.

When Rosa began buttoning up her jacket in preparation for going into the snow-filled world again, Sylvia asked, 'Are you still following up the Sadie story?'

'I suppose I am. Today's my day off but Jack, our Editor, likes reporters to be what he calls *self-starters*, and follow things up on their own, so as far as he's concerned, there's no such thing as a day off.'

'In that case, do you want to come down to Flora's place with me? I want to tell Flora about giving the money to that woman and you could talk to the girls about Sadie. They might have some ideas about who killed her,' said Sylvia.

'Flora would never let me in,' said Rosa who knew there

was no chance of her being admitted into Flora's establishment as a reporter.

'She'll be all right if I take you. We don't need to tell her you're a reporter,' said Sylvia.

'But I've seen her in the Burgh Court, she might recognize me,' Rosa protested but Sylvia only laughed.

'I doubt very much if she ever wasted as much as a glance at the press box. Go into the drawing room and wait there till I get dressed. Then I'll take you with me to Danube Street.'

When she reappeared fifteen minutes later she was wearing scarlet and black ski-wear that looked more suitable for the slopes of Zermatt than Edinburgh's New Town. She even had on dark glasses. The only thing she lacked was a pair of skis. Rosa was speechless with admiration.

Fortunately it was downhill all the way to Stockbridge and they slipped and slid, with Sylvia leading the way. She was so energetic that Rosa became even more convinced that her illness had been exaggerated. The one who seemed unfit was herself as she went panting in Sylvia's wake.

Flora Black's establishment in Danube Street was famous. It was a Georgian house in a once elegant row that was now rather rundown, but still retained remnants of grandeur with an elegant front door standing at the top of a short flight of steps, long windows and fine railings. A Christmas tree with coloured lights blazing filled one of the downstairs front windows.

Sylvia did not go to the main entrance but slipped down to the basement by a flight of iron steps and hammered on the door with her gloved fist.

It was answered by a dark-haired girl in a pink, lace-trimmed negligée. She grinned when she saw her visitor. 'Oh, it's you, Syl. Thank God you're no' a customer,' she said in a broad Edinburgh accent.

'You'll not get many of them today, Jean,' Sylvia answered, laughing too as she stepped inside.

'Ye never can tell. They'll all be fed up wi' the family after Christmas and be needin' a wee bit entertainment. It'll be as busy as the General Assembly when this snow melts,' said the girl and they both laughed again.

Rosa looked puzzled, so Sylvia turned to her and explained, 'During the General Assembly of the Church of Scotland in May the girls here are worked to death. They have queues of ministers in dog collars waiting patiently upstairs for their turn!'

'You're pulling my leg,' said Rosa but both girls shook their heads and protested they were telling the truth.

Gosh, what a story, but the paper would never print it, thought Rosa regretfully.

'Where's Flora?' Sylvia asked Jean.

'She's done a runner. The police and the press have been here all the time asking about Sadie, so she's taken herself off to see her daughter in Perth, the very respectable one that's married to an accountant. She's coming back the day after tomorrow, or so she said,' was the reply.

'I came to tell her I'd given the money to Sadie's mother,' said Sylvia.

'Oh, she knew you'd do it all right. That Jamieson woman's a waste of space. She'll have drunk it all by this time nae doot.' Jean opened a door leading off the hall and they went into a large, warm kitchen with a gas fire burning in the hearth.

Another three girls were sitting there in various stages of undress and their ages ranged from early twenties to late thirties. One was cuddling a large ginger cat, another was painting her toenails, and the third was reading a thin paperback romance with a brightly coloured picture on the cover. All were smoking.

When Sylvia walked in they looked up and smiled at her. She was obviously popular but then they saw Rosa and their faces hardened. Sylvia took over and went straight to the point. 'This is Rosa Makepeace. She's a reporter with the

76

Dispatch and she's writing about Sadie's murder. She'd like to ask you about her,'

'Aw no,' said Jean. 'Nae reporters, nae names. My man doesnae ken what I do during the day.'

'I won't mention any of your names, all I want is to hear anything you know about Sadie and any ideas you might have about who killed her. I promise I won't even say where I got my information,' Rosa said.

Sylvia chipped in: 'She's straight, she's OK.'

Rosa saw them weaken and pressed on: 'Just tell me what Sadie was like.' She thought she already knew the answer to that, but it would start them talking. Their answer was the same as Sylvia's – Sadie was young, guileless, trusting, not too bright, and with the promise of prettiness when she got a bit older and put on some weight.

'She was scared at first but Flora was good with her and picked her clients, none of the odd balls, ye ken. Some of them like wee girls like Sadie,' said the girl in the negligée.

'Didn't she mind – selling herself, that sort of thing?' Rosa asked awkwardly. It was hard to know how to phrase it.

The girl with the cat looked up angrily. 'If she minded, do you think she'd have stayed? She wasnae forced.' Her hair was as red as the fur of the cat on her lap and she looked as dangerous.

'Her mother told her to stay working with Flora till she'd a bit of money put away . . . she said they were going to live in Port Seton in one of thae wee wooden houses near the sea when she'd saved enough. Some chance!' said the girl in the negligée, who was the most approachable of them all.

'Do you think one of her clients might have killed her?' Rosa asked.

All the girls spoke together and sounded anxious, as if they were eager to banish that suspicion completely. 'Oh no! None of them are that sort. Flora's very careful who she lets in.'

The novel-reading girl added, 'Anyway Sadie was out all day before she disappeared. She could have met somebody in the street. Flora was worried when she didn't come back at night, but we thought she'd gone to see her mother.'

'But she didn't. Her mother said Sadie hadn't been there,' Rosa said.

'You can't trust a word Betty Jamieson utters. She'd not want to let on Sadie'd been there because the lassie probably took her some money and she was afraid that if Flora thought she had cash, she wouldna' let her have any more,' said the red-haired girl, staring at Rosa with bright hazel-coloured, very angry-looking eyes.

'Do you think she could have met her killer in Roxburgh Close or the High Street then?' Rosa asked.

'How do I know? I was here grafting my arse off. I only know she wasn't in this house and hadn't been since morning. Flora's soft with her but the rest of us have to graft, believe me. Sadie went off about dinner time wearing a scarf I lent her and she never came back,' snapped the girl with red hair.

'Was the scarf found on the body?' asked Rosa.

'Nothing was found on the body. I asked the policeman who came here about it but he said they found her clothes scattered across the beach but no scarf. I liked that scarf too. It came from Jenners.' The eyes still blazed.

'What was it like?' Rosa wanted to know.

'It was silk with red and white flowers on a blue background. A bonny thing. I said I want it back if they find it.'

Amazed that the loss of a scarf seemed more important to the angry girl than the brutal murder of a friend – and even more amazed that she would consider wearing it again – Rosa directed her attention to the other girls.

'What sort of men use this house?' she asked, again not sure how to phrase the question.

'Gents! Nobs. Nothing but the best. You'd be amazed if you knew who comes here. Poor souls, some of them just want to get a bit of comfort or to talk – it's often their wives' faults,' said the girl with the novel.

'Give me some names. I won't print them,' said Rosa, trying her luck, but they all laughed and the red-haired girl scoffed, 'You must be joking!'

'You can't blame her for trying,' said Sylvia, joining in the laughter, but the red-haired girl didn't laugh. She leaned towards the stranger and said balefully, 'You'd better watch yourself. You're playing with fire. If some of them hear you've been down here asking questions, you could be in trouble.'

'Oh, I'm not scared,' said Rosa with bravado. 'Besides the police will probably catch the killer soon.'

'That all depends who did it, doesn't it? Some folk in Edinburgh are above the law. Just remember that,' was the baleful reply and Rosa wondered what made this girl so hostile.

They were given cups of instant coffee – not ground beans like Sylvia's – who was sipping hers with every sign of enthusiasm as she asked, 'Any news of a funeral? Has there been any decision about that? It should be done soon because Betty won't be able to keep her hands off Flora's money for long.'

The girl in the negligée nodded. 'Jock was up in the High Street last night and somebody told him it'll be soon.'

'Who's Jock?' Rosa asked, and the girls chorused, 'Our doorman . . . the bouncer. A copper he met in a pub said they're probably releasing the body tomorrow or the next day.'

'Who'll go?' Sylvia asked.

'Flora might if the police loosen up on her, and Jock too, and some of us, but not all because the house won't be closed,' was the reply.

Rosa's surprise showed on her face and the red-haired girl grinned maliciously as she said, 'You think that's bad? Flora never even closed when her husband died. He was laid out in the parlour upstairs and we went on working down here.'

'That's true. I remember. It's always business as usual in this place. Like the Windmill,' agreed Sylvia, lifting her gloves off the floor, where she'd dropped them when they arrived. When she stood up and pulled on her ski jacket, Rosa saw again how very thin she was.

'Poor Sadie. When you hear about her funeral, let me know please,' Sylvia said to the girl in the pink negligée, who nodded and said, 'OK, I won't forget.'

When the basement door was opened to let the visitors out, freezing-cold air rushed into the house and the prospect of trudging back uphill through the snow appalled Rosa. It obviously intimidated Sylvia too for she took one look at the desolation outside, then turned back into the hall to call out, 'Jean, be an angel and ring for a taxi.'

'They'll no' come out in this weather,' was the shouted reply.

'At least try,' pleaded Sylvia in a voice that suddenly sounded desperately weary. Jean came into the narrow hall and walked past them to where a black telephone was lying on the bottom step of a stairway leading to the upper storey. 'He says he'll try as a favour to Flora,' she shouted back after a few minutes.

Miraculously the taxi got through and, slipping and sliding, took them to Queen Street. At her front door, Sylvia's enthusiasm and energy seemed to have drained away and she did not invite Rosa back up to her flat.

'Take the taxi on to your digs, I'll pay for it,' she said, leaning weakly against her door jamb, but Rosa shook her head. 'No thanks. You've been great. I'll walk home from here.'

In fact she enjoyed the slithery slide downhill because it took her back to childhood days and she did have plenty to think about.

Ten

On Wednesday morning the snow had started to melt but the roads were very slippery and dangerous, so Rosa walked to work up treacherous hills, and made poor time, with the result that she was later than usual. As soon as she got into the office there were two disappointments waiting for her – first, she discovered that Marie had still not returned to work, and second, that Mike had appropriated the Sadie story. In journalism, he said, you couldn't afford to be late or take a day off.

He had some information that he wanted to write down but he wouldn't tell her what it was. 'It's my story now, Makepeace,' he snapped.

When he wanted to begin writing, however, he couldn't find his typewriter and went storming round the desks, examining everybody's machine, but all of the other reporters had put identifying marks on theirs and guarded them jealously.

While he was angrily looking, Patricia came in and discovered that her machine was also missing, so she joined the search party. Then one of the subs called out that another typewriter had gone from his end of the room, and when Harriet arrived to prepare her Woman's Column, she threw a tantrum.

'Who's taken my typewriter? I've a deadline to meet. How am I expected to do it without a typewriter? This office is a madhouse!' she screamed with her eyes rolling manically and her hands gripping her tightly permed hair.

'Look at her, a typical menopausal spinster. That's what'll

happen to you if you don't have enough sex,' Lawrie whispered to Rosa.

For once, Jack looked frightened by the extravagance of Harriet's behaviour, so he turned to Gil for help.

Gil drew himself up to his full five foot five and surveyed the staff. 'Exactly who has lost their typewriters?' he called out.

Four hands were raised. The rest of them sat with their arms defensively round their machines. Mike looked almost as mad as Harriet, for his eyes were popping and he was padding up and down like a caged animal, so eager was he to start banging out his story about the hunt for Sadie's killer. He turned to Rosa and demanded, 'Give me your machine. It's your duty.'

'No way!' she told him and clutched the typewriter even tighter. *Serves you right*, she thought.

Jack and Gil had their heads together and muttered away until Gil announced, 'Mike, run up to that pawn shop near the council buildings and see if he's got any typewriters for sale. I saw one in his window the other day.'

Jack delved into his wallet and produced three of the large, impressive-looking bank notes printed on white paper that, going by their appearance, should be worth far more than five pounds. 'If he has any, buy them, buy them all,' he said, tossing the money to Mike.

In revenge, Mike said to Rosa, 'I can't carry more than one at a time. You'd better come too, if you're strong enough to carry a typewriter.' She got up reluctantly when she saw Jack nodding in agreement. She mustn't plead physical weakness.

The High Street pawnshop had one window looking out on to the pavement, so low down it was necessary to bend to see into it. Piled inside was a weird assortment of chipped enamel pots and pans, a plaster figure of a boy with an Alsatian dog, a trumpet, a guitar with broken strings, assorted clothes and grimy blankets, a pair of ice skates, and a framed

Victorian print showing a garland of pink roses and ivy round the slogan 'Help Me God'.

They peered at this collection through the smeared glass and Rosa said, 'I quite fancy that picture actually.'

Mike laughed bitterly and quipped, 'It would be more suitable if it said "God Help Us".' Then he pointed with a trembling hand at the back of the display. 'Look!' he shouted.

There it was, a black-lacquered portable typewriter exactly like the ones in the office. Mike was still pointing. 'Look at it. That's my machine!'

'It can't be,' said Rosa.

'It *is*,' I tell you. I put a coloured sticker on its side and it's still there. Some bugger's pawned my machine. Let's go in!'

The door had a bell above it and when he thrust his forceful way through, it set up a terrific ringing that summoned the pawnbroker from the back. He stood behind his protective metal screen and shouted out, 'What do you want?' for they looked frightening – at least Mike did because he was so big. The pawnbroker's finger was hovering over a bell on the counter. If he rang it, he'd summon policemen from the station on the other side of the road and they'd probably be arrested.

'I want that typewriter,' stormed Mike, pointing at the window.

'You can't have it. The man who brought it in might redeem it.'

'He bloody well can't. It's mine – or at least it's the *Dispatch*'s and I want it back.'

The pawnbroker was obviously intimidated by Mike's size and rage so he said, 'Calm down, son. Take it. I thought there was something dodgy about it anyway when it was brought in.'

'Have you any more?' Rosa piped up.

'I might have.'

'We're looking for another three that've gone missing from

our office,' she said.

The pawnbroker sighed deeply. 'I might have guessed. There's three more just like that one in the back, all pawned by the same man. If you give me eight pounds ten, I'll let you have the lot. I probably shouldn't have taken them but I know him. He's been in before and he always redeems his stuff in good time . . . honest, I didn't know they were nicked.'

Mike brandished the money and the deal was done, but Rosa was still curious. 'Who brought them in?' she asked.

'You're not going to report me, are you?' asked the old man and she shook her head. 'Then, all right, it was one of my regulars, a very pleasant gentleman writer. He often leaves his typewriter with me over the weekend but usually buys it back on Mondays. I'd no reason to think he wouldn't do the same again, but he was in and out of here more often than usual during the festive season.' The pawnbroker was obviously worried in case the police got involved and he was charged with receiving stolen goods.

Mike and Rosa both reassured him and she said, 'It's all right now we've got them back. What does the man who pawned them look like?'

'Tall and thin with very fair hair. Funnily spoken – colonial accent I'd say.'

'Alan!' they chorused and started to laugh. Their hilarity reassured the pawnbroker, who hauled three more portables out of his back premises and pushed them across the counter to them. 'I'll get my laddie to help you carry them down the road,' he said, glad to be rid of the incriminating goods.

On their way back to the office, they agreed not to tell Jack who stole the typewriters but he was too sharp for them, or perhaps he already had a good idea what happened to the machines. He'd known Alan longer than any of them, after all.

'OK, who pawned them?' he demanded, casting his eye round the reporters' room. Everyone looked innocent but Alan was conspicuous by his absence.

A short search turned him up, asleep like the dormouse at *Alice in Wonderland*'s tea party, with his head lying on a big table in the library. When wakened and accused, he casually owned up to pawning the office machinery. Jack took him into his office and tore a strip off him, but to everyone's surprise, did not send him packing. Alan's erudition always turned aside Jack's wrath, and it was not the first time he'd helped himself to his employer's fixtures and fittings.

Eleven

In the excitement of the typewriter hunt Rosa forgot about Marie, but just before two o'clock she slipped along to the copy room in search of her friend. The morning shift was leaving and the night girls were coming in. Thankfully there was no sign of Eileen.

'Has Marie turned up yet?' Rosa asked one of the girls who was pulling on heavy snow boots. She shook her head and said, 'No.'

'Is she ill?'

The girl shrugged. 'We don't know. She never rang in and Eileen's hopping mad. Marie'll probably get her cards when she does come back.'

'Is Lillian around?' Rosa asked.

'She's here, but she's gone to the toilet right now. She'll be back in a minute though.'

When the plump, friendly Lillian came back, she frowned when Rosa said she was worried about Marie. 'You see, I left her at the N.B. on New Year's morning but I should have driven her home and she's not been in to work since. Eileen says you know where she lives. I thought I'd go there and find out if she's OK,' Rosa explained.

Lillian nodded. 'I heard she's been off when I got in today, but I was away too – I had the flu and I've not been out of the house since Christmas. I live near Marie, so I can look in on her on my way home tonight. Give me your phone number and I'll ring you when I find out what's happened. I'm sure it's nothing serious.'

86

'That's good of you,' said Rosa and gave Mrs Ross's number to Lillian, hoping that her landlady's good mood was still lasting.

Instead of going straight home, she went with the men to the Cockburn for sandwiches and to talk about Alan's theft of the typewriters, so it was eight o'clock by the time she was back in Northumberland Street. Mrs Ross was waiting for her. The moment the front door opened, she shot out of her sanctum and said, 'That man who drives the big cars came to see you.'

She meant Iain, whom she did not like. She thought Rosa should stick with Roddy.

'Oh yes,' was the guarded reply. Rosa had expected to hear from him eventually.

'I told him I didn't know when you'd be back.' Rosa reopened the front door and looked out into the street. There was nothing parked near the house except her own lonely-looking little car.

Mrs Ross went on, 'And a girl called Lillian phoned for you. She left this number and said to tell you that Marie Lang hasn't been home since New Year's Eve.' She handed over a piece of paper with a phone number on it.

Rosa felt a spasm of disquiet as she took the note and Mrs Ross noticed her reaction, asking, 'Are you all right, dear? Who's Marie Lang?'

'It's a girl in the office. She's not been in to work since hogmanay. I should have taken her home on New Year's morning but I didn't. I'm worried about her.'

'You can use my phone if you like,' said Mrs Ross, which made Rosa realize she must look upset.

Lillian answered the call and said, 'You're right, it's a bit odd. Marie's disappeared. She lives with her sister and brother-in-law and they were expecting her back on New Year's Day but she didn't turn up. They thought she was staying with friends and didn't bother but they're getting worried now.'

They took their time, thought Rosa, but she asked Lillian, 'What's her address?' and wrote it down before she hung up. She was standing in the hall wondering if she was brave enough to drive on the treacherous, slushy roads outside when there was a knock at the door. Mrs Ross answered it and Iain was standing on the doorstep. Parked behind Rosa's car was an enormously long Armstrong Siddeley with huge chrome headlights. It looked like a duchess feeling distinctly uncomfortable in the company of a charlady.

Without waiting to find out what he wanted, she grabbed his arm. 'Thank God you've come. Take me to Sighthill,' she said.

'OK,' he replied. He'd drive anybody anywhere – especially a girl.

They were at the Binns' end of Princes Street before he asked, 'Where exactly in Sighthill are we going, by the way?'

She read out the address, which meant nothing to either of them. 'Let's just go to the housing estate and I'll ask when we get there,' she told him.

They asked five different people before they found the street where Marie lived. All the houses looked exactly the same, anonymous blocks of pebble-dashed council housing, four homes in each section – two up and two down – with square, sterile gardens where nothing but grass seemed to grow.

Marie lived on a ground floor. Lights were shining between drawn curtains at the windows and a dog barked when Rosa knocked on the door. The woman who answered it was a tired-looking, slightly older version of Marie – thin, blue-eyed and blonde – but without the younger girl's vivacity.

'I'm looking for Marie,' said Rosa and the woman sighed.

'So's everybody. She's not here. What do you want? I'm her sister and I'll tell her you called when she comes back.'

'I work with her and I'm worried because she hasn't been into the office since New Year's Eve. I was with her at the Tron and in Princes Street Gardens that night and dropped her off to wait for a taxi at the N.B. I feel very bad that I didn't bring her home in my car and hope she's all right.' Rosa didn't add that her anxiety was made worse because of Sadie Jamieson's murder.

Marie's sister looked over her shoulder at Iain's car and said in amazement, 'Is *that* your car?'

'No, mine's a Morris Minor. A friend brought me tonight,' said Rosa sharply, wondering how Marie's sister could give any thought to the sort of car she drove when her sister was missing.

The door was opened wider and the woman said, 'I'm Alice. Come in and bring your friend if you like.'

Rosa went in but didn't invite Iain, saying he could wait in the car because she wouldn't be long. Marie's sister led the way up a narrow lobby into a main room where a young man and two small children were watching television. A white dog sprawled on the hearthrug. The room was warm and tidy, home-like and comfortable.

One of the children moved along the sofa so she could sit down and she said, 'My name's Rosa Makepeace and I work at the *Dispatch*. Everyone there is wondering why Marie hasn't been to work . . .'

Alice said, 'This is my husband, Sandy Collins, and my children, Sally and Tom. We've not seen Marie for three days but we thought she was staying with one of her girl friends, maybe Kate, who lives not far away – she does that sometimes during the holidays and she doesn't have to tell us. We didn't know she hadn't been to work till her friend Lillian came in tonight and told us. We haven't a phone, you see. Marie's lived here since our mother died last year. They used to be three doors along the road but when Mum died, Marie gave up that house . . . No point paying two rents, is there?'

Rosa nodded in agreement and asked, 'Where does her friend Kate live?'

'Two streets away, not far.'

'Do you know if Marie went to Kate's when she left me?'

'Sandy went along there after Lillian called but Kate hasn't seen Marie since New Year's Eve either.' Alice's calmness was amazing, and Rosa wondered if Marie's absence from the household was a sort of pre-arranged respite for them all, allowing Marie a bit of freedom and letting Alice and Sandy enjoy being alone as a family for a bit. Having a sister around all the time must be an annoyance, especially since the house was small and anything said or done in any of the rooms would be heard in all the others. Privacy would be impossible.

'Have you reported her disappearance to the police?' she asked and they stared at her in surprise.

'But she might come back any minute,' protested Sandy.

'And she's grown up. She's not a bairn. She's often away for two or three days,' added his wife.

'How old is she?' asked Rosa.

'Twenty,' said Alice. Marie looked younger than that. Rosa remembered the childish-looking Sadie and her clients with their special tastes.

'I think you should report that she's gone missing,' she told them.

Alice nodded, 'Yes, we're going to. If she doesn't come back tonight, Sandy'll call in at the High Street police station on his way to work tomorrow morning. He's a clerk in the City Chambers, you see.' They obviously thought Rosa was fussing about nothing for they knew Marie's habits. It was probably not unusual for her to go off for a night or two, if not with the friend they knew, perhaps with another they didn't.

When Rosa left, she saw them opening the curtains and crowding into their sitting-room window as she walked down the path and climbed into Iain's magnificent car. He started the engine and she sat staring so grimly ahead that he looked sideways at her before he said, 'Cheer up. You look awful. What about going to the Peacock for a drink?'

The Peacock Inn in Newhaven had been a favourite haunt of theirs since they first started going out together. Rosa stared at him, suddenly aware that his preference for taking her to out-of-the-way places like Newhaven could be because there was little likelihood of meeting people he knew there.

Yet tonight she was lonely and worried. She badly needed someone to talk to – even him – and anyway, she was grateful for his willingness to drive her to Sighthill without asking any questions. She nodded and said, 'It seems that the only places I go to these days are pubs.'

'Could be worse,' he said and as they drove along, she gathered her wits, relaxed her expression (mindful of his statement that she looked awful), and tried to appear cool towards him though his physical presence was wreaking its usual havoc on her heart. 'Thanks for giving me a lead to Sylvia,' she said.

'Did you meet her? Quite a girl, isn't she?' he replied.

'Yes, I like her,' she said and described their outing to Danube Street through the snow.

'She seems to have made a big impression on you,' he said.

'She has. I don't care how she makes her living. I think she's got her head screwed on. She's not a loser like some of those girls,' she said, reflecting that even the toughest of the girls in Danube Street had a downtrodden vulnerability and resentment that was missing in Sylvia.

She wondered what Sadie had really been like. Was she an innocent or another cowed female who took the easy way out, another victim? Probably.

When they were settled at a quiet table in the Peacock Inn, Iain bought two drinks and draped himself casually in his chair before saying, 'What were we doing chasing around Sighthill anyway?'

'I'm worried about a girl I work with. It'll probably all blow over but I joined up with her and her friends after I left you at St Giles, and then I took her to get a taxi at the

91

N.B. Nobody seems to have set eyes on her since. She's disappeared.'

'Oh, don't worry,' he assured her. 'She'll turn up. They always do. Listen, there's something I have to tell you. That's why I went to your digs tonight.'

Of course he must have had a reason for seeking her out at Mrs Ross's, she thought, staring at him and realizing that he too was looking unusually serious.

'What is it? Have you lost your job?' she asked.

He shook his head. 'No, it's worse than that. Hold on to your hat. I'm getting married.'

It wasn't really a surprise of course, considering the way Brenda Hamilton-Prentice had behaved at St Giles. Oddly enough, her first impulse was to laugh sarcastically, but that didn't last long.

'Who's the bride?' she asked steelily, though she knew the answer to that too.

'Brenda Hamilton-Prentice. The bailie's daughter.'

She was right – *the girl in green.*

'She's pregnant of course,' she said and he nodded.

'And her father will kill you if you don't make an honest woman of her.'

This time he shook his head. 'Not really, he's against it but she's determined to marry me. He's only going along with it for her sake and because of the family's reputation. He and I don't get on. He thinks I'm after her money.'

Mr Hamilton-Prentice, town councillor and magistrate, owned a string of electrical shops around the city and, since everyone's aspiration was to own a television set, he was making a fortune. His daughter, Brenda, was his only child, his heiress.

'And aren't you after her money?' Rosa enquired nastily, lifting her glass and taking a gulp at it.

Iain shrugged. 'To be honest, it helps, but I'm not keen on getting married to anybody right now. For God's sake I'm young, only twenty-eight.'

'Old enough. And marriage will certainly restrict your social life,' she said. You could cut glass with her tone of voice. He looked even more gloomy and she leaned back in her chair to let the jibe go down before she continued, 'And don't tell me. You'll be getting married in St Giles.'

'Actually we did think about it but that takes time to arrange.'

'And time is something you don't have on your side with junior knocking at the door,' she said and laughed loudly to hide her misery.

He bristled. 'Don't be such a bitch, Rosa,' he said.

'How did you expect me to behave? Do you want me to weep? Commit hara-kiri? You've not brought me here to ask me to be a bridesmaid, have you?' she snapped back, remembering the times he'd sworn eternal love for her and she was stupid enough to half-believe him. Thank God she'd not given in and slept with him, thank God for cowardice and ignorance! The next time she saw Lawrie, she'd tell him that acne was a cheap price to pay for an escape like hers.

Iain was looking offended. 'I don't know why you're being so bitchy. You didn't take me seriously, did you? You never seemed to anyway. I brought you here tonight to explain about St Giles. I really wanted to go to the service with you and I didn't know she'd be there – she said she was having an early night . . .'

'Understandable in her condition,' said Rosa.

'I'd no idea she was pregnant till she told me out there on the pavement.' He was flustered, that was obvious. The idea of marriage and fatherhood was not appealing.

'I suppose the baby is definitely yours,' she asked and he drew himself up as if the very idea of one of his women granting her favours to someone else was unthinkable.

'Of course it is,' he said.

'And her father'll have you run out of town if you don't marry her. Don't worry, one day you'll probably be a town councillor too, a pillar of respectability, cheating on her, with her old man's business behind you – don't tell me you haven't thought about that . . .' She could map his life out for him and for the first time felt relief that there was no part in it for her.

A tide of red rose in his cheeks and he stared balefully at her. 'Give it a rest,' he said, looking over his shoulder to see if they were being overheard.

'Nobody knows you're here, do they? That's why you like it. How long has it been going on with her?' Rosa asked in a quieter tone and, relieved, he answered, 'A couple of months, ever since she came with her father to buy a car. That's when he said I cheeked him, but she stood up for me. She phoned me the next day and it went on from there.'

Her tone hardened again. 'That'll be the story of your life. *It went on from there.* Well, sorry to disappoint you but I'm not going to throw a fit of hysterics. In fact I don't give a damn.'

'You really are a hard nut,' he snapped. 'You'd better watch out or you'll turn into your friend Sylvia – so sharp you might cut yourself.'

'I'd rather be Sylvia than your intended wife, Miss Pea Brain 1956,' she said.

'You're so smart. What makes you think she's a pea brain?' he asked. They were really squaring up for a fight now.

She leaned across the table towards him and said very loudly, 'She must be a pea brain or she wouldn't be marrying you.'

'Better a pea brain than a bitch,' he retorted. 'My advice to you is find out more about the company you keep. Your friend Sylvia has some strange associates. Keep away from her, Rosa, or you might find yourself in a situation where your fancy university degree won't help you.'

They glared at each other across the table, Rosa seething with fury and rage at her own stupidity. Iain didn't look like Burt Lancaster anymore. Instead he looked like a seedy car salesman with an eye for the women. She wanted to get away from him, and with as much dignity as she could muster, she rose, grabbed her coat from the back of the chair and stalked to the door. He made no move to stop her.

Fortunately there was a taxi dropping off more customers at the entrance. When they got out, she hopped in and told the driver to take her to Northumberland Street. *That's the last time I show my face in the Peacock*, she thought.

Leaning back in the seat, she gathered her wits. It was as if Iain had stabbed her but she could not deny that her hurt was mixed with relief because the only way she would ever break with him completely would be if he did something unforgivable like this. While he went on committing half-sins, things she could not prove, he could have kept her dangling.

Thoughts tumbled around in her mind like coloured balls in a tombola and she didn't know which one to take out first, but it was a comfort at least that she had no desire to weep.

Twelve

She slept like a log, which was a relief considering the traumatic day she'd spent, and in the morning she found that a deep frost, which set in overnight, had turned the roads leading uphill from the New Town into slides of sheer ice. Trying to drive over them would be very unwise, so again she trudged up to Princes Street, passing cars slewed this way and that across the roads as she went.

The sky was a piercing blue and when she paused at the junction of George Street and Hanover Street, she was awed by the jagged black silhouette of the Old Town snaking down-hill from the Castle. Edinburgh was such a beautiful place, it was hard to believe that murders could be committed, hearts broken and bad things happen in it.

In the office, Patricia was at her desk with the morning newspapers spread out on her desk. 'Look at this,' she said pointing to the *Daily Express*. Leaning over her shoulder, Rosa read that an engagement had been announced between the film actress Grace Kelly and Prince Rainier of Monaco. Every imaginable cliché was raked up by the writers commenting on the event – starting with 'fairy-tale romance' and going on to 'Grace's Prince Charming'.

'He doesn't look much like a Prince Charming to me, more like the frog,' said Patricia sceptically, but the girls read every word of the reports because both of them were brooding over broken hearts, and took comfort in the possibility that a dream lover might be waiting for them as well.

When Rosa consulted the day's diary, she found she was

assigned to the Burgh Court, the dogsbody job. By sending her to the least important court, old Bob, the Chief Reporter, was taking her down a peg for her scoop hunting.

The court started at ten o'clock, so she walked up to the High Street police station where it was housed in a modest room on the ground floor. The press sat on a hard wooden bench with a ledge in front that had been carved with hundreds of journalists' initials over the years. Some distinguished people had left their marks on that ledge and every cub reporter felt honour bound to add to them. It was a rite of passage, surreptitiously scraping away with a penknife when the court officials were not looking.

Rosa was the only journalist in court because everyone else was out on the big story – Sadie's murder. The session began on time and a succession of trivial offenders came bobbing up from the underground cells, which were housed in ancient cellars beneath the building.

As usual, the same old names cropped up on the charge sheets because the law-breakers were almost all from families that had lived in the Old Town – often in the same rooms – for centuries. They were totally unregenerate; paid their fines or did their seven days in jail, and reappeared in court in no time at all.

The day's cases were about quarrelling women and drunken villains causing affrays in one or other of the many public houses of the district. Sometimes a friend of the accused would appear as a 'character witness' and when that happened, the court officials could be seen stifling grins of disbelief.

There was not a long list because most of the unruly New Year revellers had been dealt with during the past two days. The police were hard-pressed to find someone new to arrest and a harmless old tramp was summoned for 'committing a nuisance', which meant he'd peed in public. Remembering the stench of Fishmarket Close on New Year's Eve, Rosa reckoned he must have been very unlucky, or unusually liberal with his outpourings, to be caught, because peeing in the closes off the High Street was a fairly common habit.

At eleven fifteen, she was yawning and thinking about going back to the office when there was a commotion in the dock and an angry-looking young man appeared, struggling in the grip of one of the policemen from the dungeons. There was a bruise on his cheek, and he had a black eye. There was a dirty bandage round one of his wrists.

He was a good-looking fellow with a mop of curly black hair and flashing dark eyes that showed he might have gypsy blood. 'Listen,' he yelled at the magistrate on the bench. 'That bastard beat me up. He's the one who should be here.' With his unbandaged arm he was pointing at Boyle, the court sergeant, who stood by the dock, rock-like in his navy-blue uniform and staring straight ahead. His neatly combed blond hair and prominent nose gave him the profile of a Roman emperor.

Because of the aura of power he always exuded, both Patricia and Rosa fancied him and tried to engage him in chat without the least success. He ignored them as if they were beneath his consideration, which they found infuriating. They had a private bet of a pound on which of them would first make him smile.

There had been similar accusations of brutality against him before but, as usual, the magistrate seemed not to hear the angry prisoner's outburst, so he shouted again, 'That bastard beat me up!'

'Be quiet,' snapped the court clerk and asked the prisoner to confirm his name and address.

Rosa copied the details down – Patrick Noonan, Lady Stairs Close, the Lawnmarket. The Noonans were one of the High Street's fighting families but she hadn't seen this particular member of the clan before. He was also better dressed than the usual brawler, in a sports jacket and brown trousers, though his tie had been taken away and his open shirt collar was bloodstained.

The charge was read out – causing an affray in a public house called the Blue Blanket in the Canongate.

'Are you guilty or not guilty?' asked the clerk.

'Not guilty, and that bastard beat me up for nothing!' Again the protest was swept aside and the clerk stepped up with a Bible to administer the oath to the first witness, an oily-looking police constable who began reading from his notebook about being summoned to the pub at twenty-one hundred hours on January the third to stop a fight in the bar.

'I broke up the fight, arrested the accused and conveyed him to the cells here. He was very abusive,' he intoned.

'Well done,' said the magistrate who then looked at the man in the dock and asked, 'What have you to say for yourself?'

The prisoner was burning with indignation. 'I wasnae fighting. I was trying to stop it. It's a miscarriage of justice . . . And I want to lodge an official complaint against that bastard there!' Again he pointed at the sergeant but when he saw he was getting nowhere with the magistrate, he turned towards the body of the court and addressed Rosa in the press box.

'Listen, I was in the Blue Blanket with my brother when the fight broke out. It had naethin' to do wi' us, but that bobby picked on me and took me in. In the cells Boyle got stuck intae me. Everybody round here kens him. He likes hurting people. I was perfectly all right when I was brought in and look at me now.'

She knew he was probably a villain but for some reason felt sympathy and pity as she stared back at him. Even if he was guilty, Boyle shouldn't have beaten him up. Justified anger, however, was not enough to make the magistrate listen.

'Guilty!' he intoned and slapped down his gavel. 'I fine you twenty-five pounds or seven days in Saughton prison.'

'I've not got twenty-five quid. It's not bloody *fair* . . . !' yelled the man in the dock.

He was being pulled away when a girl suddenly stood up

in a public bench at the back of the court and called out, 'Please . . . !'

Everyone turned to stare at her and her face went deep red in embarrassment. 'Please, I want to pay his fine,' she said in a trembling voice and brought some money out of her open handbag.

The clerk beckoned to her to come forward, which she did without looking at the prisoner. With her head bent she paid the money and only then did she look at him. He was standing stock still staring at her and they exchanged a look of such affection that Rosa's heart went out to them.

The girl was neatly but not expensively dressed, and she was very nervous, so she had probably never been in a court before. Twenty-five pounds was almost certainly a lot of money for her but if she hadn't paid it, Noonan would have been in for even more ill-treatment in the cells than he had already suffered.

Rosa wondered if this was his wife, so she leant forward in an effort to hear what was being said to the clerk but could make out none of it because the girl's voice was very low.

Noonan's case was the last item of the day and as soon as the court cleared, Rosa went across to the clerk's table and copied down the name of the woman who had paid his fine. She was gathering her things up from the press box when Sergeant Boyle walked slowly towards her.

'I wouldn't write anything about Mr Noonan if I was you, Miss Makepeace,' he said, looking at a point on the wall slightly above her head. It was the first words he'd ever addressed to her but she hadn't won the bet because he hadn't cracked a smile. Yet he knew her name, and she realized he was giving her a warning.

She gave him a hard stare. 'It's not your business to tell me what I should write about, Sergeant Boyle,' she said.

Already she was thinking that she would suggest to Jack, who liked rocking official boats, that the *Dispatch* could run a piece about the protests of brutality that so often came up from the cells but were always ignored. In full sight of Boyle, she carefully underlined Noonan's name in her notebook, then walked out with the sergeant's cold stare fully on her.

In the open square outside, she was surprised to find a cluster of other reporters and photographers standing round the old Mercat Cross that stood between the police station's entrance and the back door of St Giles's. Mike was among them.

'What's going on?' she asked, running over to him.

He looked condescendingly down at her. 'Something big. There's been another murder. A body's been found apparently. They're giving out a statement soon.'

'What kind of body?' she asked, suddenly very cold.

'A *dead* body of course.'

'I mean is it a man or a woman?'

'I don't know. Go back to the office. They'll be waiting for the Burgh Court stuff.'

'There isn't anything worth using,' she said, her crusading feelings about Noonan disappearing now that this greater distraction had appeared – besides, she was filled with disquiet for reasons she did not want to examine.

Annoyed at her for moving in on his patch, Mike moved away but she stood her ground and wriggled into the front row of photographers as a uniformed inspector emerged from the police headquarters with a sheet of paper in his hand.

'Gentlemen,' he announced, ignoring Rosa, 'a female body was discovered this morning in Duddingston Loch by a man who was bird watching. As far as we have been able to ascertain, death was by strangulation, so we are conducting a second murder inquiry.'

Chaos broke out with everyone shouting at once. 'Has she been identified?' called Leo Fairley, one of the city's oldest and most respected reporters, employed by the *Daily Mail*.

'Yes, Mr Fairley,' said the inspector who was well disposed towards Leo. 'The victim is a young woman called Marie Lang, aged twenty . . .'

Rosa reeled and tasted sour bile in her mouth. *I shouldn't have left her. I should have taken her home. Oh God, I should have taken her home,* she thought.

Mike sprinted past her and she ran after him to the office. Both of them were so out of breath when they got there that they could hardly speak.

'There's been another murder,' gasped Mike, leaning both his fists on Jack's work table.

Jack visibly brightened. 'Who is it this time?' he asked.

'A girl called Marie Lang, aged twenty, found in Duddingston Loch . . .' Mike was still panting.

'Write it up,' said Jack.

'I know her. We all know her.' Rosa's voice came from behind Mike.

Jack looked at her. 'You *are* the lucky one, aren't you? OK, put it down on paper,' he said. She stood in front of him without speaking, filled with horror because her New Year's wish had worked and she was turning into living proof of his theory that some reporters have an uncanny facility to make news happen around them.

'Go and write it down,' Jack repeated.

'But it's *Marie* from our copy-taking department and it's my fault she's dead,' said Rosa and burst into tears.

Thirteen

Tears embarrassed Jack but could never distract him from a big story, and nothing was bigger than a murder. While Mike was sent off in the office car to the place where the body was found, Rosa was briefly consoled, given tea and a large white handkerchief to blow her nose, then told to write a short feature about Marie called 'The Girl I Knew . . .'

There was no point pleading off if she wanted to keep her job. Jack was her boss and he would have despised her as a weakling if she failed in her assignment. The piece, however, was written from the heart and ended with her last glimpse of Marie on the steps of the North British Hotel.

'What happened to her after that? Was the murderer waiting on the pavement? Was he in the car that followed us on our short journey from Cockburn Street to Princes Street?' Rosa wrote as the last paragraph of her story. Then she started to cry again and Gil told her to take the rest of the day off.

At half past five, she was lying on her bed in Northumberland Street trying to distract herself by reading Graham Greene's *Brighton Rock*, when Mrs Ross suddenly appeared in the bedroom door and whispered, 'Get up, Rosa, there's some police officers to see you!'

Even the police wouldn't be allowed in Rosa's room, so she went downstairs into the hall and found a uniformed policewoman and the plain-clothes officer with the impassive face whom she saw at Aberlady. The woman reminded Rosa of a terrifying girl against whom she played hockey at school and who tripped her up by sticking out her stick as she dribbled up the wing. Could it be her? But there was not a flicker of recognition on her face when she stared at Rosa.

The man held out his hand politely and said, 'Thank you for seeing us, Miss Makepeace. Your Editor gave me your address. I am Detective Sergeant Mallen, and this is WPC Henderson.'

Mrs Ross, hovering behind Rosa, and avid to hear what was going on, invited them into her private lounge. Rosa sat in one armchair by the gas fire, and the other two settled on the sofa. Mrs Ross perched on one arm of Rosa's chair but Mallen looked at her and said, 'I'm afraid this is a private matter, madam.' Looking aggrieved, she flounced out.

When the door closed behind her, Mallen said, 'I've just read your article in the afternoon edition about knowing Miss Lang. We think you must be the last person to have seen her alive.' His eyes were a very cold blue and his mouth a firm line. He looked as if he had no human feelings at all. The policewoman's eyes also seemed to have glazed over. There was not a flicker of sympathy in them.

Rosa nodded and swallowed, finding it difficult to speak. The woman regarded her speculatively as if she found it hard to believe a journalist could be moved by emotion. They both waited till she collected herself and after a while Mallen spoke again: 'Please tell me everything you remember about your meeting with Marie Lang.'

She had already written it down, but it was a relief to get it off her chest again and she went through the story from the moment she met up with the line of dancing girls outside St Giles to the time she dropped Marie off at the hotel.

Every now and again, Mallen interrupted with a question: 'Was anyone else there?'; 'Do you think she intended to meet someone after you went away?'; and finally 'Was anyone following you?'

She found herself frowning as she answered this question: 'When we drove out of Cockburn Street I thought a car pulled out and followed us, but when we got to the N.B. it passed us and headed out along Waterloo Place.'

'What sort of car?' His voice was sharp.

'I don't know. Nothing special – medium-sized, dark-coloured. I do remember one thing though. It only had one headlight working. That's an offence, isn't it?'

He nodded and said sarcastically, 'It is, but not as big an offence as murder.' She wondered if he was trying to be funny but there was absolutely no expression on his face as he pressed on: 'Are you sure about the time?'

'Yes, it was twenty past one on the N.B. clock when we got back to my car in Cockburn Street. I wanted to take Marie home but she said it was too late. I was glad I didn't have to go to Sighthill because I was tired.' Her voice cracked again and she had to fight for control for she didn't want to break down completely before these impassive people.

'Is the time important?' she managed to ask eventually.

He nodded. 'Very. The medical authorities think she died early on the morning of January first. You were probably the last person to see her alive.'

She cringed and asked, 'But what about the hotel doorman? He was standing at the top of the steps when I dropped her off. I saw him speaking to her.'

The woman had produced a notebook and was writing down Rosa's replies. She wrote good shorthand, better than Rosa's, which was described by Patricia as 'bastard Pitman's'.

When she asked about the doorman, both Mallen and the policewoman paused and stared at her. Mallen spoke first. 'After I read your newspaper piece I spoke to the N.B. doorman. He says he never saw either you or her. Neither did anyone else, so we only have your word that you took her there. I'm afraid I'll have to ask you to come with me to the station and make an official statement.'

Mrs Ross was horrified when Rosa told her she was going to the High Street station with the police.

'Do you want me to phone your father?' she asked, but Mallen shook his head and assured her, 'That won't be necessary. Miss Makepeace is only coming to help us with some information. She will be returned home in half an hour.' *Like a parcel*, thought Rosa, who was in a daze.

Mrs Ross stood at the front door staring after them as they got into a black police car and Rosa was glad the worried landlady hadn't got her father's phone number or she would be on to him straight away.

The interview room in the High Street police station was as stark and empty as a cell. It didn't take long to tell her story to a silent female stenographer and WPC Henderson, who seemed to have been appointed her escort. Mallen disappeared. Both women acted so hostile that Rosa's nervousness was supplanted by anger, and she began fizzing with resentment at the way she was being treated.

'What were you doing in the High Street when you met Miss Lang?' asked Henderson.

'I was coming out of the midnight service in St Giles,' said Rosa defiantly.

'You are religious?'

'Not really. I went to the midnight service out of curiosity.'

'Hmm, curiosity.' She obviously thought that strange and Rosa decided against mentioning Iain. Let them find out if she was alone or not. She was not going to do their work for them.

'You were particularly friendly with Miss Lang?' was the next question.

'Not *very* close but friendly, yes. I knew her through work.'

'Did you know any of her other friends?'

'Only the girls in the copy room at the office.'

'There was no pre-arrangement for you and she to meet that night?'

What on earth did they think she'd been doing? 'Of course not. We met by accident. I originally intended to go to George's café near the King's Theatre for spaghetti with some of my colleagues but I met Marie with her friends and we all went dancing.'

'After the midnight service?'

'Yes,' she said sharply.

'Why?'

'Why not? There's no law against it, is there? There were a lot of people dancing in the Gardens that night.' Rosa glared at the hostile Henderson, who shook her head as if Rosa had kicked a football into her garden, and said, 'Miss Makepeace, you should co-operate with us. We know that you were unusually worried about Miss Lang not going into work. You even went out to Sighthill to see her sister, didn't you? Why did you do that?'

How to explain that she'd had some sort of premonition that bad trouble had befallen Marie? She decided not to try.

'Because I felt that I should have taken her home. I was worried when she didn't come in to work on Monday. I felt responsible.'

The policewoman looked over at the stenographer and said, 'You say you felt responsible. Isn't that rather strong? Did you have some sort of premonition about her? You didn't know she'd been killed, did you?'

Rosa's throat tightened. 'Of course not. I was concerned about her as a friend, that's all.'

'You're not psychic or anything?' asked Henderson sarcastically. Anger flared up in Rosa and she stood up to say, 'No, I'm not psychic and I've told you all I know about that night. I had nothing to do with Marie's disappearance. Now I'm going home. Don't worry about the lift. I'd rather walk.'

Amazingly, they let her go.

The High Street was echoing and empty. Because a frost had the world in its grip again, the sky was clear and star-spangled and the pavements clear and dry. Rosa's footsteps rang out like hammer blows on the cobblestones as she headed for the News Steps near the junction with the Mound, and she went down them three at a time, propelled by fury.

107

At the bottom of the steps, she ran down to the junction of Market Street and Cockburn Street and then plunged into Waverley Station where she took the metal-gated lift up into the North British Hotel. It was quicker and easier than climbing the daunting Waverley Steps.

There were lots of smartly dressed people sitting around drinking in the hotel lounge but she strode past without looking at them, and ignored the raised eyebrows of the clerks on the reception desk who were surprised to see a furious-looking girl in red tartan trousers tearing through their marble halls. The man on duty at the front door, tall and straight in his buff livery, was the one who had been there the night she dropped Marie off beside him.

He turned to look at her as she walked up. 'Taxi, madam?' he asked.

'No,' she said and stared hard into his eyes. They were grey and shifty-looking with deeply wrinkled bags beneath them though he was only about thirty, she guessed.

He made as if to turn away from her but she said firmly, 'Wait. I want to speak to you. You remember me dropping off a blonde girl here early on New Year's morning, don't you?'

He looked back. 'No,' he said coolly. He was an accomplished liar, this one.

She ignored the denial. 'As you know, it was about half past one. I saw you watching us when I stopped my car down there on the road. It's a grey Morris Minor. You opened its door.' She pointed down the steps at the edge of the pavement and went on, 'My friend walked up the steps and stood beside you. You said you'd whistle up a taxi for her. I heard you and I'm sure you remember, though you told the police you never saw either of us. Why did you lie?'

His face beneath the brim of his top hat looked parchment pale in the ghostly light from the street lamps. 'Go away. Get the hell out of here or I'll call security,' he hissed. It was obvious he knew what she was talking about.

108

She didn't want another brush with the law so she walked down the steps to the street, but on the pavement she turned and called back at him, 'I know you saw both of us and I'll find out why you say you didn't.'

Crossing Princes Street to Register House, she stood looking around for a moment, trying to decide what to do next. Once more, she badly needed someone to talk to but had no one she could trust.

Should she ring Father? She dismissed that idea. No way would she contact Iain either. Roddy would listen but he was too far away and she didn't have a phone number for him anyway, only an address. The clock above the N.B. showed that it was ten past eight and when a couple walked past eating fish and chips out of newspaper, the smell made her suddenly realize that she was ravenously hungry. All she had eaten during the day was a cup of tea and a bacon sandwich at eleven o'clock in the office.

The thought of bacon sandwiches made her salivate and she turned back towards Waverley Station, running down the steep steps and along the overhead bridge to the back entrance. The thought of going to the Cockburn and being cross-questioned about Marie by Etta was too much for her so she headed for the Doric Tavern in Market Street. It was nearer anyway.

A search of her pockets yielded up a pound, a crumpled ten shilling note, three florins and some coppers – more than enough for a meal.

The Doric first-floor dining room was half-full and she sat at a corner table looking down into the street. The fruit and flower market opposite was shuttered and quiet but in a few hours, when the *Scotsman* presses began churning out tomorrow's newspapers, it would spring into life and lorries loaded with bouquets and baskets of fruit would block the carriageway.

Nellie came limping over. She was a typical Edinburgh waitress – tiny, under five feet tall; on the wrong side of middle age; dressed in a shabby black crêpe dress and a frilly white apron of the sort worn by French maids in farces. Poor Nellie suffered terribly from varicose veins and bunions and the way she crept about from table to table made you feel her pain.

'What'll it be?' she asked without ceremony. She was even less into pleasantries than Etta and though she knew this customer well enough, she was not prepared to acknowledge her.

'A mixed grill,' Rosa said, and then added, 'But how much is it?'

'Ten shillin's. Mak yer mind up. D'ye want it or no'?'

'Yes, please, and a whisky with ginger ale, please.' She had enough money for a reviver.

'Pushin' the boat oot, I see,' grunted Nellie as she shuffled away.

The mixed grill was enormous and well worth ten shillings. Rosa was cutting up the last tomato when heads in the room turned and Sylvia in her Persian lamb came sweeping in with another well-groomed girl dressed in a full-skirted scarlet coat. Nellie immediately became welcoming and showed them to a table on the far side of the room. As she was shrugging off her black fur, Sylvia spotted Rosa and waved. 'Come and join us,' she called.

Rosa put down the money for her bill, lifted her whisky and went over. The two newcomers were wearing low-cut, taffeta cocktail dresses – Sylvia's was pale green and her companion's black with bugle beads stitched over the bodice. They were both beautifully made up and smelt of exotic scent.

'Sit down. Meet my friend Barbara,' Sylvia said to Rosa. To Barbara she said, 'This is the newspaper reporter who wrote that story in tonight's paper about the second girl who was murdered. The one whose body was found at Duddingston.'

Barbara nodded as she drawled, 'I read it. How terrible for you . . .'

Rosa was unable to stop the words pent up inside her from

pouring out: 'The police came to my lodgings tonight and took me to the High Street for questioning.'

Sylvia's curved eyebrows soared to her hairline. 'Why?' she asked.

'Because they think I was the last person to see Marie alive. But I dropped her at the N.B. and the porter who was on that night told the police he never saw either of us. I know he did though. Why is he telling such lies? And why do the police believe him instead of me?'

Barbara sighed. 'Policemen always believe men before women, I'm afraid.'

'One of them was a woman. I'm sure she used to play hockey against me . . .' babbled Rosa. She felt as if the whisky was having a strange effect on her. Sylvia frowned as she lifted a hand to summon Nellie. 'Three malt whiskies,' she said.

Rosa protested, 'Let me get them.' She'd no idea how much three malt whiskies would cost but trusted they would not be more than a pound. Sylvia brushed her protest aside as Nellie waddled over with the drinks.

'Drink up. I can see you're worried about this,' Sylvia said sympathetically.

Rosa nodded. 'Not half!'

'Then don't be silly. You've nothing to worry about. You couldn't have killed her. I heard tonight that she'd been raped and strangled. There's no way they can accuse you of that.'

Rosa started to shake as the realization of what happened to poor Marie hit her. She'd been holding that thought back.

'But they think I've been lying about dropping her beside the doorman . . .' she whispered feebly.

'They're only checking on your story and his as well. They probably know he's lying anyway. And they haven't accused you of anything, or charged you?'

'No.'

'In that case, do nothing. Carry on as usual,' Sylvia advised.

Barbara leaned over towards Rosa and whispered, 'And

don't go out at night on your own. Don't take any chances.'

Was she being melodramatic? 'Why not?' Rosa asked.

'Because you may know more than you realize – or someone might think that you do. Your friend was killed after all and you were the last person to see her.'

'Apart from the N.B. doorman,' said Rosa bitterly.

By the time they'd drunk the malt whisky, she began feeling slightly more reassured, drawing strength from their confidence, but suddenly Sylvia stood up and announced that she and Barbara had an appointment at a casino. They both looked at Rosa who said, 'That's fine. You've made me feel better and I'm going home now. I could do with a walk.'

Sylvia groaned and struck herself on the forehead with her black-gloved hand. 'Don't you ever listen to a word that's said to you? Go home in a taxi for God's sake!'

Rosa had enough money left for a taxi fare, so she agreed but they didn't trust her and insisted on seeing her get into a black cab. As she was being driven away, she saw them hiring another cab for themselves and enviously wondered what it was like to go, all dressed up, to a casino.

She'd never been to a place like that – she only went to pubs.

Fourteen

Next morning Jack watched Rosa with unusual concentration while she told him about her police interview. 'You're sure the doorman spoke to Marie?' he said.

'I'm positive. I was pleased because he said he'd get her a taxi . . .' she told him and he nodded.

'It's a funny business. But you'd better stay away from the Marie story. I'll put Tom and Mike on to it,' he said.

Damn, that's not fair! she thought but couldn't argue.

Mike was looking very smug when she sat down at her desk and he leant over to say, 'Have you looked at the diary yet? I'm doing the funeral today.'

'What funeral?' she asked.

'Sadie Jamieson's. She's being cremated at Seafield at half past ten. Didn't you know?'

Of course she didn't and she felt a failure for losing touch with that story too because of her involvement with Marie's death. Mike had really stolen a march on her. As she turned away from him, Alan looked up from his slumped position at the end of the line of desks and said in a casual voice, 'I heard you telling Jack about taking Marie to the N.B. I saw her speaking to the doorman at the hotel that night.'

They all stared at him and he permitted himself a fleeting smile but said nothing more. Rosa's short fuse burned out first. 'What were you doing at the N.B.?' she snapped.

Alan pushed at his languid forelock of fair hair and said, 'I was quite affluent, so I decided to hire myself a room . . .'

The thought in all their minds was that Alan's unusual

113

affluence must have come from pawning the typewriters.

'You hired a room in the N.B.?' queried Mike in disbelief. It was the most expensive hotel in the city. Film stars stayed there. Danny Kaye was currently installed in one of the suites and was holding a press conference that morning.

'They have very good bathrooms, excellent-quality soap,' said Alan.

'Bugger the soap. Do you go there often?' shouted Jack from the other side of the room and Alan nodded.

'Yes, every now and again. Whenever I need a bath, I stay overnight. They do an excellent breakfast too.'

So Rosa was right in her assumption that he lived most of the time in the office. He really was an odd man.

Aware that he had everyone's attention, he sighed and squared his shoulders like an actor about to go on stage. 'Yes, as I was saying, I walked down to the hotel about one o'clock and ordered coffee and sandwiches in the lounge before I went up to my room. I was there when Marie came up the front steps and spoke to the doorman. She stood beside him for a few minutes, but the next time I looked she'd disappeared. I never thought anything about it till now,' he said.

Jack gave a horrible groan as if Alan's lack of news sense physically pained him. *There must be something about writing theatrical reviews that atrophies the scoop reaction*, thought Rosa.

'Alan,' she pleaded, 'you should go up to the police station and tell them that you saw her. That'll back me up if you do.'

'OK, I'll go now,' he said and rose to his considerable height. The whole office watched in silence as he left. He was actually quite a powerful-looking man and suddenly Rosa wondered if he could drive a car and resolved to find out the moment she had the chance. Whoever killed the two girls must have had a car.

Although Mike was now in charge of Sadie's story, Rosa was too personally involved to wash her hands of it, and besides she was convinced that the two killings were connected. She turned the charm on Mike. 'Be an angel. Let me go with you to Sadie's funeral,' she whispered to him.

He was suspicious. 'It's my story now, Makepeace,' he warned.

'I know,' she agreed, 'but it was mine at the beginning. I won't poach. I'll ask Jack if I can go, shall I?'

Before he could protest, she was over at Jack's table making her request.

Amazingly Jack seemed indulgent and thought it a good idea for her to go to the funeral. 'I've ordered the office car to take Basher and Mike, but you can go too and add the colour bits. Make sure you come back with something good,' he said.

Mike's chagrin was obvious but Rosa was beaming, not the normal reaction of someone going to a funeral. She was very well aware that Jack was trying his reporters out, seeing which one would outsmart the other. It was some sort of a test.

In the car, Mike sat in the front with the driver and lit a cigarette as if he was in charge. 'Stop at the nearest florist,' he ordered, 'I want to buy a wreath.'

When the car reached the junction of London Road and Leith Walk, he jumped out and ran into a big flower shop on the corner. Within minutes he re-emerged with a large bunch of yellow chrysanthemums wrapped in green paper.

'They're bloody expensive,' he complained, 'but I'll pay a third and you two'll have to share the rest. Put it on your expenses.'

Basher only shrugged and said laconically, 'Think again, son.' Though he was the same age as Mike, he acted like someone a generation older.

Mike looked at Rosa and said, 'Then you'll pay half, Makepeace.'

She said nothing and watched as he started writing in big black letters on a card, which would be tucked into the flowers.

'What are you putting on that?' she asked suspiciously.

He held out the card so that she could read: *In Memory of a Young Life So Tragically Ended, from an Anonymous Sympathizer.*

'Don't you think that's a bit cheesy?' she said.

He glared. 'You don't know anything about emotion, do you? This'll make them weep.'

'And then you'll put a bit in the story about it. But if I've to pay half the cost, I want it to be plural – *anonymous sympathizers*, at least,' she insisted.

At Seafield crematorium, Basher sloped off and Mike started treating the funeral like a military operation. First of all he put his floral tribute in a prominent position among the small collection of flowers behind the chapel and then came back to join Rosa and a few other reporters waiting outside the grim chapel. The others were rivals from the *Express*, the *Mail* and the *Evening News*. It bothered Mike that no one from the *Daily Telegraph* or the *Glasgow Herald* had turned up, and he whispered to Rosa, 'Where are they? Are they following up something else?' He only relaxed when representatives of those two newspapers joined the group. They chatted but never mentioned the reason for the gathering. Everyone was playing their cards very close to their chests.

As they filed into the chapel, Mike held Rosa back and whispered, 'You sit at the back and watch the people. Murderers often come to their victims' funerals. They can't keep away.'

She looked around. The only people mourning Sadie were her mother, Betty, almost respectable-looking in a black hat and coat, and her friend Nelly. There was also a shabby-looking man, who could be Jock, Flora's doorman, with two of the girls from the Danube Street house, including the cat lover with red hair. The press, and three policemen, including Mallen, made up the rest of the congregation. If Mike's theory was right, Mallen was probably watching out for the murderer. There was no sign of Sylvia or Flora.

The service was short and the minister's address was

punctuated by Betty's wailing that eerily echoed and re-echoed in the half-empty chapel. Remembering her mother's funeral, Rosa hated the moment when the coffin went sliding away between parted curtains and she closed her eyes so she didn't see it.

Suddenly she was jerked back to awareness when Betty gave an eldritch scream, put her hands on her head, knocking off her black hat and making her hair stand on end. Then she collapsed against Nelly, who held her up as they stumbled dishevelled towards the door, where they were met by a blinding onslaught of flash bulbs from a squad of photographers. The Basher was not among them. He was nowhere to be seen.

Before they were back in the car Mike was already composing his story. 'We'd better get to a phone. I've a good intro. *Mourning mother breaks down in agony of grief,*' he crowed.

'It'd be quicker to go straight to the office,' Rosa protested.

'OK, but where's the Basher? We can't go without him,' said Mike looking frantically round. He was worried that his good ideas would desert him before he got his hands on a typewriter.

'I saw him leaving in a taxi while the service was going on,' the driver said and Mike snapped, 'Bloody hell! In that case, take us back to the office. Jack'll be watching and we can't let the Basher steal a march on us by being there first.'

'We're on the same side, Mike,' Rosa reminded him.

'Don't be daft, of course we're not. In this job it's every man for himself,' he told her.

They ran into the office as if they were being chased and started to write the story, Mike doing the typing. Gil stood over him and took every sheet as it was finished. Rosa supplied the colour bits – descriptions of Betty's breakdown and what the flowers looked like. Mike, who wrote good shorthand, had a verbatim note of the minister's address in all its banality.

They argued about which hymn was played. Mike said it was 'Jerusalem' but Rosa insisted it was 'The Lord is My Shepherd'. Gil said either would do. When Rosa was dictating her last sentence about the terrible grief of the murdered girl's mother, the Basher arrived carrying a sheaf of prints, which he put down on Jack's desk.

'Bloody good!' said Jack when he looked at them.

He was so engrossed in setting out his front page that neither Mike nor Rosa dared go over and sneak a look at the pictures, so they had to wait for the paper to appear.

Basher's scoop was a photograph of Betty kneeling by the wreaths and weeping over Mike's card, the words of which were clearly visible.

'Flowers from a stranger makes bereaved mother weep . . . (picture by *Dispatch* photographer Robert McIvor)' was printed beneath the picture.

Mike was hopping mad. 'The wreath was my bloody idea and that bastard stole it,' he raved.

'Never mind,' Rosa told him. 'It got us the front page and a by-line each.'

She lifted the paper and stared at it again. The Basher must have taken the picture before the funeral started because Betty was relatively tidy, hat in place and hair neatly combed, not the tear-stained wreck she was at the end of the ceremony. She was kneeling on the ground with Nelly leaning down beside her. It was a picture to melt the hardest heart.

Sharing the front page with the story about the funeral was Tom's report about the finding of Marie's body. Rosa's spirits slumped again and the depression that had gripped her since she heard about her friend's death returned. It was the first time she'd read all the details.

Marie's body, according to the police information, was spotted yesterday morning floating in Duddingston Loch, trapped by reeds at the side of a little wall that stuck out into the water in the shadow of the church.

The man who found her – *deeply shocked Mr Thomas*

Appleby, 57, of 85 Craiglockhart Parkway – had been bird-watching through binoculars from a raised bank, when he saw what he thought was a yellow mop head sticking out of the water. He'd been hoping, without success, to spot an unusual Russian winter migrant that another bird watcher claimed to have seen on the loch, but curiosity made him decide to investigate the mop head before he went home. He poked at it with his walking stick only to find that it was the head of a blonde woman. She was almost entirely submerged in the water, trapped by the reeds, and looked as if she had been in the water for some time.

When she was pulled out by a police diving squad, it was revealed that her arms had been tied behind her back by a brightly coloured silk scarf.

Shocked, with the paper still in her hand, Rosa walked across the room to Tom's desk and said without preamble, 'Marie was tied up with a scarf. What colour was it?'

He stared at her. 'Why do you want to know?' Even Tom was becoming possessive about his stories.

'Because I was told that the other murder victim, Sadie, borrowed a silk scarf from one of the Danube Street girls . . . maybe it's the same one. Maybe the same person killed them both.'

'I don't know what colour it was,' Tom snapped, but Jack was listening so he got up, pulled his overcoat off the back of his chair and said, 'I'll go up to the station and ask though.'

Fifteen minutes later he was back in the office. 'The police say it was a blue silk scarf with red and white flowers printed on it. Does that help?' he asked slamming his notebook down on the desktop.

'Yes, yes it does. The girl in Danube Street lent Sadie a blue scarf with a red and white flower design and she was angry because it wasn't found with her body . . . She said it was expensive. It came from Jenners.'

Patricia looked up from her work and said sarcastically, 'You'd better ring her up then. One doesn't throw away a

Jenners' scarf, does one? Dry-cleaning works wonders.'

Jack, however, was delighted that they had another scoop. They were in possession of information that the police may not have. 'Write it up,' he shouted across the room, 'Makepeace, you do the stuff about the scarf going missing with Sadie. Tom, get a police statement when you tell them it's linked with the other murder.'

Fifteen

Her piece was short, so Rosa finished first, and decided to go for something to eat. In the canteen she met the Basher who was morosely chewing a filled roll. When she sat down beside him he said, 'Rotten about Marie, isn't it? She was a nice girl.'

'Was she a friend of yours too?' she asked, surprised to see him showing any feelings.

'I used to see her in the Plaza sometimes. She was a good dancer.'

She nodded sadly, remembering Marie's exuberant high kicks on New Year's morning.

'And now I've to go to Duddingston and take pictures of the place she was found,' the Basher mumbled through another bite of roll.

'Can I come with you?' she asked.

'Haven't you anything else to do?'

'I'm down in the diary for an interview with a woman who is writing a history book about some historic Edinburgh house this afternoon, but that's not till a quarter to four. You're going to Duddingston now, aren't you?' she said, looking at the canteen clock that showed the time as ten minutes past one.

The Basher stood up. 'OK. The office car is at the bottom of the steps waiting for me. You can come if you don't hang about.'

'I'll be at the car before you,' she said and ran to get her raincoat, which was hanging above the pipes in the ladies' lavatories because it had been wet when she got back from Sadie's funeral and needed drying off.

The office driver was a morose man called Ben who liked nothing better than gloom and doom. The murder of some-one from the office would keep him talking for months. Basher sat in the front beside him and Rosa climbed into the back, but before he'd even switched on the engine, Ben was off: 'Marie was a nice lassie. Very decent family. Her father was in the Navy during the war and went into the police when he was demobbed. In the Navy he was torpe-doed and they say that's what killed him eventually. Died four years ago. The mother died of a broken heart last year. Terribly unlucky family. Here's hoping they get the rat who did it.'

It was not necessary to contribute to this monologue. The Basher made assenting noises and Rosa sat staring out of the window as they drove through Holyrood Park, skirted the bottom of the Salisbury Crags, where the bad weather of the last few days had brought big rocks tumbling down into the roadway, and headed for the expanse of water that was Duddingston Loch.

Till then Rosa had always liked Duddingston because of Sir Henry Raeburn's much reproduced but delightful paint-ing of a clergyman, the Rev. Robert Walker, skating happily across the ice there in 1784. It was on display in the National Gallery and she often went in to look at it, because she felt that, like her, the Reverend Walker enjoyed the wintertime.

Today however the loch was not frozen but looked grey and sinister. Its water glittered and heaved like mercury under a sullen sky and all round the perimeter of the loch, bare stalks of reeds and undergrowth stuck up like stakes.

One or two curious rubber-neckers were hanging around on the roadway but there was no sign of any police activity except a line of red and white tape cutting off the place where Marie's body was found.

Silhouetted on the horizon were the jagged battlements of

the church steeple that stared down towards the water. Beneath the church, a little wall, beside which Marie had sheltered, jutted into the water like a pointing finger. Hefting his big camera, the Basher strode down the grassy slope towards it and surveyed the scene.

'Got to get the church in,' he muttered to himself and Rosa stood back, making no comment, because she'd learned that photographers did not react kindly to reporters making suggestions about the sort of picture they ought to take.

Several plates were snapped because the Basher was striving to capture the forlorn atmosphere of the place. He was an artist really. When he turned away to take a panoramic view across the water to Prestonfield golf course, she walked down the grass slope and along the wall. Standing on the end of it, she stared into the water, shuddering as she imagined a body lying down there.

Why? Who did it? Poor Marie. *I shouldn't have left her. I should have taken her home.* Her fists were knotted tightly in her coat pockets, with the fingernails pressing hard into the pads of her hands, and tears gathered again in her eyes.

Only Ben spoke as they drove back to the office, droning on . . . 'It's a terrible thing. He must have taken her there in a car. They should be out looking for clues but the Edinburgh polis are bloody useless. They never catch onybody for onything – unless they give themselves up . . .'

Oh shut up, shut up! Rosa wanted to shout at him but said nothing.

She was back in the office by half past two and as soon as she set foot in the door, Patricia called out, 'The police are looking for you again. You've never been so sought after, darling.'

'Where are they?' Rosa asked, looking around.

'There's only one. Jack took him into his office. Go in,' said Gil.

It was Mallen of course, still wearing his belted macintosh as he sat in a leather chair facing Jack's desk. Big Stella was bustling around, obviously intrigued, and Jack looked unusually beneficent and mild.

'Ah Rosa,' he said, 'Inspector Mallen has a few questions he wants to ask you.'

Mallen wasn't an inspector but he was flattered and didn't correct Jack, who'd certainly inflated his rank deliberately.

'Again?' she asked shortly.

'This time it's about what you wrote in the latest edition about the silk scarf,' Mallen said. 'Will you come up to the headquarters and give a statement about it?'

Jack intervened. 'Don't put yourself to any trouble, Inspector, you can speak to Miss Makepeace here. I'm sure she's done nothing wrong.'

Mallen shot a suspicious glance at him and said, 'Of course we're not suggesting she's done anything wrong, sir.'

'In that case why put her through the trauma of being interviewed for a second time in your police station?' said Jack.

Mallen gave in. 'I was wondering why you didn't mention knowing about the scarf when you were in the station last time,' he said to Rosa.

'Because I didn't know that Marie was tied up with it then,' she told him. Mallen had a peculiar effect on her. Her heart was thudding with nerves and she was grateful to Jack for his protection. It was obvious that he had no intention of leaving the room and was backing her up.

'You should have given the information to the police before publishing it in the newspaper,' snapped Mallen, who was obviously annoyed at the *Dispatch* having information that was unknown to him.

Jack interrupted: 'We're a newspaper. We're not police informers. It's not our job to find out who killed those girls. It's yours.'

Mallen ignored him and kept his eyes on Rosa. 'The scarf came from a woman in the Danube Street brothel, you say. You seem to be very friendly with prostitutes, Miss Makepeace.'

That was too much for Jack, who stood up and walked across to the door, which he opened as he told Mallen, 'That's enough. If you persist in persecuting this girl, I'll expose your tactics in my newspaper. She's only doing her job. Maybe you should go away and do yours, which is catching a murderer.'

Sixteen

In that day's diary Rosa was assigned to interview Mrs Sheila Dean, the Edinburgh housewife who was writing a book about an interesting old house. Rosa had rung her up and made an appointment for them to meet at three forty-five in Patrick Thomson's tea room, opposite the *Scotsman* building on North Bridge.

Over the telephone Mrs Dean had explained that she preferred the interview to be conducted in a public place because her husband, a barrister, did not approve of the press and she did not want a reporter to go to her home.

Rosa, who was not keen on doing the article because she knew that Bob thought it was a more suitable piece for a woman journalist than a murder investigation was, wondered what the husband would say when the piece appeared in the paper. Lawyers, especially Edinburgh lawyers, could be prickly subjects to handle, tending to pick holes in, and threatening legal action about, anything that was written about them or their families.

Patrick Thomson's was an old-established department store with a tea room on the first floor overlooking the main street. A house string quartet was playing when Rosa walked in. They were three old men – a cellist, a pianist and a violinist – and a busty, grey-haired woman in a faded-looking black dress who played a viola. They scraped out Strauss waltzes, Polish mazurkas, and pieces from *The Merry Widow*.

Though they were not first-class musicians, they were good enough to dispel the gloom of the dreary weather outside, and gathered an admiring following among the middle-class Edinburgh ladies who sat swaying gently to the familiar tunes as they sipped from china cups with genteel pinkies raised in what Rosa imagined to be Roddy's mother's style.

The interviewee was waiting at a table in a corner. She was a healthy-looking young American with long, shiny brown hair, great teeth, and an eager, enthusiastic face. She began talking even before Rosa sat down, bubbling over with information about a dilapidated Trinity mansion with which she had fallen in love and was painstakingly researching its history.

'Imagine, General Monk slept there in 1660,' she said excitedly, showing Rosa a photograph of the house. 'The trouble is that it's falling down now. No one but me seems to care. My father left me some money and I dream about buying it. What a wonderful house it would be to own, but my husband won't hear of it. He says the expense would be crippling . . .' She rattled on while Rosa made notes in a spiral notebook.

What Mrs Dean should do, she thought dispiritedly, *was buy the house and ditch the husband.*

But she was only half concentrating because she was pondering the strangeness of her job. An hour and a half ago she'd been standing at the place where her friend was murdered, and now she was taking tea and pretending to listen to this pleasant woman who had never seen anything more horrific than a dead budgie.

They parted on cordial terms, but before she left Mrs Dean asked Rosa if she could miss out her name and address when writing the story.

'That's not possible. There's no story without telling of *your* interest in the house,' Rosa said.

Mrs Dean's brow furrowed as she said, 'I thought an article might rouse interest among other antiquarians, but you see it's my husband. He doesn't like me making an exhibition of myself.'

'I'll try to write more about the house than you,' Rosa assured her.

'Well, if you do put in my name, will you please make sure to call me Mrs Ronald Dean – not Sheila. My husband is very fussy about proper forms of address.'

'All right, I'll do that.' Rosa saw this story ending up on the spike because Jack would never stand for her referring to an interviewee in such a formal way. Another problem was having to put an age in the story. There was no point even asking Mrs Ronald Dean's age because she would never agree to it being quoted. But she was too nice for Rosa to tell her that they had both wasted their afternoon. The music had been soothing, if nothing else. Rosa paid for their tea and, through the window, watched her interviewee getting on to a bus for Trinity. It would be the last she'd see of her, she was sure.

What a waste of time. She'd have been far better employed staying in the office and working on the idea of doing a piece about the brutality wreaked on prisoners in the cells beneath the court. She'd almost forgotten about that since Marie's murder, but now she was determined to suggest it to Jack. It was the sort of investigation that he liked – and old Bob hated.

When Mrs Dean's bus disappeared down the North Bridge for Princes Street, Rosa changed her mind and decided not to return to the office just yet. Instead she would do something that she shouldn't – she was going back to the North British Hotel, to speak again to the lying doorman.

Unfortunately the uniformed man standing at the top of the carpeted stairs when she got there was not thin and upright but portly and middle-aged. His face looked rubicund in the glare of the lights shining out from the reception hall and, if it wasn't so unlikely, she'd have sworn his cheeks and lips were rouged.

'I'm from the *Dispatch*. Is the other doorman not on duty today?' she asked.

He squeaked in an effete, high-pitched voice, 'Him! That bitch! He's done a runner. Just like that. Didn't turn up this morning.'

'Without telling anyone?' asked Rosa.

He nodded and leaned forward, eager to pass on gossip. 'That kind are here today and gone tomorrow, dear. He's only been with us for three months and, between you and me, I didn't think he'd last that long. He's got a record. The manager took him on as a favour to a friend, but my brother-in-law, who's a prison officer up in Saughton, came in to see me one day and recognized him. He'd just got out.'

'What was he in for?' Rosa asked.

'Thieving, housebreaking, GBH. "Don't tell on me, give me a chance," he says to me, but I think once a thief, always a thief.'

'You're probably right,' said Rosa and turned to walk away with her hopes of finding out what happened to Marie disappearing fast.

Halfway down the steps an idea struck her and she turned back to ask, 'You don't have any idea where he lived, do you?'

His little eyes, sunk in pouches of fat, looked suspicious at her persistence, and he shook his head. 'He had a room in the staff section upstairs, but he took all his stuff when he left. I know where he drinks, though. In the Blue Blanket in the Canongate.'

That was the same pub where the protesting prisoner in the Burgh Court was arrested. Rosa had never been in it but knew that it was one of the most unsavoury public houses in the entire Royal Mile, and that was saying something. No unescorted woman had a chance of getting through the door – even a woman with a man would be regarded with deep suspicion. If she went to look for the doorman there, she'd have to find a man to go with her.

'Thanks,' she called back over her shoulder and stepped down into Princes Street. Thoughts were racing madly through her head. *Did the doorman's disappearance mean that he had run away? Could he be the killer of Sadie and Marie?* It was possible. How he enticed Sadie away was a mystery, but he could have offered to drive Marie home himself if there were no taxis immediately available. She should have asked the plump doorman what hours the other man had worked and if he had access to a car. If he was guilty of murder that would explain his denial to the police that he ever saw Marie at the hotel.

There were two possible suspects for Marie's death now: the missing doorman, and, it had to be admitted, Alan; he knew her, she would have gone away with him quite confidently, and his alibi for the night she went missing was paper-thin.

But surely not? He was eccentric, none too scrupulous about how he got his hands on money, but not evil. Besides, if he did kill her, why admit to seeing her in the hotel? He didn't have to, unless he was afraid that the staff would tell the police he was there. From what he said, he was a familiar face to them. Yes, the waiters and reception staff would recognize him easily because he was far from nondescript.

She decided to keep her theories to herself – after all, she was off the story and the police were breathing down her neck. It was safer to persuade Jack to allow her to investigate Noonan's court protest.

When she hurried back to the office, she found the *Dispatch* floor in chaos. Jack was shouting and two security men in overalls stood at the newsroom door with fire extinguishers at the ready. There was a pungent smell of burning paper and her colleagues were milling around in the corridor, coughing, spluttering and laughing.

Patricia grabbed Rosa's arm and giggled. 'You've missed some really hot news! Tom knocked his pipe out in one of the ashtrays and set fire to a pile of paper . . . What a blaze, so exciting. Hot news!'

It was obvious she was enjoying the incident and so was

everyone else. It had partially lifted them out of their gloom about the fate of the universally popular Marie.

When security let them back in to rescue their possessions, the desktops were swilling in white foam dotted with charred bits of blackened foolscap.

Disconsolately Mike picked up fragments of copy paper that should have been his last story of the day. Whilst he was sweeping the remains of it into a waste-paper basket, he let out a shout, 'Hey, look at this! I thought I'd lost last week's expenses envelope but here it is, beneath all this crap.'

Miraculously the little brown paper envelope had survived the conflagration. There was a considerable sum of money inside because Mike's expenses were always grossly inflated and he had a sideline filling in claim forms for the others because he was afraid they would be too undemanding and spoil the pitch for him.

He was so pleased with his windfall that he invited his friends to the Cockburn for a drink at knocking-off time.

Rosa was included but she sat still and watched them trooping out. She waited till Jack went into his private sanctum before she knocked at his door. Stella opened it and said, 'Yeah?'

'Can I have a word with Jack, please. I have an idea for a story.'

Jack's voice rang out, 'OK, bring it in. But make it quick.'

She coughed to clear her throat and said, 'Last time I was at the Burgh Court, one of the prisoners accused the sergeant in charge of beating him up, but the magistrate didn't listen. It often happens. I think that sergeant really is brutal. I have the angry prisoner's name and address and I could follow it up through him.'

Jack glared at her. 'Prisoners are always innocent according to them and they often complain of being beaten up.'

'Yes, but I believed this one – he had a terrific shiner and blood on his shirt.'

'And you don't like run-of-the-mill stories, do you? You like hard news.'

She nodded, remembering the old house story, which would certainly not make the paper.

He shrugged. 'OK, see what you can get but I don't guarantee to use it unless you can make it stand up. It can be big trouble taking on the authorities. They don't like people asking questions. Don't imagine yourself as a crusader – you might end up with egg on your face.'

Rosa was late in arriving at the Cockburn so Mike's bonanza was almost used up by the time she got there.

'What do you want?' he asked, ruefully looking at a handful of coins, which was all he had left.

'A lemonade will do,' she said, thinking about the perilous state of her liver, and he relaxed.

Etta too actually smiled at her when she went up to the bar.'I hear the police have been giving you a hard time. Don't let them get you down. It's nothing personal. They don't like you springing surprises on them about that scarf and so on.'

So Etta had contacts in the police as well as in the press. Rosa leaned over the bar and said, 'Do you know a man called Sergeant Boyle?'

Etta's friendly expression stiffened. 'What do you want to know about him?' she asked.

'I want to know what he's like because the last time I was in court, a prisoner accused Boyle of beating him up and said that he did it to lots of prisoners – he said he enjoyed hurting people.'

'If I was that chap I'd watch my back in the dark,' said Etta.

'You mean he might have been telling the truth?'

'Folk come in here and say all sorts of things. All I can tell you is that if my daughter brought Boyle home as a prospective husband, I'd be awfy upset.'

'Thanks Etta. I'm going to ask more about him. I might get a piece out of it.'

'Sylvia's been in. She sends you her regards,' said Etta.

'Is she all right?' Rosa asked.

'Not bad,' said Etta cagily.

Rosa wondered if Sylvia's name had been brought up by Etta as a hint about who to ask next about Boyle. Perhaps she could ask Sylvia to go to the Blue Blanket with her, but she immediately rejected the idea, for the tall blonde would be like a peacock among pigeons there. And she was a woman, one of the forbidden species.

Carrying her glass of lemonade, she went over to sit with her friends who had been joined by reporters from some other papers, including the hotshot Leo Fairley. When she slipped into her chair, she asked, 'Does anybody know anything about Sergeant Boyle, the one in the Burgh Court?'

Leo leered, 'Fancy him, do you?'

Patricia said, 'Rosa and I have a bet on which of us will get him to flirt with us first.'

'Kid,' said Leo, 'forget it. He's a hard man and when he needs a woman he knows where to go. He used to be a great rugby player – Boroughmuir, if I remember – but he had a bad habit of roughing people up on the field. Even his own team were all terrified of him.'

'I think he's still roughing people up – in the cells. There was a man in court the other day who said Boyle had beaten him up. I wondered if it was true,' said Rosa.

Leo leaned across the table towards her and shook his finger reprovingly. 'No crusading,' he said, using the same words as Jack. 'Let sleeping sergeants lie, that's my advice.'

Rosa laughed, trying to pass it off. She didn't want anyone else pre-empting her story. Looking at the faces round the table she wondered if she could ask one of these men to escort her to the Blue Blanket. Not Lawrie, he would blab. Mike would steal the story. Patrick and the other boys would tell Mike, and then he'd steal the story. The Basher could cope and keep his mouth shut but he wasn't around. She'd have to ask Iain. She'd use him just as he had used her.

Patricia was beside her and it was obvious that her euphoria about the fire had worn off because she was drinking gin and tonic, which always had a depressing effect on her. She sat with her chin propped up on her hands staring bleakly into space, not taking part in the general chatter.

'What's up?' Rosa asked in a low voice.

She rolled her eyes sideways and whispered, 'It's Hugh.'

Of course. 'What's he done?' asked Rosa and Patricia's brown eyes slowly filled up with tears. 'I'm going to the lavatory. Come with me,' she said.

They stood pressed up against the wash basin beside the cubicles and Rosa listened as Patricia explained between sobs, 'He's been bothering and bothering me to sleep with him – but I've been too scared. Then he said either I do or it's off. So last night I said I would. We went to his flat in Great King Street and I took off my clothes and got into bed with him – but he did nothing, nothing at all. He lay there staring at the ceiling and smoking. It was so shaming. After three hours, I got up and went home in a taxi. He found me repulsive!'

'Did he talk to you about it?' Rosa asked.

'He told me not to be cheap when I tried to touch him.'

'The bastard!'

'No, it's me. There must be something wrong with me. I wonder if I'm deformed or repulsive, but there's nobody I can ask. Maybe I should go to bed with Lawrie first and get it over. He never rejects anybody.' She was crying pitifully and Rosa felt powerless to help because her ignorance was worse, but instinctively she knew that Hugh was playing a sadistic game.

She hugged her friend and said, 'There's nothing wrong with you. He's deliberately torturing you. Give him the push. You can have anybody you want. Mike would jump through hoops for you.' Rosa was very aware she was giving advice she wouldn't take herself.

Patricia sobbed. 'Why is it the only men who want me are men I don't want?' she asked brokenly.

'I wish I knew the answer, because that's my problem too,' said Rosa.

Though she knew she shouldn't, when she left the pub, she went back to the office to phone Iain. At least she wouldn't have any trouble losing her virginity if she were rash enough to get into bed with him, she thought as she dialled the number.

'Hey!' he exclaimed in surprise when he heard her voice. He probably thought he'd never hear from her again.

'Listen, I want you to do me a favour. I've got to go some-place that I can't go on my own. I need a man with me.'

'It's not to a ball, is it?' he asked, apprehensive that his bride-to-be would hear of it.

'No, of course not. It's to a rough pub in the Canongate.'

'That's all right then.' The Hamilton-Prentices didn't go to such places.

'Can you come now?' she asked.

'Not tonight. What about tomorrow? I'll pick you up at the Tron at half past six.'

'OK, that'll do but don't bring a fancy car. I don't want to attract attention,' she told him.

Seventeen

S aturday was the busiest day of the week for the copy-
takers because from mid-afternoon they had to try to
answer two or three phones at once. Football reporters all
over the country phoned in with results, frantically competing with racing correspondents and rugby commentators.

The afternoon edition, the *Sporting Pink*, was put out on
pale strawberry-coloured newsprint and contained all the
sporting results. One thing not much in evidence was news.
A story had to be cataclysmic to be included and even then
it could find itself stuck in the Stop Press column at the foot
of the back page.

News reporters who worked on Saturdays had a lazy day,
not bothering to hurry back to the office after lunch to write
up any run-of-the-mill stories which were assigned to them.
These could be knocked out on Monday mornings or
completely ignored if not sufficiently important.

For most of the morning, the office was almost deserted.
Saturday was Patricia's day off, so Rosa had no one to
chatter with, and, in search of amusement, she wandered
out at lunch time to walk the length of Princes Street, and
stare into the windows of the big shops – especially the
upper-class department stores Forsyths and Jenners, but
lingering longest at Greensmith Downes. Though it was not
so large as the other two, it was the smartest clothes shop
in the city.

She was gazing into one of the big windows, dazzled by
the sight of a full-skirted white ball gown with a scarlet

bolero jacket made of silk, as was the huge matching rose tucked into the waistband, when a voice said in her ear, 'Very glamorous, I agree.'

Sylvia was standing behind her, wearing her black astrakhan coat and a green scarf tied over her head and knotted on her chin. Her face was carefully made up, as usual.

'It's gorgeous,' Rosa agreed.

'Do you go to many balls?' Sylvia asked, stepping closer to the glass in order to have a better view.

Rosa laughed ruefully. 'No. I go to pubs, or, if I want to dance, to the Plaza and the Palais. I went to lots of balls when I was up at university but not to a single one since I left.'

'You'll go again some day, Cinderella. That dress would suit you. You should buy it. I'll go in with you and see what it looks like when you try it on,' said Sylvia.

Rosa grinned and pointed at the price ticket, saying, 'There's one reason I won't buy it. It's fifty-two guineas.' Her wage, though high for a woman, was seven pounds ten shillings a week, plus what Mike made on her behalf in expenses, but that was not usually more than three pounds.

Sylvia looked solemnly back at her. In spite of the make-up, her eyes were tired and pouched. 'Live life while you can,' she said solemnly. 'Come on, let's go in.'

The women in the evening dress department obviously knew her and bustled expectantly round them. Though Rosa protested, the white dress was retrieved from the window, and it was her size. She touched its beautifully accordion-pleated skirt with reverence but common sense told her to fight off the impulse even to try it on. 'I'd never wear it. It'll hang in my wardrobe till it goes out of fashion,' she said and refused all their blandishments to put on the dress because she didn't want to be tempted.

Sylvia shrugged good-humouredly. 'You're a real Scottish Calvinist at heart, aren't you? You don't approve of self-indulgence,' she said as they walked out of the hushed store.

On the pavement of Princes Street she said, 'I'm going for a coffee. Care to join me? There's a good café in the basement of the tobacco shop along the road.'

'Yes, I know it. Let's go.'

When they were seated, Sylvia lit a cigarette and drew in the smoke with a huge breath before she said, 'You should have bought that dress, you know.'

Rosa laughed. 'Perhaps.' She remembered Etta's hint that Sylvia might help her in her enquiries about Boyle, and leaned across the table to say in a more solemn voice, 'I wonder if I could ask you something.'

Sylvia's reply was: 'Try.'

'Do you know anything about Boyle, the police sergeant in the Burgh Court?'

Sylvia stared at her over the rim of her coffee cup. 'I know one thing – stay away from him.'

'That's all right. I've no designs on him. It's because I'm doing a piece about the way prisoners in the cells are beaten up before they appear in court. They often accuse him . . .' said Rosa.

Sylvia nodded. 'I believe them. He's trouble. His wife was killed in a road accident a few years ago and people say he became very bitter afterwards but I think he must have been nasty from the start. He used to go to Flora's but she banned him after he beat up one of the girls. I've heard that he picks up rough trade in Leith nowadays.'

'He always looks so calm and controlled,' said Rosa, surprised.

'Believe me, they're the worst kind. My advice is not to start asking questions about him. You could find it'd be like turning over an ant hill,' said Sylvia sipping her coffee.

Then she closed her eyes for a moment and sighed, 'God, I'm tired.'

'Have you been very busy?' Rosa asked and then wondered if it was a tactful question.

'Sort of. I've a friend up from London and he talks all the time. He even shouts out to me when he's in the bath. It's very exhausting.'

A pang of envy seized Rosa. When not at work, most of the time she lived in total silence. For company she played the radio on the Home Service so she could have another voice in her life, but Mrs Ross insisted that it was kept very low which meant that it was barely audible.

Sylvia drank her coffee in one swallow and signalled for another before she went on: 'Hal, my friend, is writing a book and he likes to read bits out to me.'

'What's it about?' asked Rosa. Many of her colleagues claimed to be writing books and had to be restrained from reading them aloud too.

Sylvia laughed. 'It's about a man who's living off his girl-friend's immoral earnings. It's meant to be funny.'

Rosa stared. She couldn't help it. Surely someone who lived off a woman was a pimp? 'Like Porgy and Bess,' she suggested.

Sylvia grimaced. 'Hardly! This is a comedy.'

'I hope your friend doesn't live off you,' Rosa ventured. Surprisingly Sylvia didn't seem offended.

'In fact, he does, off me and another girl in London. He's comparing business in the two capital cities, he says.'

Rosa was flummoxed. The only question that came into her head was, 'Which one's winning?'

'London at the moment. My expenses are not so high as the Mayfair girl, but the clients here are not so generous either.' Sylvia could have been speaking about buying and selling potatoes.

Now Rosa needed another coffee, so she waved to the waitress, who came over with it. Sylvia saw her confusion and laughed. 'You really are an innocent, aren't you?' she said.

'Yes, I suppose I am, but, like Etta says, I'm working on it,' Rosa told her.

Sylvia ground out her cigarette in the ashtray before immediately lighting another, inhaling the smoke as if her life depended on it.

'Why do you do it?' Rosa asked, abandoning caution.

'Do what? Smoke?' The hazel eyes were narrowed.

'No, not smoke. Why do you give your friend money you earn?'

'Because we're partners. We're in business together. I've known him since I was a girl and I love him, I expect. I suppose that technically he's a pimp because we share my earnings but he doesn't beat me up or take all my money or anything like that. His parents know my parents – they're all terribly respectable and have no idea what we're doing. They think I'm an interior decorator.'

She would have made a very good interior decorator, thought Rosa, remembering the elegant flat. She was amazed at the frank way Sylvia was answering her questions.

'How did it start?' she asked, intrigued.

Sylvia frowned and twirled the cigarette around in her fingers. 'We used to talk about making a lot of money. Hal was working for a stockbroker at the time and saw how some people have absolute piles of the stuff. But you need money to make money and our problem was how to get our hands on the start-up fund. He's a younger son with nothing to inherit and my parents sent me to a good girls' school and expected me to repay the investment by making a good marriage. We needed to do something with a quick, big return. Like robbing banks, Hal said!' She laughed again at the memory. 'I didn't want him doing that,' she went on, 'so it was my idea for us to rent a flat where I could entertain a few clients. I never had any trouble finding them. I'd been fighting off my father's friends – sometimes literally – since I was fifteen. We planned to make enough money to buy a yacht and sail around the world.

'Because our parents knew a lot of people in London and might find out what we were doing, we decided to bring sin

140

to the provinces and I set up in Edinburgh. I arrived here in Festival time four years ago and, through well-connected contacts of Hal's, I was up and running within a week.'

Her face was pensive as she went on. 'It was so easy. All my clients were very polite and paid me handsomely. But a year ago I started feeling under the weather. When I went for a check-up they found that I've got this bloody illness . . . It's cut down on my earning capacity . . .' Her voice trailed off.

'What rotten luck,' Rosa said and really meant it.

Sylvia saw that the reaction was sincere and went on again: 'I can't keep up the pace any more but Hal's determined I'll have my trip round the world, so he's taken a flat in Mayfair and hired another girl to do there what I do here. He's also writing his book and he's sure it'll earn us a fortune. One of his friends is already interested in making it into a film.'

'When is this world trip going to happen?' Rosa asked, hoping it was soon.

'Next year. The cash is piling up and he's put it into a Swiss bank.'

'I hope he's trustworthy,' said Rosa, her cautious streak coming out again.

Sylvia laughed. 'Don't come all Calvinistic on me again, Rosa. It doesn't really matter any longer if he isn't, because, frankly, I don't think I'll last another year.'

'You shouldn't say things like that. You should be more positive,' Rosa protested but Sylvia gave her a gimlet look and said, 'Why? It's easier if I'm realistic. Don't flannel me. I don't believe in happy endings. I just want to be happy *now*, in this moment. You should adopt that philosophy too.'

A sense of bleakness almost overwhelmed Rosa as she said, 'I'm beginning not to believe in happy endings either. Everything has been so bleak lately. Those senseless murders! There must be so many evil people walking about. I watch people and wonder what they're really thinking.

Even the worst villains probably look all right when you pass them in the street. I keep thinking about the men I know, and wondering if they could have killed Sadie and Marie. Could they be capable of doing something as ghastly as that?'

'I thought you'd been taken off those stories,' said Sylvia.

'Officially I have. The men seem to have taken them over. Jack's allowing me to investigate brutality against people in the police cells instead but I can't stop thinking about the murders and I'm still following them up in my own time.'

Sylvia leaned towards her, dropped her voice and said with great intensity, 'Rosa, I've told you this before. Keep out of the brutality story – and the murders. There's vested interests involved. The police and big business in this city hang together. They'll gang up on you.'

'But surely if crimes have been committed, they'll be discovered and punished in the end?' Rosa asked.

Sylvia sighed at her naivety. 'You haven't a chance against them. If you're a man and one of them, that's fine. If not – don't antagonize them. Take care. Please keep out of it, Rosa.'

With their third coffees, the waitress had brought a plate of biscuits but Sylvia only ate one bite out of hers and shoved the rest to the side of her plate. Her hands were shaking as she lit yet another cigarette. 'Keep well out of it,' she said again, and stood up to bring their meeting to an end.

Both looking serious, they left the café and walked slowly along to Hanover Street, where their paths divided.

As Sylvia looked in the direction of her flat, her spirits visibly lightened. 'Nearly home,' she said, as if she had been forcing herself through an ordeal. 'I hope Hal has a bottle of champagne on ice for me.'

At half past six Rosa was waiting on the pavement outside the Tron Church with her coat collar turned up against the cold and her hands shoved into her jacket pockets. Amazingly Iain turned up on time and drew up beside her in a little

black and cream Hillman California car. 'Is this ordinary
enough for you?' he asked as he leaned over to open the
passenger door.

'It'll do,' she said as she climbed in. He was looking so
dangerously dashing in a thick blue fisherman's sweater that
she had to harden her heart against him.

'Where are we going?' he wanted to know.

'The Blue Blanket. It's on the right-hand side of the road,
near Huntly House.'

'God no! That's a dump.' His face showed his disinclina-
tion for patronizing the pub, so it must be bad.

'I warned you that it's rough.'

He pulled a face. 'Rough is an understatement, believe
me. What do you want to go there for?'

'Because the doorman from the N.B., the one who says I
didn't drop Marie off beside him on New Year's morning,
drinks there,' she told him.

'He must have a lead-lined stomach then. Make sure you
don't drink anything that doesn't come out of a sealed bottle.
They keep a big carboy full of dregs from the glasses on the
bar. You can buy a glassful for sixpence,' he said darkly and
her stomach heaved at the thought.

They parked a bit up the road from the pub and walked
down towards it. It was a shabby-looking establishment, the
sort of drinking den that Burke and Hare would have patronized, and Rosa quailed when they pushed the front door open
into a small room with a curving bar. The stench of sour beer
mixed with Jeyes Fluid wafted out to hit them. There was
sawdust on the floor and no attempt had been made to create
a feeling of comfort or a pleasant ambience. Three tramp-
like men were leaning on the bar and another two sat in the
shadows on rough wooden benches alongside it. The men at
the bar looked round in surprise when Rosa walked in.

'Nae wimmen,' snapped the barman.

'Have you a snug?' asked Iain.

The barman motioned with his chin to a little enclosure

at the end of the bar. 'In there,' he said frostily.

Behind the wooden partition were three chairs and a shaky table. Iain leant on the small segment of the bar behind the partition and shouted, 'Two bottled beers, please.'

They were shoved through without ceremony. Rosa went up to stand beside Iain and found that by staring into a segment of the mirror at the back of the bar, she could see what was going on in the main room next door. The North British doorman was not there but one of the figures on the dimly lit bench was Sergeant Boyle.

'What's the name of the guy you're looking for?' Iain whispered to her.

'I don't know.' She kicked herself for being so stupid as not to find that out from the other doorman. Jack would kill her if he knew. She felt confused by seeing Boyle, as if her two quests for information were being deliberately muddled up.

Iain, unaware of her confusion, wanted to help her, so he leaned forward on the wooden bar and called to the barman, 'I'm looking for somebody.'

'Oh yeah?'

'He works as doorman at the N.B.'

'You mean Duncan Skinner?'

Iain looked at Rosa, who shrugged to tell him she didn't know the doorman's name. 'Say he's tall and thin, about thirty,' she whispered, deciding to ignore Boyle, who may not have seen her come in.

Iain passed on the description and the barman grunted, 'That's Duncan. He's no' been in the night though.'

'Was he in last night?'

'Might have been. Depends what ye want wi' him.'

'Nothing much, private business,' said Iain lightly. 'I owe him some money and I want to pay it back.'

The barman grinned wolfishly and said, 'Gie it tae me and I'll pass it on.'

'Oh yeah, that's likely. I'm not a halfwit. Where does he live?' said Iain jovially.

'I've nae idea. He comes in, gets pissed, and disappears.'

Rosa, looking in the mirror, saw no movement from any of the men in the bar. Boyle was still slumped at the end of the bench. She plucked at Iain's sleeve and said on impulse, 'Ask him if he knows a man called Noonan who was in a fight here the other night.'

He repeated the request and the barman suddenly popped through the partition and stared at her. 'Whit exactly are ye after?' he demanded.

She said, 'I work for the *Dispatch* and was in the Burgh Court the day before yesterday when a man called Noonan came up from the cells. He said he'd been beaten up after being wrongly arrested in here the night before.'

The barman seemed to soften towards her. Lowering his voice, he almost whispered, 'Yeah, he was hauled in for naethin' and I heard they'd given him a going over. It's just because his family have a name for fighting, but he's been in the Army and he's tryin' to go straight. Not gettin' a bloody chance though, is he?'

While he was speaking to them, his eye was on the people in the main pub. Suddenly there was the noise of a chair being scraped over the floor and in the mirror's reflection, Rosa saw Boyle stand up and make his way to the bar.

At that moment the doorman seemed to freeze, his growing co-operation disappearing. Hurriedly he stepped away from the snug, saying loudly, 'I dinna ken whit ye're after but I think you should get the hell oot o' my shop.'

In the mirror above his shoulder Rosa could see the hard-faced sergeant standing at the bar with a pound note in his hand. Iain and she drank their beer hurriedly before they stepped out from behind the partition and walked towards the door.

As she passed, Boyle turned to stare, again not quite at her. 'Miss Makepeace,' he said in a low, flat voice, 'keep off my back.'

Completely confused and scared by the hostility of his gaze, she followed Iain to the car. Boyle was warning her, she knew. Someone must have told him that she was planning to write about his brutality. Who was the informant? So far she'd only told Jack, Etta and Sylvia. Who had talked? Probably Etta who had friends in the force. Back in the Hillman, Iain said, 'Let's go to the Sheep's Heid in Duddingston for a proper drink.'

She'd still been shaking, but now she shuddered as if she was in the grip of a high fever. 'Duddingston! No thanks!'

'OK, sorry, I forgot about your friend. Any place you like then. I've missed you.'

She shook her head firmly. Common sense was coming back and she knew there was no way she could allow things to drift back to the old situation between them.

'When are you getting married?' she asked, as much as a reminder to him as to herself.

He shrugged and stared at the car windscreen. 'The weekend after next.'

'In St Giles?'

'No, in the register office in Queen Street.'

'A quiet wedding,' she said.

'Listen, Rosa, I really like you and I don't want us to stop being friends. We could meet every now and again,' he said, turning towards her but she shook her head.

'No, I'm not into that.'

She knew that the only way she could cure herself of her fixation with him was by total ruthlessness. Like a surgical operation.

He accepted what she said because of the finality of her tone. 'I'll drop you home,' he offered.

'No, drop me on the Bridges. My car's parked beside the office and I've something to do,' she told him.

In fact the prospect of the lonely weekend looming ahead of her was so depressing that for a moment she considered driving down to Selkirk to visit her father, but she noticed that the sky over the Forth in front of her had taken on the colour of beaten pewter and she could smell snow in the wind.

Up the Yarrow valley where her father lived, drifts could bank up within an hour. One winter they had been snowed in for six weeks. If she stayed away from work even for six days, she would definitely be fired.

Yet what was the alternative? An endless weekend shut up in Mrs Ross's, lying on her bed and reading books. Then she remembered that Jacques Tati's film *Monsieur Hulot's Holiday* was playing at the Cameo in Tollcross.

That's where I'll go, she thought with a surge of relief as if she'd been let off a punishment.

One of the first pieces she wrote for the *Dispatch* was an interview with Tati when he came to Edinburgh for last year's Festival. She had been hideously nervous and inexperienced and knew nothing about him or what he had done – a cardinal sin in the eyes of most celebrities, who expected interviewers to be fully informed about their life histories. But Tati was the soul of courtesy and a kindly provider of information. He bought her a drink and, because he'd broken his arm and was wearing a plaster cast, he invited her to add her name to a selection of famous signatures scrawled all over it. She became his fan for life.

His maladroit behaviour on the screen of the little cinema that smelt of cigarette smoke cheered her up. In a way Hulot reminded her of her father and when she emerged from the Cameo, her mood had lightened. Perhaps a younger Jacques Tati would suddenly appear and transform her existence.

On her way home she made a detour by a Stockbridge Italian café to buy her supper, crisp golden fish and chips wrapped up in newspaper. She hid the warm package in her handbag because Mrs Ross would ban it from the house if she caught a whiff of it.

Rosa had nearly reached the sanctuary of the staircase leading up to her room when the landlady emerged from her sitting room and said, 'There's been a phone call for you, dear.'

Guiltily shifting the handbag to her far-away hand, Rosa asked, 'Did the caller say who it was?'

Iain? The back of her neck prickled. Surely not: he seemed to accept that it was all over between them. When would her fixation with him stop bothering her?

When she saw how Mrs Ross was beaming, she knew it wasn't him though.

'No, it was that nice doctor. He says he'll ring back at ten o'clock. I thought you'd be in by then.'

Roddy. What a pity there was no surge of sexual excitement. A glance at her watch showed it was five to ten.

'I'll listen for the phone,' she said but Mrs Ross shook her head.

'No, go on up. I'll get it and call you. I do like talking to him. He gave me some good advice this afternoon about how to stop my chilblains itching.'

Poor Roddy, thought Rosa, fighting the impulse to laugh. Mrs Ross was probably saving up her ailments for every time he called.

There wasn't even enough time to unwrap her supper when he rang, exactly on time, and she wished he wasn't so reliable. If he kept her dangling, he'd probably have more success.

His voice was solemn when Mrs Ross handed over the phone and Rosa knew that she'd stand listening behind her sitting-room door while the conversation lasted.

'I've got a new posting,' he said.

'Have you? A good one I hope.'

'It's to Cyprus, Nicosia. We're flying out tomorrow.'

'To Nicosia! Gosh, that's quick.'

'There's been some trouble there, Greeks shooting Turks and vice versa. We're going out to try to calm things down.'

'Take care of yourself, Roddy,' she said and realized that she really meant it. Then she added in an effort at lightness, 'At least you'll get some good weather. It's starting to snow again here.' Through the glass fanlight at the top of the front door she could see snowflakes drifting down like goose feathers.

'I'll miss you, Rosa,' said Roddy.

'I'll miss you too,' she told him and was surprised to realize that she was telling the truth. He was so trustworthy. He'd make a wonderful psychiatrist because he had a huge capacity for listening and not condemning.

'Do you mean that?' he persisted. *Don't push it, Roddy*, she thought, and said lightly, 'Of course I do. Bring back some lemons.'

'Lemons?'

'They grow there.'

His voice grew formal again and he said, 'Of course,' which made her feel a bitch.

When she hung up, Mrs Ross immediately opened the sitting-room door and asked, 'Is the doctor going away?'

'Yes, to Nicosia.'

'I do hope he'll be all right,' she said fervently.

'So do I,' Rosa told her.

In her room, at last she hungrily ate the lukewarm fish and chips with the window open to get rid of any smell. When she finished, she carefully folded up the sheets of newspaper in which she'd carried her supper home intending to stick them into a street dustbin next morning so Mrs Ross didn't find the incriminating evidence.

As she was putting the paper into her coat pocket, she saw that it was the outside pages of the last edition of the *Evening News*. Out of habit and professional interest, she cast her eye over the copy, looking to see if they'd covered the same stories as the *Dispatch*. At the foot of the back page there was a Stop Press column printed sideways. She turned it round to read:

'The body of a man was found this morning in the Dean Gardens. It is thought he either fell or jumped from the Dean Bridge. His name has not been released.'

She felt her hands prickle and realized what Shakespeare

149

meant when he wrote the lines about knowing when something evil was about by the pricking of your thumbs. The stark stop press announcement made her heart jump into her throat and set all her journalistic antennae twitching violently.

Eighteen

The Dean Gardens in Stockbridge were walled and private. Only subscribers had keys for the two entrances, which were a wooden door set in thick stone walls at one end of the property, and a gate with high iron railings at the other. The Gardens themselves were several acres of paradise tucked away within the city. There were many decorative trees, shrubs, drifts of spring flowers in the early months of the year, and banks of pink and purple rhododendrons later on. Inhabitants of the houses round about strolled along the twisting paths, exercising their dogs and communing with nature, but that privilege cost them a considerable sum of money each year.

Lying as they did on the north side of the Water of Leith, the Gardens swept steeply down in terraces from the elevation of Anne Street into the valley. Towering 106 feet above them and the river, were the four elegant arches of Thomas Telford's 1829 Dean Bridge, which carried the Queensferry Road on its way from central Edinburgh to South Queensferry. In 1912, the bridge's parapets were topped with fierce-looking spikes of iron, because from the day it was finished, its height made it a standing temptation to would-be suicides. In spite of the spikes however, every year a few determined people managed to plunge off it to their deaths among the clustering trees far below.

On Sunday morning, the sky was clear and the previous night's frozen snow still frosted the streets, turning the bare branches of trees into meshes of lace. Wrapped up in her pea jacket and a woollen hat, Rosa trudged to the Gardens wondering if she knew anyone who might possess a key to them.

Most of her acquaintance was not so refined and she had decided that her only hope of gaining entry was to lurk by the wooden door at the end of Anne Street and slip in behind an unsuspecting keyholder.

Then she remembered that Jean Noble, an ex-colleague of her Great Aunt Fanny, lived in a basement flat in Clarendon Crescent, where the Dean Gardens ended. Miss Noble had always been friendly towards Rosa, so she decided to call on her.

When she rang Miss Noble's doorbell, she was recognized at once and invited inside. 'It's Fanny's niece! How nice to see you. Come in.'

Feeling awkward, Rosa edged into the little lobby and said, 'I hope I'm not intruding, but I was wondering if you're a keyholder to the Gardens.'

The old lady's ruddy face beamed. 'Of course I am, my dear. I love going there. Now that I haven't a garden of my own, it's my personal haven. In fact I was just about to put on my boots and go walking in the snow. Would you like to come with me? You live in Northumberland Street, don't you? It's rather dark and gloomy there, I always think. Not a green thing in sight, and you must miss that because you're a country girl.'

Rosa had planned to come clean about her real reason for going into the Gardens but did not want to spoil Miss Noble's innocent enthusiasm for the outing. She obviously did not know that a body had been found there only yesterday.

'I was hoping to get into the Gardens and I'd love to walk with you,' she said a little lamely.

'Wait till I put on my heavy clothes then, and get my camera. The Gardens will be looking lovely today,' Miss Noble cried as she disappeared into a back room. When she returned she was wrapped up like an Eskimo with only her eyes and the tip of her nose showing. A Rolex camera was slung around her neck.

She patted it with a gloved hand and said, 'This is my pride and joy. I'm a member of a camera club and, though I say it myself, I take some beautiful pictures.'

Then she handed Rosa a big key and said cheerfully, 'That's the Gardens key. Let's go before the weather changes again. How's your great-aunt?'

'Very well,' Rosa said, though Fanny never admitted to good health, and was always suffering from some unspecified ailment or other.

Miss Noble shot her a sceptical glance as if she saw through this deception. 'That's good,' she said and gave a surprisingly girlish giggle that made Rosa warm to her so much that her conscience made her decide to come clean.

'Actually, Miss Noble, I was wondering if you saw the bit in the news last night about a body being found in the Gardens. You know I work for the *Dispatch,* don't you? We don't work on Sundays but I thought I'd check that story out . . .'

To Rosa's relief, Miss Noble was not at all shocked. 'Dear me, another one! People often jump off that bridge, you know. The police don't usually publicize the cases because they think it encourages other poor souls to do the same,' she said in a matter-of-fact voice.

'Yes, I know that,' Rosa agreed. Unless the person concerned was very prominent or the story very unusual, most newspapers operated a no-suicides policy – at least they did not follow the stories up – which explained why there was no mention of the Dean Gardens body in any of the Sunday papers.

They walked quickly along the Crescent and when they reached the iron railings, Miss Noble said, in a school-mistressy manner, 'Come on, open the gate. I'll snap some snow scenes and you can go nosing around if that's what you have in mind.'

Inside the Gardens Miss Noble headed along a tree-lined path till they were in sight of the bridge and then she stopped. 'I'm going no farther. Come back and find me here when you're finished,' she told Rosa, who walked on, leaving the old lady focusing her camera on a trio of berry-laden holly bushes crowned with snow. It was only a short distance till the bridge loomed over her. An uneasy silence brooded over the scene and there was not a soul about.

Looking around, she saw, off to the right where the under-growth was thickest, that some small trees and shrubs had been trampled down by many feet, and branches had been broken off recently. In the middle of a thicket of rhododen-drons there was a cordoned-off area where the bushes were completely flattened.

She looked up and found that the middle stone arch of the bridge was immediately above her head. Instinctively she flinched. Dejected and a little scared she turned to walk back to where she had left Miss Noble, but, turning a bend in the path, she met a man leaning on a huge sweeping brush; a wheelbarrow and shovel stood by his side.

Miss Noble was coming along from the other direction and waving as she called out, 'There you are, Rosa! I was looking for you. This is my friend Tommy Nisbet, one of the gardeners here. I've just been talking to him and he tells me he found the body of that poor man yesterday morning.'

'How awful for you,' Rosa said to the man, but he obvi-ously didn't require sympathy.

His eyes sparkled as he said, 'They're aye loupin' aff that bridge. What a daft thing to do. The policeman thought he must have been drunk because there was an awful smell of whisky aff him. He was deid when I found him in the bushes. I saw some of the rhodies were flattened when I was sweep-ing away the snow from the big steps. Oh aye, I thought to myself, another yin's jumped.'

'What time was that?' Rosa asked.

'About ten o'clock. I was clearing the snow for folk who

like to walk through the gairdens in the morning when I came on him. This is my fifth and I've been workin' here for twenty years. They put spikes on the top of the bridge parapet but that daesnae stop them. I cam in the day to tidy up a wee bit – it doesnae do to have all thae broken branches lying aboot.' Tommy was being very officious and enjoying every moment of his few minutes of fame.

'What did you do when you found the body?' Rosa asked.

'I legged it down to the phone box at the end of Hamilton Place and phoned the police. An ambulance came first and then a police car,' he said.

'Did they have any idea when he jumped?' was Rosa's next question.

He shrugged. 'During the night. They usually go over when it's dark.'

Even in the middle of the night, there was usually some traffic over that bridge. Had anyone seen a man climbing up on the parapet in order to jump to his death?

The most important question was burning on her lips however: 'Was he identified?' she asked and Tommy nodded vigorously.

'Oh aye. He had stuff on him and the police found out who he was quick enough. Duncan Skinner was his name.'

It was as if something exploded inside her head. She saw stars. Her legs started to shake and her heart thudded in her ears. It was very frightening to have another awful premonition that turned out to be justified.

Weakly she sat down on Tommy's wheelbarrow and Miss Noble anxiously asked, 'Are you all right, my dear? Did you know him?'

'Yes. At least I didn't *know* him exactly, but I know who he is – was . . . I've spoken to him . . . He was a doorman at the North British Hotel . . .' Her voice trailed off.

It was all too much of a coincidence. Something awful was going on. The blue sky seemed to have darkened and the surrounding trees no longer looked beautiful – they

looked evil and threatening. She remembered Sylvia's warning to keep away from the whole business; yet she kept being
dragged back in.

'Are the police sure he jumped?' she asked Tommy.

'Hoo else wid he get ower that bridge?' said Tommy in a
reasonable voice.

'He could have been pushed.'

'That's no' very likely. The parapet's high and he'd be a
guid weight. He wasnae a wee fella.'

That was true. He'd been tall, strong and straight, certainly
not a wee fellow, but he was thin and probably not too heavy.

Miss Noble closed the viewing aperture of her camera, put
a hand under Rosa's elbow and said briskly, 'You're very
white. You've had a shock and it's getting cold. Come back
with me and have a hot drink.'

Weakly, Rosa followed her along the path and up the hill
again. At the gate Miss Noble stuck out her hand for the key.
Locking the gate behind them, she gently propelled her
charge along the road to her flat.

In her cosy sitting room she said, 'Take off your boots
and sit down,' and pointed to a deep armchair drawn up in
front of a glowing coal fire. Wordlessly Rosa did as she was
told and a few moments later a warm glass was put into her
hand. 'Drink that. It's a hot whisky mac. You look as if you
need it,' Miss Noble told her.

A generous slug of whisky had been mixed with ginger
wine and hot water and when she drank it down she felt the
blood starting to flow in her veins again. Jean Noble sat in
the opposite chair staring at her guest. In spite of her age,
her eyes were still piercingly blue and full of unspoken
questions.

'You see, I spoke to Skinner, the dead man, only a couple
of days ago,' Rosa explained. The old lady nodded in silent
encouragement so Rosa went on to tell her the whole story:
how she was sure that he had seen Marie at the hotel but
later denied it to the police.

'Then he disappeared, and now he's dead,' she said.

'It sounds very fishy. Do you think he killed your friend and committed suicide out of remorse?' Miss Noble asked.

'He might have. But he'd have had to leave his post at the hotel door that night, and nobody says he did that. He may have seen who picked Marie up though, because she obviously went away with somebody.'

'But why would that make him kill himself?' was Miss Noble's next question.

'I don't know. Maybe he didn't commit suicide. Maybe he was pushed over the bridge in spite of what your gardener friend said.' Rosa gave another huge shiver and felt the muscles in her legs and back contract in a spasm of nervous pain. *What am I getting myself into?* she thought.

Miss Noble added more whisky to both their glasses and said briskly, 'Don't worry. It had nothing to do with you.'

'But it might have. I saw him talking to Marie – and even though the police didn't seem to believe me, I directed attention to him. If he was pushed over the bridge it might have been because he knew more than he told the police.'

'Come, come, you're being fanciful. There's no suggestion he was pushed. I think it's more likely that he had too much to drink and did away with himself. In fact, he might have killed that poor girl and realized how evil he was! Tommy said the body reeked of whisky and people do strange things when they're drunk. Did he have a family? He may have had other problems you know nothing about,' said Miss Noble in a sensible tone.

Rosa shook her head. 'I don't think he had any family. He lived in the hotel staff quarters, and the other doorman said he wasn't long out of prison.'

Miss Noble clucked her tongue. 'Prison! He could have any amount of problems. It might have nothing to do with your dead friend. Are you feeling better yet? Would you like something to eat?'

Rosa shook her head. Her stomach was churning too much

to receive food but the whisky was reviving her and clearing her head. The heat of the fire warmed her feet and when she bent down to pull on her boots again in preparation for leaving, Miss Noble put a hand on her shoulder and said, 'Don't feel personally involved with this, Rosa. I'm sure it has nothing to do with you and it sounds like a messy business. In fact, I don't know what you're doing working on a newspaper anyway. A girl with a degree like yours could be doing any kind of job. Your aunt is always talking about how clever you are. She's very proud of you and she'd be distressed if she knew about this, but don't worry, I'm not going to tell her.'

Fanny, proud of her? Rosa was astonished because her aunt had never shown any sign of it.

'But I like my job. In fact I love it. There's nothing else I'd rather be doing,' she told her.

Miss Noble sighed in sympathy. 'Of course, you're young. I suppose at your age I wanted adventure too – in fact I joined the suffragettes, you know, and was arrested once, but they let me go. If you're determined to go on working in newspapers, do take care.'

Everybody is telling me the same thing! What do they think is going to happen to me? Rosa asked herself.

Miss Noble insisted on accompanying her to the gate of the Gardens and unlocking it so she could take the shortcut back along its paths to Stockbridge and her lodgings. As she ran beneath the overhanging trees, she looked back over her shoulder and waved to the old lady who was standing at the gate watching her go. In farewell Miss Noble raised both hands with the thumbs up like an encouraging spectator at a football match.

Safely out of the Gardens and heading along Hamilton Place, she spotted the phone box from which Tommy had phoned the police. Suddenly it was imperative for her to tell someone else about the dead doorman. She had to get it off her chest. Amazingly there was no one in the box, and there was even an undamaged phone book, so she flipped through it till she found *Playfair, S.*, with an address in Queen Street.

Putting in a couple of pennies, she dialled the number and waited while it rang out. The breath was coming shortly in her chest and she felt giddy. After five rings, Sylvia answered. She sounded guarded.

'Sylvia, it's me, Rosa Makepeace. I've been in Dean Gardens and found out that Duncan Skinner, the doorman who saw me drop Marie off at the North British, jumped off the Dean Bridge into the Gardens yesterday. They say it was suicide – but he might have been pushed.' She knew her voice sounded hysterical but she couldn't help it.

For what seemed like ages there was total silence from Sylvia's end.

'Sylvia, are you still there?' Rosa half shouted.

'Yes, I heard you. I'm thinking. Where are you now?'

'In the phone box in Hamilton Place. I've just come back from Dean Gardens.'

'For God's sake go home and stay there. The man probably killed himself. I told you to keep out of this business,' Sylvia snapped and hung up.

Rosa stood holding the dead receiver for a few moments and then hung up too. She felt foolish. There was nothing else to do but go home and huddle over her gas fire till tomorrow – but then she was going to write this story, no matter how often she was advised to keep quiet. She must get it down on paper because she was probably the only person, certainly the only journalist, who could make the connection between a run-of-the-mill suicide and Marie's murder.

Nineteen

Next morning she was 'on the Calls' again so she shut herself in one of the phone booths and rang round to the police, the fire brigade and the ambulance service.

Her call to the police brought in nothing significant, but when she contacted the ambulance service, which was usually more friendly and informative, she asked, 'What about the body found in the Dean Gardens on Saturday? Is there anything on it?'

The man at the other end of the line rustled through some papers before he said, 'Yes, that was reported at nine twenty-nine a.m. on Saturday morning. He was dead on arrival at the E.R.I.'

'Have you a full report?' she persisted. 'There was no mention of it either yesterday or today in the morning papers.'

'Not much,' was the reply.

'Has the body been identified?' she asked, half-hoping that Tommy's information was wrong, though that wasn't likely.

'Yes. He was Duncan Skinner, age twenty-nine, of eighty-nine St Stephen's Street, Stockbridge. But you shouldn't be putting in anything about him because the police don't like publicizing details of how people kill themselves. It always gives somebody else the same idea.'

Age 29, she thought. *Younger than he looked.*

'I know about that. I'm interested because I might know him.'

'Did you?' asked the ambulance man.

'No, it's not the man I know,' she lied.

Her next call was to the police. 'Can you give me any details about the death of Duncan Skinner in Dean Gardens? The *News* had a bit in their Stop Press on Saturday night about a body being found in the bushes there.'

More papers rustled. 'It was a suicide. He jumped off the bridge.'

'Were there any witnesses?'

'Only the gardener who found the body.'

'No one on the roadway over the bridge saw anything?' she persisted.

'Nobody's come forward.' The voice at the other end was dismissive.

'Have you put up any notices asking for witnesses?'

A sharp note came into the policeman's voice. 'Why should we? He jumped off. Lots of people do the same and we don't make a big thing about it. His family have been informed.'

'Did they say there was any reason for him killing himself?'

'Listen, I don't know any more about his reasons than you do. It's not our policy to publicize suicides like this,' he snapped and hung up.

Without asking anyone's advice or talking about what she was planning to do, she sat down at her typewriter and wrote a report about Duncan Skinner's death. When it was finished she laid it on Jack's desk without saying anything and went to the canteen for a cup of coffee. Within fifteen minutes, Gil came along and tapped her on the shoulder.

'Jack wants you,' he said.

'Where did you get all this?' Jack asked. He was standing against the window with her copy in his hand.

'I went to Dean Gardens yesterday and spoke to the man who found the body. I checked up on its identity this morning. It's the N.B. doorman right enough,' she told him.

'How did you know about a body being found in the Gardens?' he asked.

'The *News* had a bit in their Stop Press on Saturday night.'
Jack glared at his reporting staff. 'We missed it. Who was on the Calls on Saturday?'

All heads, including Rosa's, dropped. Nobody would admit to missing a story.

Jack switched his interest back to her. 'Has the *News* got this?' he asked, waving the sheet of paper.

'Well I didn't tell them and as far as I can see they didn't follow up their original story – probably because it was a suicide,' she replied.

'You're sure it's the man you've named. You're sure he's the doorman from the N.B.?'

'Yes. Positive. I've got his home address too and I could go down there now and check him out if you like.' In other words, she was saying, this is my story again.

'OK. Get going,' he said. Once again he seemed slightly bemused by her facility for being around when things happened – so was she, come to that.

She didn't seem to do anything to deserve these scoops. They came her way on their own and she was beginning to wish they wouldn't.

St Stephen's Street in Stockbridge was narrow and lined on both sides by gloomy tenements. An imposing church stood at the eastern end but after that, the quality of the architecture went downhill. Number 89 turned out to be a flat-fronted building with a public house in the basement and a pawnbroker on the ground floor. A bell rang when she pushed open the pawnshop door and asked where the Skinners lived.

A cadaverous woman behind the pawnshop counter said nothing, only pointed above her head with one hand and then stuck out three fingers. Rosa wondered if she was a mute but took her gesture to mean the third floor.

Two doors opened on to the third floor landing. One had a brass plate with the name McPhail incised on it. The other was unadorned, so she tapped loudly at it. For a long time there was silence and when she was about to give up, she heard the clattering of keys inside and the door creaked open.

A bent old man in a collarless white shirt stood in the lobby staring at her. 'What do you want?' he asked. His accent was not local. In fact he sounded like a Londoner.

'I'm from the *Dispatch*. I want to ask you about Duncan,' she said quickly.

One of the astonishing things she learned early in her journalistic career was how often traumatized people were prepared to talk to the press, even in times of deepest trouble. They seemed to regard a sympathetic reporter as a sort of confessor.

The old man called over his shoulder, 'Jess, it's a girl from the newspapers.'

A woman's voice came back. 'Ask her in then.'

Their sitting room was meticulously clean and tidy with two high-backed chairs drawn up to the fire. On the mantelpiece was a trio of framed photographs, one of them of Duncan Skinner, looking young and carefree.

A dumpy, grey-haired woman rose from one of the chairs and turned towards the visitor. 'Did you know our Duncan?' she asked. Her accent was not local either.

'I met him in the N.B., but I didn't really know him,' Rosa admitted.

The old couple sighed in unison. 'What we can't understand is why he did it,' said the woman.

'Are you his parents?' Rosa asked for they seemed old to have fathered a man of Duncan's age.

'Oh no, we're his mother's parents. He lived with us off and on after his mother went away. Sit down,' said the woman, patting the seat of an upright chair near her.

Rosa perched on it and looked from one to the other. They were solemn-faced but neither seemed overwhelmed by grief.

'What did the police tell you?' she asked.

'They said he jumped off Dean Bridge,' the old man replied.

'It must have been an awful shock.'

He shook his head. 'We're used to getting shocks from Duncan but this is the worst of all.'

'Does his mother know – or his father?'

'No. His mother's in America. She went off with a GI during the war, and God knows where his father is, or even who he was. We came up here when I was offered a job in the docks at the beginning of the war and we brought the boy because he'd be safer up here than in London because of the bombing. She never took him back.' The old man's voice was hard.

'How old was he when he came to live with you?'

'Thirteen. But after he grew up he was only here now and again. By the time we got him he was too old for us to make him listen to anything we said.'

'He lived with us when he wasn't in jail,' added the dead man's grandmother. It was obvious that their grandson had been a bitter disappointment to them.

Rosa listened as the couple took turns in talking, telling of how a grandson who originally seemed to be everything they wanted – good-looking and clever – fell in with a bad crowd and 'went to the dogs'.

'He was very easily led,' said Mrs Skinner with a sigh.

'When did you last see him?' Rosa asked.

'He came in about tea time on Friday night with his suit-case and dumped it down. He'd given up his job in the hotel, he said—'

'And it was a good job. The best one he'd had for a long time. The wage wasn't all that great but he got a free room and all his food,' put in the old man.

'On Saturday he didn't get up till midday but then he got dressed and said he was off to meet somebody. He was very cheerful. We'd no idea he was thinking of killing himself.' Mr Skinner's face looked puzzled as he stared at the photo-graph above his wife's head.

'He didn't say anything about who he was meeting or where?' Rosa asked.

'He told us it was about another job, a better one than at the hotel. He went off saying he'd be back at night but the next thing we knew was on Saturday morning with the police knocking on the door to tell us what had happened. They said he was drunk. That was funny because Duncan wasn't a heavy drinker. That was one vice he didn't have. He'd take a beer but whisky made him sick and he never touched it,' the grandmother explained.

'I told the policeman so but he insisted Duncan must have been drunk because there was a strong smell of whisky from his body when he was found,' added her husband.

'He didn't leave a note?' Rosa enquired and they shook their heads in unison.

'The police helped us to look in his suitcase and there was nothing in it except his clothes and some money . . .' There was another pause while they looked at each other, obviously considering whether or not to tell her more. She kept silent because silence is the best way of making people talk. They feel it is necessary to fill the void with words.

The grandfather spoke first. 'It was a shock to find he had so much money.'

Rosa only nodded, and, sure enough, more information came out. Mr Skinner said, 'He had a big envelope stuffed with bank notes. I counted them – a hundred quid in new five pound notes. He got big tips in his hotel job but we didn't know he was making as much as that.'

His wife said with a sigh, 'The police say the money's ours because there's no report of it being stolen and we're his next of kin. He has nobody else except his mother and we haven't heard from her for years. It's a terrible way to come into an inheritance though, isn't it?'

Rosa felt sorry for them because she guessed they were feeling far more desolate than they pretended, but the journalistic impulse prevailed and by the time she was back in the office, she had the story of Duncan Skinner half-written in her head:

Mysterious suicide of hotel doorman – very cheerful and looking forward to a new job hours before he killed himself – a teetotaller who reeked of whisky when he was found dead – a man on a low wage who left one hundred pounds in new bank notes in a suitcase with his grandparents

Most important of all from her point of view was that he was almost certainly the only person to have seen Marie go off with her killer. His knowledge could have put him in danger, and how had he come by so much money? Was it possible that Marie's killer had paid him to keep his mouth shut and then leave his job? Was a cover-up going on?

Skinner's importance as a witness in the Marie murder had to be included in any story she wrote but without stressing it too much. It could be done by stating it as a negative . . . *Duncan Skinner, who was on duty at the North British Hotel door on New Year's morning when Marie Lang, the girl found murdered at Duddingston Loch, disappeared from there, told the police he had never seen her.*

It was too late for her story to appear in the first edition. It made the next one however, and appeared on the front page with her by-line. When the *Evening News* came out, Jack was delighted to find they had not followed up the suicide story, apart from a small paragraph at the bottom of an inside column giving the dead man's name, age and address. Once again the *Dispatch* had a scoop.

Their paper was hardly out on the street when Jack's phone started ringing.

He lifted the receiver and listened for a little while, as his face grew redder and redder. It was obvious that the caller was annoying him and his notorious temper was about to erupt.

Suddenly he yelled, 'Shut up! I'm running a newspaper, not an advertising sheet. If you ad men want to tell me what to put in the paper, you can take it over completely.' Then he slammed the phone back into its cradle and stormed out, en route to the executive floor to continue the battle.

Rosa quailed because she felt sure that the Duncan Skinner piece had started this new row. Her growing conviction about a conspiracy among important people in the city seemed even more possible and all the warnings she'd been receiving came rushing back into her mind but she could not ignore a story of such significance no matter how often she was advised to walk away. After all, a liking for sailing close to the wind was one of the reasons people became newspaper reporters.

After work, the reporters drifted into the Cockburn because they were all anxious to talk about Jack's war with the bosses.

Mike had overheard Gil telling one of the senior subs that Jack was so furious about the efforts being made to censor his coverage of news stories he was considering resigning. Apparently some of the *Scotsman* board members thought that the *Dispatch* was becoming too provocative and there had been complaints from important citizens. In spite of Rosa's misgivings about the Skinner piece, none of those complaints were directed at any particular story, only at the 'general tone' of the paper.

Mulling over this, they sat in the bar as gloomily as if they were at a wake, for nobody was in the mood for drunken revelry. Their Editor might be capable of flaying them with words, but he was stimulating to work for and, if they survived his regime, he was providing them with experience which would qualify them for working on any top-flight newspaper in the English-speaking world.

Life with Jack was exciting, and they were of a type and at an age when excitement was more necessary than food.

Patrick piped up: 'If Jack goes on the way he's heading, he won't be with us much longer. We should make the best of it while we've got him.'

'I'd miss the old bastard,' said Mike and they all nodded in agreement.

'Save your cuttings,' said Lawrie. 'I'm already writing off for other jobs.'

They rounded on him as if he was a traitor but he threw

167

up his hands and said, 'I'm realistic, that's all.'

'I can't understand what they're complaining about. Management should be pleased because we're scooping every other paper right now,' complained Tony.

Patricia snorted, 'They think scoops are vulgar. All they worry about is increasing the advertising revenue. Jack's way of rocking the boat must be upsetting somebody with influence. His stories aren't directed at the right sort of people. He appeals to the masses and they don't buy their clothes in Greensmith Downes or get big television sets from Mr Hamilton-Prentice.' Her tone of voice was scathing.

She was right, of course. The city wasn't prepared to stomach Jack's aggressive journalism. Typical Morningside ladies like Roddy's mother, in their tea-table chat, would say, 'But the *Dispatch* is so common! It's full of horrible things like murders and suicides. That sort of thing's all right for London perhaps but this is *Edinburgh*.'

Rosa stood up and wound her long muffler round her neck. 'I'm going home,' she said and turned for the door. It seemed that the only thing for her to do was hole up with her misery, but her way was blocked. Iain was standing in the passage between the tables looking at her.

'I'm glad I caught you. I want to speak to you,' he said.

When will my heart stop jumping with anticipation every time I see him? she thought but did not reveal how taken aback she felt, because all she said was, 'What about?' in a surly tone.

Gently he tucked her scarf closer round her neck and said, 'I've a car outside. I'll tell you there.' She wondered what he wanted because he had never been so solicitous to her before.

The wedding's off – she's not pregnant after all, was her next confused thought as she walked with him to the door, deliberately not looking at frowning Patricia or across to the bar, where Etta's disapproving eyes were following her.

True to form, he was driving a long, black Jaguar with a

silver cougar springing from the bonnet. 'What happened to the little Hillman?' she asked.

'Don't you like this?' he asked as she sank into the squashy leather seat. The interior of the car smelt of luxury.

'I liked the Hillman better,' she said.

'You enjoy being contrary, don't you?' he said and switched on the engine that purred like a contented cat.

'This is a work car, of course,' she said. Iain's employer, Frank Calder, was the biggest dealer in top-quality cars in the city.

'I'm delivering it for a client,' he concurred.

'And you're making a detour to see me. Why exactly?'

'Because I want to talk to you. Where would you like to go? I was thinking the Maybury Roadhouse might be a nice place to have a drink.'

Another out-of-the-way place, she thought sceptically.

'That's quite a detour. I presume your client is not in any great hurry to get his car,' she said, but in fact the idea of going to the Maybury pleased her. It was an expensive and sophisticated roadhouse on the far west of the city, at the start of the road to Glasgow, and was a particular favourite of Rosa's because of its magnificent Art Deco architecture. The bleached lime interiors and scalloped glass wall lights, the murals of thin huntresses leading greyhounds on leads, were all very evocative of the 1930s. Going in there was like being transported back to the Jazz Age.

Neither Iain nor she mentioned his wedding as they swept along the city streets. Princes Street looked like a dressed-up courtesan under the gleam of yellow street lights and the interior of the car was luxuriously warm and comfortable.

They talked stiffly to each other about the places they passed, and current items of news. Grace Kelly and Prince Rainier engaged their interest for a bit until they realized that they were touching on a sensitive area – a wedding. Then Rosa rapidly changed the subject by telling him that a friend of hers has been posted to Nicosia with the Army.

He frowned. 'Poor sod. They're shooting British soldiers like pigeons out there.'

'Are they really?' She felt a spasm of apprehension for Roddy. He'd leave a big gap in her life.

Because it was early, not yet six thirty, there were only a few cars drawn up in the Maybury forecourt. They pushed open the wonderful gilt bronze doors and entered a world of golden light, the downstairs lounge. A staircase curved elegantly up to a balcony encircling the first floor and Rosa stared about, as delighted with the place as she'd been the first time Iain took her there.

A pianist tinkled out a medley of tunes on a white grand piano. He was playing Gershwin's 'Let's Call the Whole Thing Off'. Very suitable, she thought.

Iain was going out of his way to be charming. He even took her coat and pulled out one of the tub chairs so she could sit down. 'What would you like to drink?' he asked solicitously.

'What sort of cocktails were popular when this place was built?' she asked.

'I'll ask if they do a White Lady,' he said and, miraculously, they did.

He was drinking whisky and sat with his glass in his hand staring at her for a few moments before he came to the point. 'I'm worried about you,' he said eventually.

It was so patently unlikely that she was immediately on the defensive.

'Really? There's nothing wrong with me.' Surely he didn't think she was suffering from a broken heart?

'You're fine at the moment maybe, but you're playing with fire. If I tell you something will you promise on your honour not to write about it?' he went on, lowering his voice.

'You sound like spy – or a Boy Scout,' she quipped.

'Don't make jokes. This isn't funny. If you don't give me your word, I can't tell you.' His face was unusually solemn.

'It isn't illegal or anything like that, is it?'

'No. Will you promise?'

'I don't know. At least give me a hint what it's about.'

'It concerns those stories you've been following up.'

The pianist switched to 'I Got Rhythm' and she sat up straight, antennae twanging. 'What about them?' she asked. He was up to something.

'Some people don't like them. They're putting pressure on the newspaper board to have them stopped.'

'They can't stop news!' she protested.

'Yes, they can. They don't want so much to be made of those murders. Every time they think it's dying down, you pop up with another revelation. The doorman's suicide was the last straw. Nobody else publicized that. Only you and the *Dispatch*.'

'You mean everybody else was silenced? But it's important. Skinner was a witness to Marie's disappearance. He was very significant.'

'You made it sound as if you think he was bumped off,' said Iain.

'He might have been! He lied about not seeing Marie, but I saw her speaking to him and so did Alan.'

Iain groaned. 'Listen to you. That's what I mean. Maybe he *forgot* he saw her. He must have seen hundreds of women that night. You jump to conclusions to get a good story. Everybody else ignored his death because the guy killed himself.'

She refused to give in. 'What makes you so sure he did kill himself? He wasn't depressed. He had plenty of money. He wasn't ill. He was young.' On her fingers she ticked off the reasons against Skinner killing himself.

'He was drunk,' said Iain.

'That's not been proved. He was a beer drinker, that's true, but he never touched whisky though his body reeked of it when it was found beneath the bridge. I think that's very suspicious. Whisky could have been poured over him to make it look as if he was drunk,' she snapped back.

He reached over and took her hand. 'Rosa,' he said very earnestly, 'Stop it. I've been told to ask you to stop. I'm afraid that if you don't, something unpleasant might happen to you. You'd just be another unfortunate girl who fell in with the wrong sort. Already your articles have made it clear that you're sympathetic to people like Sylvia Playfair and the Danube Street girls. Your character could be blackened.'

'As long as it's not my eye,' she said flippantly.

'It could be that too. Perhaps even worse,' he replied. His tone sobered her and she stopped talking to stare at him. He was very much in earnest. 'Who told you to shut me up?' she whispered.

'Hamilton-Prentice and Big Calder, who owns the car showroom. And they're not the only ones. They all use Flora Black's place and they're worried sick, so they're ganging up. They're talking about withdrawing their advertising from the *Dispatch* and giving it all to the *News*. If they and all their friends do that, they could force your paper to close.'

'Why should your future father-in-law want to do such a thing?'

'That's what you mustn't talk about. He and some of his mates have a nice little thing going with Flora. They pay her fines and she supplies them with special girls, the sort they like. It's been going on for years. Calder likes to be beaten and Hamilton-Prentice likes them young – Sadie was one of his. When the girl gets too old, Flora finds him another one. I warn you if you write a word about this, I'll deny I told you anything. You could be sued for thousands because the lawyers'll gang up against you too. You haven't a chance.' His face was hard. It was obvious that he was intent on making her back off.

'My God, one of those men didn't kill Sadie by mistake or anything like that, surely?' she gasped.

He shook his head vigorously. 'Of course not. None of the men I know had anything to do with her death. It's been a shock to all of them – but she was just a tart, Rosa. She wasn't important. They've all had to cut their ties with Flora but she'll not split on them because she knows that when it dies down – and it will – they'll go back again. The trouble is you and your paper are being blamed for it not dying down.'

She felt colour flaming into her face. 'That's horrible. Just a tart – not important! Two girls were murdered, for God's sake. We're not talking about dead pets. Sadie's killing was terrible enough, but the reason I'm personally involved and so angry is because of Marie. She wasn't a tart. She wasn't being hired out by Flora. I'm partly to blame for her dying. Am I supposed to walk away and pretend that her killing was just bad luck?'

'Keep your voice down, don't get excited,' Iain whispered, looking around.

She said loudly back, 'Are you afraid some important person will hear us? Some friend of Calder or Hamilton-Prentice. Your father-in-law to be sits on the bench, doesn't he? He must have friends in high places, including the police. Has he succeeded in shutting them up too?'

'He has friends in the police and in the law,' Iain agreed cautiously.

'I suppose I should have realized that nobody's been very anxious to get to the bottom of those killings. The police haven't exactly been working overtime, have they? They'd be quite happy if these two cases were shoved under the carpet and joined the great unsolved. That's what all this is about really, isn't it? We should all look the other way and let it be forgotten,' she said bitterly.

'Hamilton-Prentice and his pals are as worried as anybody about who did it. They think one of their associates might have lost the plot – but they don't know who. There's quite a lot of them involved. Whoever it was may have gone a bit mad and acquired a taste for killing after he picked up Sadie. I think the police are following up leads but what they find will probably never get out,' said Iain.

'Even if they find out who it is? Not if I can help it. Even if they know who was so insane that not only did he strangle Sadie and Marie, but chucked Skinner over a bridge as well? I'll do my damned best to prevent that. What sort of friends do you go around with?' she hissed.

He stared grimly back at her as he said, 'If he's found, he can be got rid of quietly. Put away in a mental hospital or something because he's obviously bonkers. That's why you should play possum for a bit.'

'Shoving him in Carstairs won't satisfy me. I'd rather see the bastard hanged,' snapped Rosa. The gin in the White Lady had gone to her head and she hardly knew what she was saying. Indistinctly she heard the pianist switch to a Cole Porter medley and the tune he was playing was 'Night and Day'. It used to make her feel as if the pit of her stomach was about to fall out if she was with Iain when she heard it, but now she realized that she was more interested in the pursuit of justice than in her love affair.

'I can't promise anything. I won't promise anything. You can tell your friends that I'm not going to stop asking questions,' she told him.

At that moment she was suddenly struck by the idea that Iain might be the killer. Where did he go after she ran away from him at the Tron? The way she felt now, no one was free of suspicion.

'Promise not to talk to anyone about what I've told you. If you do, you might get hurt and I really don't want that to happen,' he said earnestly.

'Are you threatening me?' she asked and he looked genuinely astonished as he said, 'Of course not. Get a grip of yourself. I'm only telling you all this for your own good.'

'And to try to make me stop.' But, she thought, perhaps he was not acting purely from self-interest after all. She calmed down a bit.

'Please don't make trouble, Rosa,' he went on.

She nodded because it was the easiest way to make him

stop. 'All right, don't worry, I won't. If the truth comes out, it'll not be because you told me. Maybe Nemesis – or the Edinburgh police – will catch up with whoever is guilty without my help.'

'I don't believe Hamilton-Prentice would commit a murder or turn a blind eye if anyone was killed. I don't like him, but he's not evil – he's just arrogant, and so's Calder,' Iain told her as if he was trying to reassure himself and apologize to her.

'That may be true, but someone started this by killing Sadie, and you're telling me that Hamilton-Prentice knew her,' she said.

He nodded. 'He did and he's bloody terrified that it'll all get out. The people who vote for him in the council elections would never look at him again if they knew the truth.'

'I can't say that worries me,' she snapped.

'Don't start all that again. He's not any worse than some of the others,' said Iain, suddenly defensive. 'Even the Lord Provost isn't lily white. Ask your precious friend Sylvia about him.'

She gaped, genuinely taken aback. The Lord Provost, Sir George Gideon, was a church-going bachelor who was frequently photographed attending charity functions where he was fawned upon by adoring women. People said he never married because his mother, who lived with him and was still very sprightly, was not keen on sharing her home with another woman.

'Gideon and Sylvia?' Rosa gasped.

Ian nodded. 'Him and a couple of others. She's more expensive and much more classy than Flora's girls.'

In the silence between them she realized that the pianist was now playing 'My Heart Belongs to Daddy', and she didn't know whether to laugh or cry.

'I have to get out of here,' she said, standing up. She no longer had the stomach for spending the rest of the evening in a roadhouse, no matter how elegant it was.

While he drove her back to Northumberland Street they talked very little and she could tell that he was regretting telling her so much. *When is he going to say it's all a pack of lies and to forget it?* she thought, but he didn't.

As the car stopped outside Mrs Ross's, she looked round its sumptuous interior and asked, 'By the way, who owns this magnificent machine?'

'My future father-in-law,' he said.

'A bribe or a wedding present to you?' she asked sarcastically.

'To his daughter, not to me,' he replied.

She stepped out on to the pavement, and leaned down to say sweetly through the window, 'Never mind. If you're a good boy, perhaps she'll let you drive it sometimes – even if you've failed in your errand.'

He drove away without looking back at her and she stood on the pavement edge watching him go. The Jaguar really was a magnificent car. Her own little jalopy sat patiently under the lamppost and she went over to unlock the door and slip into its womb-like interior. There she felt safe.

Twenty

B ecause she did not want to have the story of Duncan Skinner taken over by someone else again, Rosa changed her day off with Patrick, and on Tuesday she was in the office early.

When she consulted the diary, she was disappointed to see that Mike and Tom were assigned to Marie's funeral. It was bad enough to know that she was being steered away from a big story, but she wanted to go to that funeral to say good-bye to her friend. She couldn't rid herself of the guilty conviction that she was partly responsible for Marie's death.

Jack was nowhere to be seen – he was still upstairs rowing with management – and there was no point pleading with Bob Langton to be allowed to go, so she stuck her head round Jack's office door and hissed at Big Stella who was banging away on a typewriter. She looked up with her eyebrows raised when Rosa asked, 'Where's Jack?' and replied, 'Upstairs with the Managing Director. He'll be back soon.'

'I want to ask him for permission to go to Marie's funeral.'

'You're a sucker for punishment,' Stella replied in her broad Aussie accent.

'Will you ask for me?'

Stella shrugged. 'I might. Depends on the mood he's in when he comes back. Sometimes those guys up there drive him bananas, always bitching about money and going on about not antagonizing the advertisers.'

'Try to ask him, Stella,' Rosa pleaded.

The funeral was to be held at a church in Lanark Road at

two o'clock, and she passed a boring morning doing rewrites from the morning papers. By twelve thirty she'd heard nothing and Jack hadn't returned, so she'd almost given up hope when Stella came through the office like an opera diva and paused at Rosa's desk to whisper, 'Take a long lunch hour, kid. But no news-gathering. You're not officially on the story.'

Rosa looked over to Patricia who sat opposite and asked, 'Where are you going for lunch?'

The reply was a question: 'The Chinky?' When they were in funds they sometimes went to a Chinese restaurant off Chambers Street, behind the University Old Quad. The food was genuine Chinese and they considered the ambience exotic because there were lots of paper lanterns and painted scrolls with elegant black lettering on them. Neither of them knew anything about China but were fascinated by the place, its enigmatic proprietor and his waxen-faced wife.

'OK, the Chinky. My car's outside,' she told Patricia.

'We don't need a car for the Chinky.'

'Oh, yes, we do. Today we do.'

When they were out on the street, Patricia wanted to know, 'What's going on?'

'Will you come with me to Marie's funeral?' Rosa asked.

'But I thought we were going for a Chinese meal. Anyway Mike and Tom are on that story,' Patricia said.

'We'll be there as ordinary mourners. I want to pay my respects to Marie – I feel so guilty, you see,' Rosa explained.

Patricia put a hand on her friend's arm and said earnestly, 'Look, it's not your fault. Get that out of your head.'

But Rosa was not reassured. 'It *is* my fault. If I'd taken her home she would still be alive.'

Patricia sighed. 'Have it your own way. You're obviously set on breast-beating. It's a good thing I'm wearing my black coat if I'm going to a funeral, but you're not very suitably dressed, are you?' Rosa was still wearing the tartan trousers and navy pea jacket with shiny brass buttons.

'Nobody will notice us,' she said.

Patricia shook her head. 'Don't be daft. Everybody there will be noticed, by the police if by no one else. Where's the funeral anyway?'

'In a church on the Lanark Road. I'm not sure what it's called but we'll find it easily. There'll be a big crowd. Thanks, Patricia. I don't think I could bear it on my own.'

'Goodbye sweet and sour pork – hello, sackcloth and ashes,' said Patricia as she climbed into the car.

Rosa was right about the funeral church being easy to find because there was a long line of parked cars outside and Mike was hanging about the gate having a last smoke before he went inside. She didn't want him to see them, so she waited till he disappeared before they squashed in at the back of the crowded church.

The contrast with Sadie Jamieson's funeral was striking. An organ was playing softly and a mound of flowers was piled high on top of the coffin. It was heartbreaking to realize that the girl who had been dancing in Princes Street Gardens a few days ago was lying dead beneath the wreaths.

All the way through the ceremony, Rosa wept and Patricia held her hand. Her terrible feelings of remorse and anger were unassuaged by the service. She wanted vengeance on whoever had done such a terrible thing.

Marie's sister and brother-in-law led the family mourners out, followed by a large crowd of people, among whom were several town councillors including Mr Hamilton-Prentice, and a contingent of police officers, Mallen and Sergeant Boyle among them. When Boyle passed her pew, Rosa shrank back behind Patricia in the hope that he would not spot her, but he cast a ferocious glance in her direction, and she heard in memory his voice saying, 'Get off my back, Miss Makepeace.'

Thankfully, by the time Patricia and Rosa left the church, most of the congregation – including Mike and Tom as well as Boyle and Mallen – had dispersed.

'My God,' said Patricia, 'that was heartbreaking. I don't

know about you but I need a drink and you must be dehydrated after all that weeping.'

There was a small bar on the other side of the road and there were still ten minutes to go before afternoon closing time, so they headed for it. The bar was clean and friendly, and many of the people who had been in the church were already there. Patricia bought two lagers and they found seats on a long bench beneath the window of the cocktail bar. They barely raised the glasses to their lips when someone greeted them – 'Isn't it awful, isn't it sad? I still can't believe it.' The speaker was Marie's friend Lillian from the copy-takers' room.

Her eyes and face were swollen with weeping and she left her party to sit beside the girls. 'It was good of you to come. She was one of my best friends. I can't believe she's dead. I can hardly bear it,' she said with her voice breaking again.

'It was a big funeral,' said Patricia, who took over because Rosa was on the verge of weeping again and unable to speak.

Lillian nodded. 'Yes, it's affected everybody. The Langs are a well-known family round here. Marie's father was a police constable and her brother-in-law works in the City Chambers.'

That explains all the town councillors at the funeral, thought Rosa, wiping her eyes. She had forgotten about Sandy's connection with the City Chambers.

Lillian was still talking: 'Marie's father had a lot of friends in the force and they always turn out for colleagues. My dad's one too and so's our neighbour, Bob Mallen. They're desperate to get the man who killed her.'

'Is Sergeant Mallen your neighbour?' Rosa asked, her curiosity awakened.

Lillian nodded. 'Yes, he's a decent guy and he's really cut up about Marie because he's known her since she was a kid. It's the same with Sergeant Boyle. When his wife was alive he lived near Marie's parents but he's moved away since she was killed – that's another tragedy.'

Mallen had never given any indication that he had a

personal interest in the case – but he was probably trained not to. It was surprising that the hard man Boyle felt enough for the dead girl to turn up at her funeral too. It didn't seem like him, Rosa thought. Perhaps he had a soft side underneath.

'What happened to his wife?' she asked.

'She had a car accident three or four years ago,' Lillian told her. 'Drove off the road on the Lang Whang one night when she was coming back from visiting her mother who lived in Lanark. He nearly went demented when he was told – they had no kids, just lived for each other.'

A slight feeling of sympathy for Boyle stirred in Rosa. Grief might have hardened him.

When she and Patricia returned to the office, Jack was in one of his high furies, cursing up a storm and yelling at everyone in sight.

'It's good of you girls to pay us a visit,' he shouted when they tried to slip in without being noticed. As they pulled out their chairs to start working, he asked sarcastically, 'Will you be good enough to tell me what you are doing today?'

'I'm reviewing some books,' said Patricia smartly, and Rosa told him she was still working on the feature about police brutality, which she had actually abandoned for the past few days.

'You're taking your time about it,' he said and she started to bang out words as fast as she could, using as much purple prose as possible, but she did not have enough material for a decent piece. There were still too many enquiries to be made before the story could take proper shape. To give herself time to think and plan, as soon as Jack's attention was diverted from her, she slipped out of the office to have a cup of coffee in the canteen.

Stella was at a table in the corner, smoking with Lawrie, who was fascinated by the frank way she talked about sex. 'You and I should get together,' he said, trying to grab her hand and ignoring Rosa.

Stella threw back her head and gave a bellowing laugh. 'I only tangle with the big boys. Get back into your playpen, sonny,' she said.

Discomfited, Lawrie remembered he had a phone call to make and left the girls on their own.

'Jack's in a foul mood. What's up with him?' Rosa asked Stella.

'The bosses are still on his case. They think his way of sensationalizing stories is antagonizing the advertisers. He's furious because he's a newsman – he says that's what they hired him for, and they're just jumped-up office boys who never read anything but balance sheets. He despises them because they're scared of shocking Edinburgh's bigwigs.'

Was the management's antagonism made worse by the persistence he was showing pursuing the murder stories? Rosa wondered. *Whose toes was he standing on?*

'But he has transformed the paper,' she said. 'It was a boring rag before he took it over. Now it runs new stories and breaks scoops that make the nationals sit up.' If Jack was to leave, all the excitement would disappear, and Patricia and she would be relegated to cookery demonstrations and reporting society weddings. She couldn't bear it, she'd have to leave the paper.

'You'd better start collecting your cuttings, kid, because if they push him much more, he'll be off,' said Stella.

That warning plunged Rosa into gloom and by the time the last edition went on the street, she drifted disconsolately to the Cockburn with the others, not in search of alcohol but for mutual commiseration and companionship. It was bitterly cold outside and a grey miasma of mist hung over the Old Town, wreathing the tops of tall tenement buildings, and drifting ghostlike into the mouths of dank closes. The bleakness of the weather even infiltrated the bar and they sat around in gloom, making desultory conversation.

When Mike started talking about the murders, Rosa felt a rush of fear and dread that made goose pimples prickle on

182

the backs of her hands and arms. She didn't want to hear any more about it tonight, she wanted to forget all that evil for a little while. Almost desperately she looked at Patricia and asked, 'What are you doing tonight?'

'I can tell you one thing, I'm not staying here till closing time talking about death and disaster. We drink far too much anyway. We'll have eighty-year-old livers by the time we're twenty-five if we go on like this,' Patricia snapped. She was depressed too – for different reasons.

'What can we do? Go to the pictures?' Rosa certainly didn't want to go back to her bedsitter and watch the gas fire popping.

'What about going dancing at the Plaza?' suggested Tony, the minister's son who loved dancing and swept across the Plaza floor like Rudolf Valentino, doing fancy twirls and turns which thoroughly confused his partners.

Patricia and Rosa shook their heads vehemently. A night at the Plaza after Marie's funeral was very unsuitable.

'I think I'll go to the Press Club,' Patricia announced and Rosa could tell from the set of her jaw that she had made up her mind about this some time ago. She was hoping to meet Hugh Maling there of course, because he was a Press Club regular, at least when he was not in Milne's Bar in Rose Street hanging around the Edinburgh literati in the hope that one of them would speak to him – even if it was only to ask him the time.

'But they don't allow women in the Press Club bar,' Rosa protested. She only went there occasionally because she felt it was demeaning to have to ask a man to fetch her drinks even though she was a member and paid a sub like every-one else. In spite of protests, the Press Club stayed stuck in the Bob Langton era and, like him, showed no wish for a change.

Patricia said, almost coaxing, 'There's sure to be some-one there who'll fetch our drinks for us.' Hugh, she hoped.

It was obvious she was set on going but wanted Rosa's

company. It would be difficult to sit in the lounge alone. *She went with me to the funeral, so I'll have to go with her to the Press Club*, Rosa thought in resignation.

She drove her car along Princes Street to Binns Corner, and parked outside the Press Club in Rutland Street. Once inside, Patricia's first port of call was the ladies' lavatory, where she commandeered the mirror and started to expertly repair her maquillage. She painted on her face like an artist, touching up a bit here, brushing down an errant eyebrow hair there, and when she finished she looked glittering and sophisticated, at least ten years older than her real age.

'If Hugh's here, play hard to get,' Rosa said suddenly as she watched this transformation. 'And don't go to bed with him tonight, even if he asks you.'

But she knew she was wasting her breath. Patricia had set her heart on him.

The lounge, with its line of leather-covered benches snaking round the walls, was empty and unwelcoming, though through the serving hatch they could see a cluster of men propping up the bar. Leo Fairley was one of them and Patricia called to him, 'Leo, fetch us a drink, will you?'

Leo took her money and come back quickly with two glasses of Babycham, which the girls had opted to drink because they mistakenly thought it was non-alcoholic.

'Hi, ladies,' he said, standing over them. 'Anything else I can get you?'

Rosa glowered. 'You can smuggle us into the bar with the rest of the journalists. We do the same job, we should have the same privileges.'

He laughed. 'Oh Miss Makepeace, you are set on making your mark, aren't you? But I hear that you've stirred up so much trouble with the police, that your Editor has taken you off the murders.'

She felt her face reddening. 'I haven't stirred up any trouble,' she protested.

'Yes, you have. You've got up the noses of the police by

putting stuff in your stories that you didn't tell them. They say you've been making it up and putting words into people's mouths. Your management is twisting the Editor's arm to keep you quiet.'

It was a confirmation of her own fears and she stared at him in consternation. He was one of the most highly regarded newsmen in the city, a confidant of many policemen, but not normally hostile to women journalists. Anything Leo told you usually turned out to be correct.

Though he could he incisive and cutting in print, in private life he was a pleasant person who pursued the unlikely hobby of writing verse, not significant, philosophical poetry like Alan's, but rhyming couplets about trees in springtime and the flowers growing in Princes Street Gardens.

One of his latest efforts, which had appeared in the *News*, was a rhapsody about autumn geraniums in the beds around the Floral Clock in the Gardens.

'Everything I've written about the murders has been absolutely true,' Rosa said flatly. Leo patted her arm in a fatherly way. 'I don't doubt it, but keep your head down right now. You were getting too involved and that doesn't make for impartiality – or safety.'

When he went off, Patricia looked at her fuming friend over the rim of her glass and said, 'Keep cool, Rosa. It'll pass.'

Then her eyes switched away to the serving hatch again. Framed in it was the back view of the man she adored. He was wearing a ginger-coloured tweed jacket with leather patches on the elbows and his curly brown hair was tumbled forward in the style of Dylan Thomas. Rosa wouldn't put it past him to have contrived the similarity. *But Patricia is much too vulnerable to play the part of Caitlin*, she thought. In spite of surface sophistication, her friend was insecure and needy underneath.

Patricia suddenly rose and went over to the hatch. 'Hugh,' she called out sweetly but he ignored her at first and it took what seemed like a long time before he turned round. When he did, he was not smiling.

'Be an angel and bring us through two Babychams,' Patricia said, pushing a ten shilling note across the ledge of the hatch.

Again he didn't hurry but eventually he came through with two glasses in his hand. 'What a vulgar thing to drink,' he said, putting them down on the table, keeping the change, Rosa noted. He had a posh-Scottish accent because his father was a clergyman with a large church in Aberdeen and he had been educated at Loretto, one of the Scottish public schools.

Patricia slid along the bench to make room so he could sit beside her, which he did after going back to the hatch and taking his pint of beer off the ledge.

'What have you two newshounds been writing about today?' he asked condescendingly.

'We went to the funeral of the second murdered girl,' Patricia told him and he pulled a face.

'Ugh! And one or other of you knocked out three paragraphs of deathless prose about it, I suppose?' was his next scoffing statement.

'No. She was a friend. We went as mourners, not as reporters,' said Rosa shortly.

'Does that mean you're going straight, Miss Makepeace? The police will be pleased,' he said, looking at her with frank dislike in his eyes.

'What do you mean by that?' It was impossible to pretend politeness towards him and she sensed that Patricia didn't care how rude she was – surrogate aggression probably.

'I mean that your gutter press tactics have antagonized the city powers-that-be,' he said with a smirk.

Rosa leaned forward and said, 'At least I'm a real reporter, not a pseudo hanger-on who picks holes in the work of other people when he's not capable of writing anything original himself.'

Ouch! That hurt. She could tell by his face.

'You've certainly got the common touch,' he countered, 'but you're only a dilettante. One of these days you'll snare some unsuspecting man and settle down to producing a brood of children – you've got the right sort of hips for it.'

'Hips! What have hips got to do with it?' she snapped.

'They mark you as a brood mare, if nothing else,' he said. That ended it. She couldn't think of a sufficiently cutting put-down and the only thing to do was get up and leave, knowing that she was doomed to brood all night about the smart quips that she ought to have said but didn't.

She sat fuming in her car for what seemed like a long time until a glance at her watch told her it was five past nine. Too early to go to bed, yet too late to find alternative amusement, so she switched on the engine and considered her options.

Marie still haunted her mind. *I shouldn't have left her, I shouldn't have left her*, she kept thinking. But Marie was a sensible girl, not the sort to go off with a stranger. She must have known the man who picked her up.

Was it Alan?

Was it Skinner?

Or Hamilton-Prentice? Her brother-in-law worked for him but how well did she know him?

Rosa thought about Marie's family at the funeral – Alice and Sandy Collins both looked stricken and confused. They would be back at home now, trying to come to terms with what had happened. She should have given them her sympathy and respects at the ceremony but was too overcome to do so – *Go and see them now, go and say how sorry you are*, ordered a voice in her head. Without thinking, she switched on the car engine and headed for Sighthill.

The curtains of the little council house were drawn and it looked desolate and grieving when she knocked at the door. Alice answered and recognized her visitor immediately but her face registered reluctance to speak, so Rosa said hurriedly,

'I'm not here on business. I've come to say how sorry I am about Marie. I came to give you my sympathy. I hope you are all right.' She felt tremendous pity for the thin, careworn-looking girl.

'Sandy's out. He's gone to see his mother and tell her about the funeral,' said Alice, holding the door half-closed.

Rosa backed away. 'I'm so sorry. I don't want to intrude. I know it's a bad time but I feel so guilty about leaving Marie on her own that night . . .'

Alice suddenly relented. 'Oh, come on in,' she said and opened the door wider. 'The bairns are in bed. All this has been upsetting for them. They loved their auntie.' Her voice broke and she seemed close to tears. So was Rosa, who said with absolute sincerity, 'It's awful, really awful. I wish I could help find out who did it.'

Alice shook her head slowly and looked at her visitor as if wondering what to say to her. What eventually came out was: 'Fancy a cup of tea?'

'Yes, I'd love one.'

She followed Marie's sister into a tiny kitchenette and while they waited for the kettle to boil on top of the gas stove, Alice said, 'I shouldn't be doing this. A friend in the police told me not to talk to the press, and especially not to you.'

'Really? Did he say why?'

'He told us that you're only interested in making your name and are using Marie's murder to do it.'

Rosa flushed. The charge of cynical self-interest was often levied against journalists, but in this case she felt it was completely unjustified.

'I assure you that's not true as far as Marie is concerned,' she said.

Alice nodded while she poured boiling water over the tea leaves in a big china pot. 'I thought it was a bit unfair. After all, you came here asking about Marie even before we knew she was dead.'

'Who said that about me anyway?' Rosa asked.

'Jim Boyle.'

'Him! Why should he get involved?' Rosa said bitterly. Boyle had his knife into her because he almost certainly knew by now that she was investigating his regime at the court. Someone in whom she had confided must have told him – but who? Etta probably.

'He's involved because he knows the family. Our father was in the police, you see, and all his friends are desperate to catch Marie's killer. They're taking it very personally.'

Though she did not say so, Rosa thought that their desperation had not yielded much in the way of results so far. They were hampered by their self-interest and the interference of people with influence. There was much more to this story than met the eye.

A mug of steaming tea was handed over and Rosa took it thinking, *When they're trying to bridge a gap with you, people like Sylvia give you real coffee; people like Alice make tea.*

Alice was obviously eager to talk. 'The police have been very decent to us. In the beginning, some of the CID men thought Sandy might be involved because most murders are done by family members. He was taken in for questioning, but Peter Mallen and Jim Boyle were very kind and both phoned to tell me not to worry because it was only routine. They brought him home that night and we haven't been bothered since,' she said.

This was news to Rosa, who thought that Sandy was lucky to escape 'questioning' without at least a black eye if Boyle was involved, but only nodded in encouragement.

'You see, Peter's always been a friend of ours and Jim lived next door to my parents for a while. Marie used to play with his dog. It was killed in the crash with his wife . . . Other folk have been very kind too. Mr Hamilton-Prentice, the town councillor with all the television shops, sent a huge wreath to the funeral, and told Sandy that if we needed help with anything, we only had to ask. Sandy works as his clerk

189

in the City Chambers, arranges his appointments and things like that.'

'Did Mr Hamilton-Prentice know Marie too?' Rosa wanted to know, remembering that he also had a link with Sadie through the Danube Street brothel. The name of Hamilton-Prentice, the family's patron, should definitely be added to her list of suspects.

'Yes, he knew her, but not very well. They met when we went to staff Christmas parties and things like that. He was concerned for Sandy when he heard that the police were questioning him. He said he'd tell them to lay off because he knew Sandy wouldn't hurt a fly.'

'But doesn't your husband have an alibi for New Year's Eve?' Rosa asked.

Alice shook her head. 'That was the trouble. He went out of here about half past eleven to visit his mother and see the New Year in with her. He's her only child and he always does that. I couldn't go because Marie was out and there was nobody to sit with the bairns. His friend lent him a car but it broke down at his mother's place and he didn't get back till half past three because he had to walk all the way home from Lochend Road. There were no buses and he couldn't get a taxi.'

'But surely his mother will vouch for him?' said Rosa and Alice shook her head again, tossing her hair back. When she did that she looked uncannily like Marie. 'Not her. She's losing her memory. She's not too bad when you're talking to her but she can't remember things you said or anything like that once you've gone away. She's aye saying that she hasn't seen Sandy for weeks, but he goes to her place every second day to check up on her. He's awful fond of her.'

'Why did the car break down?' Rosa asked.

Alice frowned as if that question was irrelevant. 'An electrical fault he said. All it needed was a new fuse or something. I don't know anything about cars but Sandy's friend went and got it back from Lochend Road next day.'

Rosa remembered how enthusiastically Sandy had looked out of the window at Iain's Armstrong Siddeley, and also remembered the car with only one light working. That could have had an electrical fault. *Oh, don't let Sandy be involved in the killing of his sister-in-law!* she thought.

But he couldn't have had anything to do with the deaths of Sadie and Duncan Skinner, could he? There was nothing to connect him with them. Everything was becoming more confusing by the hour.

Twenty-One

That night Rosa was plagued by horrible nightmares of Marie lying beneath the water of Duddingston Loch with the yellow hair that was so like her sister's floating out around her.

On waking early next morning she felt badly in need of doing something to stop herself brooding and decided that, if possible, she would slip away from the office at lunch time without saying where she was going. Research for the brutality story could be her excuse.

From time to time, when things were quiet, she often took French leave, and visited the National Gallery or the Portrait Gallery, wandering round looking at the paintings, but after such a miserable night, she knew she would not be in the mood for that.

Nor would she feel like window-shopping in case she was driven mad with longing by the sight of the white ball gown, especially since she knew there was little chance of going to a ball. That gown deserved to be worn in the Assembly Rooms or the George Hotel, where people like the Lord Provost and the Hamilton-Prentices took the floor.

What an enormous travesty Edinburgh *respectability* was, she thought as she lay curled in bed steeling herself to get up and face the cold. As far as morals were concerned, the dancing milkmen and brewery labourers who packed the Palais on Saturday nights were saints compared to some of the ostensibly respectable people she'd been hearing about recently.

Getting up, she quickly ate a banana sliced up in corn-flakes and started to dress, pondering if the tartan trousers would survive another day without going to the dry clean-ers. But the knees were badly pouched and dirty puddles of melting snow, through which she'd trudged recently, had left a tidemark round the hems so they did not stand up to inspec-tion. She dressed instead in an old pencil skirt with thick brown wool stockings and a Fair Isle sweater that had shrunk in the wash. Over the top of this unattractive get-up, she put on her beloved reporter's raincoat, a cream-coloured macin-tosh with leather-covered buttons, epaulettes, flaps over the breast and a belt that she tied in a tight knot round her waist instead of threading its end properly through the leather-covered buckle. On her head she wore a wide-brimmed felt hat which made her feel like Ingrid Bergman in *Casablanca*.

As she looked at her reflection in the mirror, she thought how shocked Great-aunt Fanny would be to see her looking like an extra in a Hollywood film. What a good idea! When she took the afternoon off, she'd go to visit Fanny. She hadn't seen the old lady for a long time and ought to apologize for exploiting her aunt's friendship with Miss Noble in order to get into Dean Gardens. Fanny would be sure to hear about that soon, if she had not heard already.

Patricia was off – sick, said Bob Langton with grim satis-faction – but everything was quiet and no one noticed her slipping out of the office at one o'clock. The car needed petrol and she had little money in her purse, so it was a relief to ride westwards on the top of a bus going past the zoo and know that she was not going anywhere near a church, a crematorium, Duddingston Loch or Sighthill. She wished she could be like the Basher and take unpleasant things in her stride in a more professional way.

The bus carried her through the centre of Corstorphine, past a line of shops that included a post office, a butcher's, a newsagent and a fishmonger. There was also a large garage, one of a chain owned by the firm that employed Iain. A

Daimler was drawn up idling on its forecourt and she turned her head away for she did not want to catch a glimpse of him if he was in it.

Fanny lived in an anonymous bungalow, one of hundreds that looked the same and formed terraces of streets laid out like rows of vines in a French vineyard along the face of a hill that looked south across the valley. It was not far from the zoo and sometimes, when Rosa visited, she heard wild animals roaring in the distance.

What would happen if a pride of lions escaped? she wondered. *Perhaps they would gobble up the inhabitants of Corstorphine before they were recaptured. What a story!* A laugh rose up inside her and she realized it was the first time she had felt like laughing for days.

She jumped off the bus and crossed the street to face the steep climb to the top of the hill. It was another typical Edinburgh obstacle course. Fanny tackled it every day though she was well over seventy and suffered from what she referred to as 'my tubes'. How long would she manage to go on negotiating this Everest-like climb from the main road to her home? Rosa wondered.

When she puffed up to the bungalow's porch and rang the bell, she saw her great-aunt's shadowy figure hovering behind the frosted glass panel of the door, obviously debating whether to open it or not. Rosa shouted through the letter box, 'Aunt Fanny, it's me, it's Rosa. Let me in.'

Bolts and chains rattled and the door opened. 'Come in quickly and close the door before the cold air gets in,' said Fanny, hauling her visitor inside.

It was difficult to know why she was so worried about the introduction of cold air because the interior of the house was hardly warmer than the street outside. A three-bar electric fire, with only a single bar burning, sat in the hearth of her sitting room. On the seat of her chair was a plaid travelling rug which she wrapped around herself in the evening when she watched the little plastic Baird television set – her greatest luxury.

She surveyed Rosa with her usual semi-affectionate disapproval. 'Why don't you belt your coat properly?' she asked. There was no point telling her that casual elegance was the aim. Rosa wanted to look like a newshound from *The Front Page* but Fanny would never have heard of it. In her world there was only tidy and untidy – and Rosa was untidy.

'I thought you might come today. Take off that awful coat and sit down. Would you like a cup of tea?' she said.

Rosa looked surprised, wondering if the old lady had become psychic. Why imagine she was coming today when she only visited her great-aunt three or four times a year and hardly ever during the week?

'A cup of tea would be lovely. Will I make it?' she offered but Fanny shook her head because, once, when Rosa was thirteen, she'd made tea for Fanny and broken the handle off a china teacup. She'd never been entrusted with the task since.

As she retreated into her scullery, Rosa shouted after her, 'Why did you think you'd see me today? Have you started reading the runes?'

'Of course not. It was because of your friend coming here. Did he catch up with you?' Fanny called back.

Rosa walked into the little hall and stared at her aunt's back through the open kitchen door. 'What friend?' she asked in surprise.

'The man who was here asking for you this morning.'

This morning? Rosa shivered. She had never given anyone Fanny's name and address as a contact. Not even Iain or Roddy. Why should a man turn up here, claiming to be a friend and asking for her?

'What did he look like?' she wanted to know.

'Quite tall, wearing a raincoat, and a felt hat. Fair, I'd say. In his thirties maybe but I'm not good about ages.'

Alan hadn't been in the office that morning. It was his day off so it might have been him. Or was it Mallen? The description fitted him and he could have been tracking her down to ask more questions. The description fitted either him or Alan. Or was it Iain? She might have told him more than she remembered and he knew she had an aunt somewhere in Corstorphine. But why should he bother?

'When you say fair, what do you mean exactly?' she asked. Iain's hair was light brown but certainly not blond.

'I mean his skin. He wasn't swarthy,' Fanny snapped. That didn't help much. Even Mike couldn't be described as 'swarthy'. Lawrie might though. She snapped out of speculation, reminding herself that the caller was *not* swarthy.

'When exactly was he here?' she asked next.

'Between eleven and half past. He knocked on the front door and asked if you were with me or if I was expecting you. He'd been to your lodgings and missed you.' At half past eleven she was in the office and could have been found there, as any of her colleagues – and Mrs Ross – well knew. Whoever was looking for her at Fanny's must have had some ulterior motive in checking up on *her*, not Rosa.

'Did he say what he wanted?' she asked, trying hard to keep her voice casual.

'He was very pleasant and polite. He said he wanted to catch up with you about something to do with your work and thought you might be here. He wouldn't come in, just spoke to me on the doorstep. He didn't take off his hat but it was raining a bit, so I don't suppose I can blame him for that. I said I hadn't seen you and he asked if I thought you might be at your father's, so I gave him that phone number and address.'

'I don't suppose you asked him for identification – or a warrant card,' Rosa said and Fanny looked astonished.

'A warrant card! What's that? What will I say if he comes back?' she asked.

'Tell him I've gone to China,' Rosa snapped.

Fanny actually laughed because she thought it was a joke but Rosa didn't find the situation funny. She was worried. Why was someone tracking down her relatives? How did he find Fanny's address? She didn't want to worry the old lady by showing disquiet, so she pretended to dismiss the whole thing while they drank their tea.

In spite of her apparent lack of warmth it was obvious that Fanny was pleased to see her but too reticent to show it. While they sat companionably together, Rosa felt a surge of affection for the old lady and asked, 'How are you, Aunt Fanny? Does this weather affect your chest?'

She shrugged her thin shoulders and said, 'My chest'll never be any better,' and Rosa was suddenly overwhelmed by a desire to hug her. She was her great-aunt after all, the last link with her mother. Tentatively she put out a hand and stroked the woollen-clad arm. Fanny looked surprised but did not draw away or move towards her.

'It's a very nice surprise to see you, Rosa, but I think you need a new jersey. That one's too tight,' she said, though in a softer tone.

Part of Rosa's mind was still worrying about the mystery caller, wondering if his visit was connected in some way with Skinner and how he'd tracked down Fanny. Jean Noble was a possible source of information, for she was one of the few people who knew about the connection between Fanny and Rosa. Could she have told the mystery man?

'Have you seen your friend Miss Noble recently?' she enquired while Fanny was replenishing the teapot.

The old lady shook her head. 'No, but she rang me up the other day to say she'd seen you.'

I might have guessed that bit of news would be passed on, thought Rosa, and asked, 'What did she say?'

'She said you'd dropped in to visit her on Sunday and were looking very well.'

'Was that all?'

Fanny looked suspicious. 'Yes, what else did you expect her to say?' So Miss Noble hadn't revealed that Rosa was on the trail of a man who'd committed suicide. *Thank you, Miss Noble*, she thought.

197

'Didn't she tell you we went walking together in the Dean Gardens?' she asked.

'Did you? How nice. She loves those gardens. That's why she stays on in that expensive flat of hers,' said Fanny, rattling a shovel-shaped spoon in the sugar bowl.

When Rosa was passed a second cup of tea, Fanny made a concession and switched on all the bars of the fire so they ate ginger biscuits and sipped tea in relative comfort. Fanny wanted the latest news of Rosa's father but there was not much information to give and she knew that to talk about the snowmobile would be unwise.

'He's all right. Working away,' said Rosa and Fanny shook her head in despair as she always did when the subject of Rosa's father came up. Though well-mannered, and well-educated, he was feckless and had been Rosa's mother's greatest mistake, in Fanny's opinion. She was always beadily watching her great niece trying to detect whether she'd inherited any or all of his failings.

As the room warmed up, Rosa relaxed and stuck her legs out towards the electric fire and Fanny talked about what she'd been watching on the television.

'What's My Line?' was her favourite and she loathed Gilbert Harding but admired Lady Barnet. She also revered the Queen, Prince Philip, Princess Margaret and the Queen Mother.

Because she had no television set, Rosa was not much good at talking on that subject but was able to say that in November she was sent to follow Princess Margaret around during one of her official visits to Edinburgh. Fanny clasped her hands. 'How lucky you are! What was she wearing?'

'A pale-blue satin coat and dress, with a little hat,' Rosa told her.

Fanny's eyes shone. 'That must have gone beautifully with her complexion.'

'Yes, it did.' Rosa remembered the Basher saying that the Princess looked like a 'kewpie doll'. Margaret had been thoroughly unpleasant, not only to the press, but to everyone else she met that day. It would have been cruel to tell Fanny that, however, and Rosa left her aunt's illusions intact.

Before she went back to town, Fanny insisted that they share her evening meal of corned beef and mashed potatoes, and then tried to press a ten-shilling note into her great-niece's hand but it was refused, with Rosa saying, 'Honestly, I don't need any money.' Great-aunt Fanny still thought of her as a little girl and would be genuinely amazed to hear how much she earned.

It was dark when she left and all the way back to the city in the bus, she puzzled about how the mystery man managed to connect her, Rosa Makepeace, with Miss Fanny Allardyce in Corstorphine.

Who fitted his description? It was so vague that it could have been almost anyone. Alan was only just in his thirties but looked older and haggard. Rosa couldn't remember ever seeing him wearing a hat and kicked herself for having forgotten to ask Fanny about the man's accent. If he'd been Australian, she probably would have said so though. However, by now she had worked out that whoever it was must have got the lead to Fanny through Jean Noble.

The bus went along Princes Street and up the Bridges, so she stayed on board till they reached the stop outside P.T.'s, opposite the *Scotsman* building. Then she jumped off, crossed the road and hurried through an arcade of shops to the Cockburn. On the way she looked at her watch and saw it was half past eight.

The Cockburn's phone box was a cubicle at the foot of the stairs that led upstairs to the bar but a search through the book did not turn up any number for a J. Noble in Clarendon Crescent.

Only a few of her colleagues were in the bar, with their heads together discussing the day's events. They moved over to allow her to sit at the table, and Patrick said, 'Jack's been acting very strangely all afternoon and we wonder what he's up to.'

'Why? What's he done?' Rosa asked.

'He hardly came out of his office except to call Gil in every now and again. They're planning something. Stella says they've been writing a storming leader for tomorrow's paper,' said Mike.

'Did Stella type the leader out for him? If she did, she'll know what he's written,' Rosa suggested.

'No, he did it himself. He was grunting and groaning away all the time but in the end he seemed very pleased. He even took it down to the stone himself. He didn't want to take the risk of a single word being changed.' Mike seemed to know a lot about it, which was not a surprise since he was suspected of having a dalliance with Stella, but he was very much a reserve player on her team for she was currently involved with MacGillivray from the photo desk, the Chief Sub and the man who wrote the motoring column. These rivals all loathed each other and often almost came to blows.

'Mike's waiting for dead men's shoes, and judging by the way they're carrying on, he should have a fitting soon,' Patricia once said.

Now he was leaning back in his chair and throwing out his hands as he said, 'Roll on tomorrow. I've a feeling we're in for a lively time and I like a bit of excitement.' Rosa leaned across and asked sweetly, 'Oh good. By the way, what size are your feet, Mike?'

He said, 'Ten,' and couldn't understand why they all exploded with laughter.

Twenty-Two

The *Dispatch* staff spent Thursday morning doing normal things – the Calls, rewriting pieces from the morning papers, checking up on running stories, going to the High Street law courts, drinking tea or coffee, smoking, flirting, nursing hangovers, or gossiping in corners.

Gil asked Rosa how her story about police brutality was progressing, so she couldn't leave the office to call on Jean Noble.

Jack was still shut up in his office, drafting the wording of the news vendors' advertising sheets. Normally that job was left to the circulation department, but today he'd taken it over. After a couple of hours Stella came out round-eyed and whispered to Mike, 'He's blasting the police force!'

A few minutes before midday, Colin, the copy boy, came up from the presses and threw a bundle of copies of the first edition on to Jack's table. All the reporters rushed to grab one.

They were not disappointed. There was a huge black banner headline along the top of the first page:

EDINBURGH POLICE CONDEMNED! See Page 2.

In a concerted rustle, as if it had been orchestrated, everyone turned over the front page and started reading Jack's editorial that ran down the inside of the second page. He had really gone to town. In sonorous phrases he condemned what he called the *lethargy* and *indifference* of the Edinburgh Police force.

The brutal killings of two young girls are being conveniently shoved under the carpet. The police have followed no leads, and found no suspects. A killer is walking free, able to kill again, he thundered in print and went on to ask why various leads discovered by the reporters of his newspaper had been ignored, and why the apparent suicide of a witness was not considered significant.

The rate-payers of this city have a right to expect more from their police force. The guardians of the law, who should be protecting young girls like Sadie Jamieson and Marie Lang from evil, are failing in their duty. If the Edinburgh force is incapable of positive action in this very serious situation, they should call in assistance from other more active and intelligent police authorities.

On and on it went, listing aspects of the cases which had been uncovered because of the activities of *Dispatch* reporters – the fact that Alan saw Marie in the N.B.; Rosa's discovery that the silk scarf used to tie up Marie also figured in Sadie's murder; the puzzle of why no official appeal for witnesses to Skinner's suicide had been issued.

Only in Edinburgh can a man jump to his death from a very public place and the police make no effort to find out if anyone saw him do it . . . Jack wrote and then launched into a list of other unsolved murders committed in the city over the past five years. The list was impressive and made a devastating condemnation.

The staff, breathlessly reading the paper, knew that the leader was written by a man in a white heat of indignation and anger. He was hitting back at the entrenched powers that wanted him silenced. His glove was thrown into the ring, challenging his enemies to take it up.

'This is going to set the cat among the pigeons,' said Tom when he laid his newspaper down.

He was right. Within half an hour all the telephones were ringing at once and when the receivers were picked up, loud, indignant voices were heard shouting out in rage. Rosa happened to pick up a phone that had the Chief Constable on the other end.

'Let me speak to your Editor,' he spluttered, and when the call was transferred to Jack she heard him saying, 'Then write us a letter giving your point of view. I'll give you the front page tomorrow.'

He was ensuring a massive rise in circulation for the *Dispatch* because this row would run and run.

Before Rosa went back to Mrs Ross's that evening, she drove her car to Jean Noble's and found the old lady at home. She beamed when she saw Rosa at the door, and eagerly pulled her inside.

'I want to thank you for not shocking or alarming Fanny by telling her about me going into the Gardens to find out about that suicide, but I also wondered if anyone has been asking you about me,' Rosa explained.

'Sit down, have a sherry,' Miss Noble said, almost pushing the girl into a chair.

Rosa didn't like sherry. It was too liverish for her, but Miss Noble was so obviously looking forward to having one herself that she accepted.

Bustling about in her wall cupboard to bring out a bottle of Bristol Cream and two glasses, Jean Noble spoke over her shoulder. 'Yes, how strange, a man came to see me the day before yesterday. He wanted to know how to find you. He knew where you live in Northumberland Street but you weren't there apparently and he asked if I had any idea about your family – could you be away visiting them or something like that? I said that the only family you have as far as I know is your great-aunt and your father but I didn't know your dad's address, so I told the man where Fanny lives.'

As she was handed a brimming glass, Rosa said doubtfully, 'He went to see her too and it's all very odd. If I'm not at work or in the Cockburn Hotel, I'm usually in my digs and if anyone went there asking for me, Mrs Ross would have told me so. That man couldn't have been telling you the truth. Did you ask why he wanted to see me? Didn't he give you any explanation?'

'No, I didn't ask. He sounded very plausible.' Miss Noble did not seem concerned and sipped her sherry with every sign of carefree appreciation.

'What did he look like? Describe him for me please,' Rosa asked.

Jean Noble frowned. 'Not too tall, but not short either. Wearing a fawn raincoat, a hat and suede shoes, I noticed. A strong sort of face. Very polite.'

'What age?'

'I'm not good at guessing people's ages, but he wasn't old, not as old as me anyway. Between thirty and forty I'd guess.'

'Anything unusual about his accent?'

The answer was a shake of the head. 'No, he sounded perfectly ordinary. Scots, of course. If it worries you, I'm sorry I spoke to him, but he seemed to know you. He even knew that we had been in the Gardens together. I think that's what he wanted to talk to you about . . . He was extremely courteous.'

It was amazing for Rosa to realize – not for the first time – how gullible people could be. Anyone acting in a confident way could often wheedle their way through closed doors.

She said, 'He was very polite to Fanny too and she gave him my father's address. There's something odd about it. He could have got hold of me very easily without sneaking around. If he comes back, don't talk to him again and, whatever you do, don't let him in.'

A feeling of dread filled her and she hoped that whoever the mystery man may be, he wouldn't hurt or frighten either of those innocent old women. She didn't want that on her conscience as well. It was bad enough feeling such awful guilt about Marie.

'But, my dear, he didn't *try* to come in here. He stayed happily on my doorstep,' Jean Noble reassured her.

'That's good. Don't even answer the door to him in future. Would you mind phoning Fanny for me and warning her not to answer the door to him either?' Rosa asked, adding, 'By the way, I couldn't find you in the phone book under J. Noble.'

Jean smiled. 'That's because I'm under my given names "Victoria Jean" – my father said he named me after his carriage, not the Queen, and that put me off using the name. Who wants to be called after a horse-drawn buggy? I'll phone Fanny of course but I don't want you to worry. That man was very polite, and very respectable. I'm sure there's nothing sinister about his visit.'

In spite of her misgivings, Rosa forced herself to smile back and agree: 'You're probably right. It's just that so many awful things have happened recently. As I told you, Marie Lang, who was found in Duddingston Loch, was a friend of mine and that's made me very cautious and suspicious.'

'Quite right too,' agreed Miss Noble and filled their sherry glasses again.

Driving home, Rosa passed Sylvia's house. There were lights in her windows but, remembering Sylvia's irritation when she phoned up from Hamilton Place, she did not stop because she did not want to be a nuisance. Anyway she was preoccupied by thoughts about the man who seemed to be checking up on her.

If any of the people she worked with wanted to know about her family, all they had to do was ask, and why should they bother anyway?

If the mystery man was from the police, surely they had other methods of checking up on her? It wasn't as if she'd robbed a bank. She didn't see any reason for someone going around asking about her family.

All the thinking she was doing made her ravenously hungry, so she decided to make a detour down Leith Walk to buy more fish and chips, which seemed to provide the major part of her diet these days.

Sitting in the car eating them, she decided to spend the

rest of the evening at the pictures again, and drove to the top of Regent Road to a small cinema which was showing *The Blackboard Jungle*.

The *Scotsman*'s letter columns, which attracted all the 'Pro Bono Publico' letter writers in the city, had been full of condemnations of this film, which they claimed was bad for the morals and behaviour of the young. She didn't care about that. What attracted her was the star, Glenn Ford, who she thought was really sexy-looking.

The dimple in his chin drove her mad.

Another reason for wanting to go to the film was the sound-track. The theme music was Bill Haley's 'Rock Around the Clock', which had caused a great outcry in America. Newspapers reported that it drove young audiences into a frenzy, making them leave their seats and jive up and down the aisles.

Apparently, American parents and morality crusaders feared that this new music would drive their children to lives of corruption and licentiousness. Rosa felt that she could do with a bit of corrupting so she was determined to see *The Blackboard Jungle*.

After parking her car, she headed along the pavement to the cinema door. Standing at the kiosk waiting to buy her ticket, she almost jumped out of her boots when a voice behind her said softly, 'Ah hah, going to the wicked *Blackboard Jungle*, are you?'

She whipped round in surprise with her heart thudding. Alan was standing there and, in a panicky moment, she wondered if *he* was the one who'd been tracking her down.

Her eyes scanned his face, looking for signs of evil intent, but he was smiling pleasantly. 'Going to rock along the back row all on your own?' he asked again.

'Yes, I might. But I wouldn't have thought that *The Blackboard Jungle* was your sort of thing,' she gabbled. The last review he'd written was about an Edinburgh University production of *The Duchess of Malfi*.

He smiled. 'I like to let my hair down too sometimes and tonight I've time to kill, so I thought I'd come along to see what all the fuss is about.'

'Me too,' she told him.

'Let's go together then. I've two free passes and can get you in for nothing,' he said. Feeling like a rabbit hypnotized by a snake, she accepted this offer and followed him into the dark auditorium. Walking down the dark passageway towards their seats, she decided that she'd yell like a stuck pig if he as much as moved an arm towards her. The business with Fanny and Jean Noble had unnerved her more than she realized.

As usual, once he settled into his seat, Alan seemed so relaxed that he was almost unconscious. The only sign that he was actually awake was the fact that he lit one cigarette after the other and they watched the screen through drifting wreaths of his exhaled smoke.

In spite of the tension that still held her in its grip, she enjoyed the film – not so much for the plot or the acting, which was hard-hitting enough – but for the music, which set her blood tingling. It was easy to understand how it could spark off teenage riots because as it throbbed through the auditorium, she was seized by a wish to jump out of her seat and go jiving down the aisle. Even Alan's feet were tapping on the floor beside hers. It had got to him too.

Bill Haley was making music that you could dance to by yourself. There was no need to wait for a partner. Nobody would ever need to be a wallflower again. What a liberation, what a wonderful cure for the blues! It would certainly cause a social revolution, though not the sort that the do-gooders dreaded.

Both Alan and Rosa felt full of energy and goodwill when they left the cinema. Back on the darkened street, they smiled at each other in a spirit of camaraderie. Rosa's whole body was still vibrating with the need to dance and she said, 'Wasn't that great!'

Alan nodded. 'Very hard-hitting. I didn't think much of the music though.'

Why did you tap your feet then? she thought but decided it was probably beneath his intellectual level to admit to liking Bill Haley.

'It's ten fifteen. Where are you going now?' he asked, and, immediately all her fears, which the music had softened, came rushing back.

'I'm going home,' she said quickly.

'Is that far?' he enquired and she hurriedly shook her head. 'Not really, only to Northumberland Street – anyway I've got the car.'

He nodded and said, 'That's good. I was going to ask you to give me a lift because I'm running late for my next appointment.'

She remembered that whoever killed the girls must have taken them away in a car.

'Don't you have a car?' she asked him.

'No. I enjoy driving at home but the roads here are bloody. Not like Australia. Anyway, I couldn't afford to run a car here. If I want to go anywhere, I hire one. I went to the Highlands last month and it was spectacular!'

He made two words out of 'spec – tacular' but she was not interested in his enthusiastic opinion of the mountains, for she was registering the fact that, in spite of being so hard-up that he pawned typewriters, he was amazingly lavish with his money, spending it on luxuries like staying in the N.B. and hiring cars. She wondered if the police investigating the murders had checked up on car-hire firms.

When they reached her car, she stopped with a hand on its door, reluctant to let him into the passenger seat. Sanctuary lay inside. In there she'd be safe, like a kernel in a nutshell.

Alan looked down at her beloved vehicle and said, 'I like these little cars. They're very reliable, I believe. Will you give me a lift then? I'm only going to London Road and, like I said, I'm running late.'

Hell! she thought, but how could she refuse? He'd given her a free ticket to the cinema and, as he knew, her route home took her along London Road. Her fears came rushing back, only to be slightly assuaged by his pleasant smile.

'Which end of London Road?' she asked, stalling.

'The Leith Walk end.' That was the way she had to go. There was no excuse. 'All right, hop in,' she said and slipped into the driving seat, reaching over to unlock the passenger door.

If he gets difficult, I'll crash the car, she thought and started to worry about how to do that without damaging the paintwork too much.

For something to say to lighten her mood, she remarked, 'The only person I know who lives in London Road is big Stella.'

He stared at her for a few moments, frowned and then laughed as he said, 'Makepeace, the police who complain about you are dead right. You're too nosy for your own good.'

Suddenly she felt like laughing. Her fears took flight as she thought, *Oh no! Not Alan as well!* He was human after all if he'd fallen for earth mother Stella, whose conquests were so numerous that if they all found out about each other, there would be duels at dawn and the staff would be decimated.

'It's a pleasure to take you to London Road, Alan,' she said with a grin. He grinned impishly back and suddenly she liked him very much.

Twenty-Three

Though at first they were inclined to ignore it, the police seized on the death of Duncan Skinner almost with relief.

Nettled by Jack's condemnations of their apparent inability to find anyone for the girls' murders, Skinner made a possible scapegoat. What they had to do was link him with Sadie.

A statement was issued saying investigations into his movements before he died were in hand and posters were published showing a big photograph of him beside one of Sadie. Anyone who had seen them together on December 30th, and the 31st, was asked to contact the C.I.D. in the High Street station.

It was tacitly suggested that his suicide might have been an act of remorse, and, being dead, he was in no position to protest against this theory, which, of course, exonerated the police from the charge that they'd been sitting on their hands.

Rosa was not allowed to attend any of the police press briefings, and that irked her, but she decided that the official decision to withdraw her from the story did not mean she had to stop being interested in the murders and in Skinner. It would be cowardly to lose interest because everyone warned her against involvement, and the attempts to silence her had the opposite effect to what was intended, only combining to whet her appetite for interference rather than quell it. *I'll show them!* she thought, as she pretended to be totally engrossed in her brutality piece, which, in fact, was getting nowhere.

At eleven o'clock on Friday morning, with a great clatter, Mike rushed out of one of the phone booths and announced in a loud voice, 'We can forget about Skinner as the murderer. They've pulled in somebody else! I've just been told there's a briefing in the High Street station in half an hour.'

'Get up there then and let's have all the details pronto. I'll keep the front page for you,' said Jack, ignoring Rosa's pleading look,

But it's my story, she thought, *I should be going up there too!*

That didn't help her however and she had to wait impatiently till Mike, scarlet faced, came back with his scoop.

'They've arrested a local guy. I've got his name. They're holding him for questioning but they're pretty sure he's their man,' he gasped and threw himself into a chair.

Obliging Patrick, who, unique among the reporters, was a touch-typist, hurried over and sat down at the typewriter, ready to take dictation. Mike adopted a dramatic attitude and began to declaim, *'Edinburgh Police today announced that they are holding a local man for questioning in connection with the killings of two young women – 17-year-old Sadie Jamieson and 20-year-old Marie Lang, who were both found strangled over the New Year weekend.*

'His name was given as Patrick Noonan, 24, of Flat 28, James Court, Lady Stairs Close. Noonan, who was recently demobbed after serving two years in the Army, is a member of a well-known High Street family.'

Mike broke off the dictation to tell his audience, 'Somebody phoned in and identified him because of the police appeal poster. They're pretty sure he's their man because he's got a record and so do most of the rest of his relatives. Mallen says they're a pack of rogues.'

Rosa, indignant, turned round in her chair to speak to Jack, who stared back at her with his eyebrows raised when she protested, 'But it's all too pat. It has to be a fix! They've only run him in because they need to pin it on somebody.

They had it in for him because he had a run-in with the police when he was up in court last week.'

'Don't tell me you know this guy too?' Jack asked in a tone of disbelief.

'No, not personally, but he was the one I told you about – the one who got beaten up in the cells. Last Wednesday, he came up on a charge of fighting in the Blue Blanket and I wrote down what he said, his name and everything. He's the one I'm writing the brutality piece about!'

She opened her desk drawer and pulled out her spiral reporter's notebook. Noonan's name and address were written at the top of one of the pages, followed by a verbatim note of his accusation against Sergeant Boyle.

'Listen to this,' she said and read aloud the transcript, '*I wasn't fighting. I was trying to stop it. It's a miscarriage of justice . . . And I want to lodge an official complaint against that bastard there!' Points at the sergeant. 'I was demobbed last week and I was celebrating in the Blue Blanket when the fight broke out. It had nothin' to do wi' me but they took me in anyway. In the cells that bastard got stuck into me. I want a doctor. Everybody round here kens him. He likes hurting people.*'

'I wrote that down at the time because I felt he was telling the truth. People like him are not the sort who have friends in high places or can hire a lawyer, so they often get beaten up,' she told Jack, who looked interested and asked, 'What happened to him? Was he sent down on the fighting charge?'

'No. He was given the option of a £25 pound fine or seven days in Saughton. He paid the fine.' She deliberately said nothing about the girl who stepped up with the money for Noonan because she didn't want Mike to be sent off chasing after her. She was determined to check this one herself. In fact she shouldn't have been so idle. She was remiss in not checking on Noonan days ago because she'd been diverted by the Skinner business.

'But the police have information against him,' protested

Mike who wanted the police to get their man.

'We don't know how strong that is, and they're probably grasping at straws. Rosa, you've got Noonan's address. Go up there now and speak to whoever is living there,' said Jack. Then he added, 'Where's Tom?'

'I left him up in the station talking to his police pals,' Mike said. Tom's sources of information among the police were invaluable in matters like this. They told him things to suit their own purposes and he passed them on without attribution.

Almost immediately Tom himself came through the door and sat down at his desk sighing deeply because he was aware that everyone was watching him.

'Well, what did you get?' asked Jack.

Tom took out his notebook and peered at what was written in it. 'Patrick Noonan's been in trouble since he was a little lad. He has three brothers and they've all served time. He went to Borstal for joyriding, breaking into shops and stealing cigarettes when he was eleven. He's been up before the magistrate three times since for getting drunk and resisting arrest. Things have been quieter for the past two years because he signed on in the Army after his last stint in jail, but now he's back and the police say he's been making trouble again. Fighting in the Blue Blanket was the most recent thing and that was only last week.'

Murdering two girls is a bit more than making trouble, thought Rosa.

Jack frowned and said, 'His record is very minor and run-of-the-mill though. The sort of guys who strangle girls aren't usually the ones who draw attention to themselves by breaking into shops, fighting in pubs and stealing cigarettes.'

Rosa nodded in agreement because Noonan hadn't looked a really evil type to her.

'It was the appeal for witnesses that pulled him in. Somebody phoned up and said they saw him with Sadie Jamieson in the High Street on the night she disappeared.

Apparently he hasn't an alibi for the time Marie went missing either. The police reckon if they can get him on one charge, he's almost certainly guilty of the other as well because of the scarf that was used to tie Marie up,' said Tom wearily.

'Who saw him with Sadie?' Jack asked.

Tom shook his head. 'They're not going to tell us that, are they? The Noonans are a tough bunch and not above putting pressure on whoever it is, but the police say their witness is very reliable.'

'Then it must be another policeman. They only think of their own kind as reliable,' quipped Gil.

They were still talking when Rosa quietly slipped out before Jack could detail someone else to go with her. *This is my story*, she thought, and felt like saying, in the style of Captain Oates, 'I am going out and may be some time . . .'

It was very cold and grey out on Cockburn Street, and she shuddered, hunching her shoulders inside her raincoat as she ran up the sloping close into the High Street where she paused to look up and down in both directions.

If it wasn't for the occasional passing car and the clothes of the people around her, the Old Town in January 1956 could be Edinburgh during any winter of the past five hundred years.

If a cavalcade of gorgeously clad horsemen, with the Earl of Bothwell at their head, were to come sweeping down the cobbles on their way to Holyrood, they'd recognize the closes and alleys, the buildings and courtyards they passed. They'd see little change in St Giles or in the tall tenements that leaned into the street. There was a surreal, out-of-time feeling about Edinburgh in winter that made fantasies like that seem possible.

Perhaps I'm a ghost too, she thought, and looked down at her clothes to reassure herself that she was not wearing a long skirt of fustian and wooden pattens.

Pulling herself together, she headed on up the High Street

with a glance at the Tron clock, which told her it was ten minutes past one. Crossing George IV Bridge into the Lawnmarket, she ran into a wide entry with prettily carved blue wooden curlicues at each end of its overhead beam. This was Lady Stairs Close, and, as she expected, there was a crowd of reporters standing around the paved courtyard.

Surrounded by tall, bleak buildings, the yard looked incredibly gloomy and sterile because there was not a tree, a clump of grass, a window box or a pot of shrubs to be seen. The grim Old Town had little time or money for such fripperies.

Rosa joined the crowd, and tagged on to Leo Fairley, asking him, 'Which one's the Noonans' flat, Leo?'

He pointed at a window halfway up James Court, a tenement on the left where James Boswell once lived with his long-suffering wife and family. 'Over there,' he said. 'But they've done a runner.'

'Has anybody asked the neighbours where they are?'

Leo looked at her as if she was a halfwit. 'Is that the next thing to do? So good of you to tell us,' he asked sarcastically, and she flushed but didn't withdraw. Instead she hung around while the other reporters drew a blank with their enquiries among the Noonans' neighbours before making their way to a nearby café called the Pop Inn. She tagged along.

The glass of the café door was steamed up and when Leo pushed it open, there were already several pressmen at the tables. People moved over so they could all sit down and discuss the progress of their enquiries. Everyone was being very cagey.

Rosa sat next to Ken Jones, the man from the *Daily Telegraph,* who was talking about the police. 'The CID are like dogs with two tails about Patrick Noonan's arrest. Skinner didn't really fill the bill and the senior officers have been breathing down their necks to get somebody for killing those girls.'

Leo Fairley added darkly, 'Lucky for them that they got a lead to Noonan then.'

Rosa guessed that, like her, he suspected the charge to be a fix.

'They've a definite sighting of him with the first girl, the little hooker, on the day she disappeared,' Ken reminded him.

'Who saw them together exactly?' Leo asked.

'Some member of the public apparently. He phoned in with the information and they've checked it out. Noonan and the girl were seen walking down the Canongate about seven o'clock on Old Year's night. The informant said she was wearing the scarf that was used to tie up the second girl.'

Rosa shivered. Glancing out of the window, she saw that the afternoon shadows were already gathering outside. Darkness came early to Edinburgh in January. She wondered if she was sickening for something because she felt strangely detached and out of time, just as she had done when she imagined the Earl of Bothwell riding down the High Street.

'They still have to stick the second murder on him though. Has Noonan got an alibi for when the other girl disappeared?' asked a BBC man, who was carrying a heavy tape recorder with a mike hanging round his neck.

Ken told him, 'Apparently not. They've asked him about that and he's not been able to say where he was or what he was doing. They're bringing him up to answer the first charge in court tomorrow morning. He'll be remanded and we'll hear what he has to say then.'

All the reporters scribbled down the details in their notebooks, satisfied, or apparently satisfied with what they'd heard although it was certain they were all planning their own ways of tracking down the Noonan family.

Suddenly Rosa spoke up. 'You're sure it's Patrick Noonan, are you? There's other Noonans in the High Street.'

'Yes, it's definitely Patrick,' said Ken Jones.

Rosa nodded and went on, 'That's odd because I was in the Burgh Court the other day when he was charged with fighting in a pub. It was that place called the Blue Blanket down in the Canongate. He's a regular there apparently.'

She looked around with big innocent eyes as she let this bit of information out. The men looked at her in surprise, trying to hide their interest but she knew that they had succumbed to her red herring. One by one they drifted off and she knew that their next port of call would be the Blue Blanket – and they had to hurry because it closed at half past two. She wondered if anyone at the table apart from herself knew about the girl who paid Noonan's £25 fine but said nothing. She'd keep that detail to herself.

When the last of the men got up from the table to go back to their offices, she walked out of the Pop Inn with them and didn't even turn her head when they passed the open alley-way that led into Lady Stair's Close and the Noonan family home.

Ten minutes later, having dodged down a close, run to the bottom of Cockburn Street and back up the News steps, she was once again in the middle of the paved close, wondering what to do.

A woman came down a flight of outside stairs with a shopping bag in her hand and Rosa ran towards her, asking, 'I'm looking for the Noonans. Where have they gone?'

The woman had a thin, tired face. She looked calculat-ingly at Rosa and discounted her – a girl – as being any danger.

'They're with the Kennedys of course,' she said pointing at the building behind her. It had a jutting-out tower-like wing which was entered by a nail-studded wooden door that opened on to a twisting stair.

Because she assumed that Rosa knew the Kennedys and where they lived, it was important not to ask which floor they were on. The big door opened at a push and she started climbing the stairs.

None of the doors had nameplates. Probably the residents didn't need them because their families had lived there for so long. They were as rooted in the building as the moss on the slates.

Rosa climbed seven floors, right to the top, then stood and listened. Total silence, but somewhere down below people were talking. She went down one floor – still silence. Then another, and this time she heard raised voices behind a closed door on the left. She knocked and struck lucky because it was answered by a young man who looked very like, and was almost as handsome as, Patrick Noonan. It had to be his brother.

There was no point lying. She launched into her intro-duction, apologizing for intruding, giving her name and the name of her paper, at the same time putting out a hand to stop him closing the door.

'Please listen. I think your brother has been set up because I was in court the other day when he said the sergeant there had beaten him up. I felt very sympathetic because I've heard other people complaining about that man Boyle and I believed what your brother said,' she told him.

Noonan's brother hesitated, which showed her that she had scored an advantage, so she kept on talking. 'I don't mind telling you I was very sceptical when I heard that the police have charged your brother with murder. He didn't strike me as the kind who does things like that.'

'Sceptical, is it?' he said. 'As far as we're concerned, it's a bloody lie. He says he didn't do it and now we're wonder-ing how to get him off.' He had a broad Scottish intonation to his voice but didn't speak in as slurring a local dialect as Sadie's mother.

'Have you engaged a lawyer for him?' asked Rosa, look-ing down the stairs behind her, worried in case any of the other reporters suddenly appeared.

The brother glared at her. 'The only lawyers we know are the ones that hang around the Sheriff Court and none of them are any bloody good.'

She nodded in agreement because she knew the kind of

advocates who were appointed to defend the cases of the poor. Incompetent was the kindest word that could be applied to many of them. The thought struck her that if their one-time neighbour James Boswell was still alive, he would be easily persuaded to take on Noonan's case. He was good at standing up for underdogs.

'There's a lawyer called Fenwick who takes difficult cases. You should go to see him,' she said, but without much hope. She'd seen Fenwick in action and he was impressive, but always appeared on behalf of influential clients, whom he invariably got off. His fees were probably enormous, but he might be persuaded to take on a high-profile fight if there was a chance of scoring off the police, for whom he seemed to have scant respect.

A voice from inside the flat called out, 'Who's that, Lawrence?'

'A lassie from the papers, Mum,' he called back.

Silence. He looked coldly at Rosa but suddenly the voice called out again, 'Let her in.' He opened the door wider and said, 'Come in and tell our mum about Fenwick. She's been very cut up by all this.'

A tall, thin woman with a mass of black hair like her sons', tied at the back of her head in a loose knot, was standing in a door leading from one room to another. Her face was very white and her arms were outstretched, with the hands touching the door jambs on each side. Her stance made it look as if she was being crucified.

'I heard what you were saying, but say it again,' she told Rosa who went through her spiel again – including the piece about Fenwick.

'Do you know him?' asked Mrs Noonan. Rosa shook her head and admitted she'd only seen him in the Sheriff Court where she'd gone to sit in on cases being covered by more experienced reporters.

'I think it's worth your while going to see him though. Your son's case will be very controversial. It seems to me that the police haven't much in the way of evidence against him except that he was seen walking down the street with Sadie Jamieson on the day she disappeared. It doesn't seem enough to hang a murder charge on,' she said, aware that Mrs Noonan's eyes stayed fixed on her face all the time she was speaking.

When the older woman spoke again, she had a resonant, musical voice. 'All my bairns, including Paddy and Lawrence here, have known Sadie Jamieson since she was wee. My lassies used to bring her in for a bite to eat when her mother was on the bash. Why shouldn't Paddy walk down the street with her? The police are pinning this on him because of what he and Lawrence did to that bullying sod Boyle. I knew that would lead to trouble.'

She dropped her arms wearily and walked into the main room where she sat down on a wooden chair. Another woman standing at the sink came over to put a hand on her shoulder and her son leaned down too, asking, 'Are you all right, Mum?'

She shook her head at him but kept her eyes on Rosa, who looked from one to the other of the women and asked, 'What did they do to Boyle?'

'He had it coming,' said Lawrence defensively.

'They beat him up two nights ago,' said Mrs Noonan bleakly.

Lawrence looked at Rosa and shrugged. 'Paddy and me waited for him in the Blue Blanket and did him over. We marked him. He's got the best shiner I've ever seen and I bet his ribs are giving him hell too. Serves him bloody right.'

Rosa was surprised at his frankness but realized that it was a sign of acceptance. They must have known she had no intention of informing on them.

'Did Boyle make an official complaint about being attacked? He's police after all,' she wanted to know.

'He never saw us. We waited in the lavatory and jumped him when he was peeing. We dropped a coat over his head and filled him in without ever saying a word. It was a pleasure.' He made a punching gesture with a balled fist as he spoke and it was obvious that he had enjoyed hitting Boyle, who, Rosa agreed, got what was coming to him.

'He probably suspects who did it though,' she suggested.

'He might, but half of Edinburgh has it in for him. A lot of blokes would have helped if they'd known what we were doing. Even Billy the Blue Blanket barman would have liked a kick at him. Boyle's not going to talk about what happened because he'd hate to admit to taking a hammering. A hard man like him!'

Mrs Noonan spoke up in a peremptory voice, 'He'll wait his chance, but that's not our biggest worry at the moment. Paddy admits he met Sadie in the High Street on the last afternoon of the year and walked up to Regent Road with her. She told him she was going to meet a friend at Jock's Lodge but so far nobody's come up to say they saw her there.' She looked around with a pitiful look on her face and added in a quavering tone, 'My Paddy could hang if they can't pin it on somebody else.'

'Aw no,' sobbed the other woman, whom Rosa assumed was a Kennedy.

'You must get a lawyer. And surely there's some way of establishing alibis for Paddy for the times both of the girls disappeared, because there's two of them, remember. If he can be cleared of suspicion for one death, the police won't be able to pin the other on him. The same man seems to have killed them both. Just because he was seen with Sadie, what was he doing when Marie disappeared?' said Rosa.

'We thought of that,' said Lawrence.

'And can your brother drive a car? The girls must have been driven to the places their bodies were found,' Rosa asked him, but then she remembered the joyriding charge – of course he could drive.

Lawrence said, 'Yes, he drove lorries in the Army and when he was younger, he was up in court on a charge of nicking a car just to drive around. He was a kid at the time . . .'

'But he doesn't have a car, I suppose?'

The mother and son shook their heads and she said, 'Of course not, and he's given up stealing them as well. He was trying to go straight. He'd even got a job working in the brewery down beside Holyrood Palace. It's not fair!'

'When did the police arrest him for the murders?' Rosa asked.

'Late last night . . . about two in the morning. They came to the flat and took him away. When the newspapermen started knocking on the door at dinner time, we moved over here to my sister-in-law,' Mrs Noonan said. Rosa could imagine the press invasion. There had been at least a dozen of them in Lady Stair's Close by the time she got there.

'Does the girl who paid his fine in the Burgh Court know that he's been arrested?' she asked, remembering the slim, dark-haired girl with the anxious-looking face.

Everyone in the room looked hostile and Mrs Noonan asked, 'What girl?'

'Come on. I saw her. The girl who paid his £25 fine for fighting in the pub,' Rosa told them.

'A girl paid his fine? He said he borrowed it,' said his mother in a surprised tone.

'Well, maybe he did, but she was a thin girl with dark-brown hair. She was sitting in the court when he came up from the cells, so she must have known he was on a charge. She seemed to know him well. Perhaps she could give him an alibi for the time one or other of the dead girls disappeared. Have you asked her?' Rosa suggested.

The mother looked at Lawrence and they nodded to each other in silent confirmation. 'That's her,' said Lawrence.

Mrs Noonan shook her dark head. 'We've heard about her but I've never met her. He never brought her here.'

'She might be able to help. Have you told the police about her?' Rosa persisted.

'They'll know about her already if she paid his fine like you say,' said Lawrence.

'If you like I'll go to see her. It's possible she hasn't heard about his arrest, and she might be able to help,' Rosa said, thanking her stars that she'd copied the name and address down from the court records.

'I doubt it. Paddy didn't want us to have anything to do with her. I don't think we're grand enough. It was Mary this and Mary that, Mary's nice house and Mary's fancy cooking,' said Mrs Noonan bitterly.

'But you knew about her?' Rosa asked and was answered by a nod.

'Oh aye, we knew. He's been trying to sort himself out ever since he met her.'

'So she's called Mary. I only had her initial. She might be able to help,' said Rosa, thinking how lucky that she was the only reporter in the Burgh Court that day. With any luck she would have Mary all to herself.

One of the advantages of leading a lonely existence, living alone and having no close family was that no one was waiting for you to come home; and no one would be annoyed if you didn't turn up for supper. Instead of going to the Cockburn as usual on Friday night, she climbed into her car and drove to Willowbrae Road.

It was a long road, lined by ultra-respectable middle-class bungalows, as different as it was possible to be from the myriad flats of the Lawnmarket. Yet Rosa would prefer to live up in the Old Town than down here in prim suburbia. She liked the feeling of walking in the footsteps of people from the past, even though a lot of them had been villains.

She was looking for number 164, so she drove slowly trying to make out the numbers nailed on the doors or gates, but it was growing dark and trying to pinpoint a particular house was difficult.

Eventually she tracked it down on the other side of the road and a few hundred feet along from a pair of telephone boxes. Every bungalow in the road was surrounded by its

223

own patch of garden and this one's plot was tidy and sterile-looking with two empty beds of turned-over earth running alongside a concrete path. In the summer, the beds would be planted out with mathematically spaced clumps of annuals – geraniums, salvias and petunias. Two squares of dead-looking grass filled the spaces beneath the front windows and a line of leggy cotoneaster shrubs fenced off the garden from the street. It was all so unexciting that Rosa was surprised that a girl who lived in such a place could be associated with a rough diamond like Patrick Noonan.

The only light shining out from number 164 was a faint glimmer behind a glass panel in the front door.

The door bell shrilled hysterically somewhere inside and after a short wait, a shadow showed behind the glass door and a female voice called out, 'Is that you, Derek? What are you doing back so soon? Why don't you use your key?'

'No. It's Rosa Makepeace,' Rosa shouted back. Her name sounded as if she'd made it up, she realized.

'I don't know you. What do you want?' asked the other voice suspiciously.

'I've come to speak to Mary,' shouted Rosa.

'I'm Mary and I don't know you,' was the sharp reply.

'It's about Patrick Noonan.' That did it. There was silence from the other side of the door and, after a pause, a key was turned in the lock. The girl who opened the door was the one that Rosa saw in court, about twenty-five, not very tall, thin and anxious-looking with neatly combed short brown hair and no make-up.

Although it was only five o'clock she was wearing a pink padded dressing gown with the belt tied tightly round her narrow waist, and she looked very clean, almost antiseptic. Rosa was struck by the conviction that she worked as a nurse.

'What do you want?' Mary Callendar asked, staring at her visitor – hostility seemed to spark off her.

'Have you heard that Patrick Noonan's been arrested?' Rosa asked.

The girl's knees seemed to buckle slightly.

'I read it in the *News* tonight,' she whispered as if she was afraid of being overheard though there was no one on the street near them.

Rosa lowered her voice too as she said, 'I'm a reporter on the *Dispatch* and I came to see you because the police are trying to pin the murder charge on Patrick Noonan. His mother and brother are very worried and they thought that you might be able to provide him with alibis for the times the dead girls disappeared. *They* can't because he wasn't at home during either of the important times. They wondered if he was with you, and I had your address because I was in court the day you paid his fine for fighting in that pub . . .'

Mary reached out and quickly pulled her visitor into the lobby, closing the door behind her. 'This is awful. I can't do that. Derek, my husband, doesn't know about us. I haven't told him yet and he mustn't find out like this . . .' Her voice quavered and her lips trembled.

Rosa's face showed her surprise. Noonan's girlfriend was married! This was probably her own house, not that of her parents as Rosa had assumed. A quick look round showed that the furnishings were as careful and uninspiring as the garden. A fawn carpet covered the floor of the narrow lobby and the walls were painted pale cream with a line of framed prints of roses along one side. Lady Stair's Close was a world away.

It would seem like another world to Paddy, and Mary Callendar must have had some sort of a brainstorm when she took up with him.

'Can't you help him?' Rosa asked and Mary shook her head.

'How can I? Oh, I'm so worried. I've been out of my mind with worry since I read the paper and I don't know what to do. You see we were together on Old Year's night but I can't go to the police and say so for Derek's sake. He was working away from home and doesn't know . . .'

'If you don't give Noonan an alibi, he might be convicted of a murder he didn't commit,' Rosa told her firmly and was disconcerted when the girl burst into noisy tears.

'I know that. I've been thinking and thinking about it. I don't know what to do. Paddy was with me all New Year's Eve, all night and right up till lunchtime the next day. I work shifts, you see, and Derek was driving his lorry to London. He subcontracts for a big haulier in Musselburgh.'

'Maybe Noonan'll tell the police he was with you and all you'll have to do is confirm his statement,' Rosa suggested.

But Mary shook her head and said, 'No, I'm sure he won't. I've made him promise not to tell anyone about us till we're ready. I'm surprised he told his family anything because he said he wouldn't. This is all such a mess. I've been trying to get up enough courage to break it to Derek. Patrick and I have been saving money so we can go away together – perhaps to Australia. They'll take me because I'm a nurse.' She was twisting her hands together as she wept in anguish.

At least I was right about her job, thought Rosa, but Australia might not accept Noonan because of his record. Mary hadn't thought of that, however. The affair with dashing-looking Noonan probably got out of control and now she was in confusion because her hand was being forced. She seemed glad to talk to Rosa because it was probably the first time she'd been able to talk about it with anyone.

'They wouldn't hang someone for a murder they didn't commit, would they?' she asked, desperately seeking reassurance.

Rosa shook her head. 'I'm afraid they might. They're desperate to blame it on anyone and they have a witness who saw your Patrick with Sadie Jamieson, the first girl who was killed, on the day she disappeared. If he can't explain what he was doing when Marie went missing from the North British Hotel, he won't have much of a defence – and that was the night he spent with you.'

'Oh God, how terrible, how awful!' Mary groaned, covering her face with her hands. 'I really love him. He's so handsome and so sweet to me. He wants to lead a decent life and did well in the Army. It's just when he's with his family that he goes astray. That's why we thought that Australia was a good idea.'

Rosa nodded. The High Street probably did drag its people back no matter how hard they tried to get away. Perhaps even Australia wasn't far enough to go to escape its toils.

Still weeping, the girl walked into a room at the side of the lobby and Rosa followed into the sparsely furnished sitting room that looked as if it was lived in by people who were unsure of themselves and ill at ease with each other. Occupying most of the floor space was an enormous couch and two fat chairs covered with green moquette upholstery fabric that had incised leaf patterns cut into its surface. A gleaming walnut cocktail cabinet that screamed 'wedding present from loving parents' occupied the wall behind the couch and a gas fire burned in the hearth. The colour scheme was the same as the hall and above the fireplace hung a solitary picture, a print of a Burmese girl in a cream sarong, sitting with her knees bent and her feet sticking out to one side. Munnings, Rosa thought, but she appreciated him better as a painter of horses.

'I don't know what to do,' the girl said again, sitting down on the arm of the sofa and staring at Rosa. It was obvious she was asking for advice but there was no guarantee she'd take it.

Rosa guessed that in the first rush of romance, the idea of running away with a lover seemed very attractive, but now, when things were becoming messy, she was frightened of cutting herself off from everything she knew and took for granted.

The bright light, shining down from an overhead glass bowl fitting, showed that Mary had flawless, pale skin and sweeping eyelashes, her features were finely chiselled and, even in distress, she had an air of great dignity and reserve. Hers was the sort of beauty that was not immediately striking – in fact Rosa originally thought her plain – but her appeal crept up on you and took you by surprise.

'I think if you have information that might clear Mr Noonan, you should make it known to the police,' Rosa said firmly and formally.

'But it'll all come out in the newspapers. My parents and the neighbours will read it. I'll have to give evidence in court. Derek will go mad.'

'Don't you want to get Noonan off?'

'Of course I do. I love him,' was the broken reply. 'I didn't know what it was like to love somebody like that before I met him – but I'm sorry for my husband. He's a good man. He doesn't deserve this.'

'But if you were going to Australia, you'd have to tell him then, wouldn't you?' Or were they just going to disappear one day?

'Oh yes, of course, but I thought Patrick and I could tell him together. Then we'd go away.'

'Have you any children?' Rosa asked, wondering if the thought of leaving them was too much for Mary, but there was no sign of children in this obsessively tidy house, no toys, no pram in the hall, no chipped paint anywhere.

She shook her head. 'No, not yet. We were waiting. We've only been married three years and I'm still working because we're buying this house on a mortgage. I'm a staff nurse in the casualty department at the Royal Infirmary. That's how I met Patrick. He came in one night when I was on duty. He'd cut his hand and had to be stitched up.'

Young men from the High Street were as familiar visitors at the Royal Infirmary Accident and Emergency Department as they were to the local courts. Noonan with his mass of black curls would make a big impression on this sheltered, repressed girl.

'Was that how you got to know each other?' Rosa asked.

228

'Yes. We bumped into each other in the street a couple of days later and he recognized me. We went for a coffee, and started to meet when I was between shifts. It was so exciting. The more we saw of each other, the worse it got. He promised he'd go straight for my sake . . . I really believed him.'

'His mother said he was trying to go straight,' Rosa agreed. She didn't know whom to feel most sorry for – Noonan, Mary or the absent Derek.

'Have you a family who might help or give you advice – a father and mother, I mean? Or a best friend?' she asked next.

Mary shook her head. 'My parents live in Ayr and they'd be very shocked if I told them I'd taken a lover.'

'Lots of people do that nowadays,' said Rosa, slightly enviously.

'Not the sort of people we know,' replied Mary.

'Well, I can't advise you but I think Patrick Noonan needs an alibi and a good lawyer,' said Rosa and told Mary about Fenwick.

The girl listened with interest and then said, 'He'd cost a lot of money, I expect, but I've been saving my salary so we can go off together. I have quite a lot in the bank.'

Contributing to Noonan's defence fund might be her way of signing off. The passion between them probably wouldn't last anyway for they were too different.

'That's good but you might not have to spend your money. I think your evidence would do the trick, providing you're brave enough to make a statement. Noonan's mother and brother are going to try to get Fenwick interested and I suspect they'll be able to raise enough money if they have to. You ought to get in touch with them and go to see him too. Tell him you can provide Patrick with an alibi. Explain the situation and let him handle it from there on. I'm sure he'll be able to give you good advice,' Rosa said. This situation was beginning to tire her and she felt she was arguing against implacability.

Mary Callendar listened, calmed down a little, straightened her shoulders and said, 'Perhaps that's what I'll do.'

'Don't leave it too long,' said Rosa, heading for the door. Mary let her out and didn't say goodbye as she walked back down the prim-looking garden path, reflecting on the incongruity of Patrick Noonan and that girl getting together and the even greater improbability of them staying together.

Love took so many different forms and caused so much trouble. Patricia and Hugh, Alan and Stella, herself and Iain, Sylvia and her Hal . . . there was no way of predicting who would fall for whom or why.

Thinking about love was so depressing that she decided to find some cheerful company for the rest of the night. The bar at the Cockburn was deserted, however, and Etta said that Mike and the boys had gone dancing at the Plaza. Patricia was at the Press Club 'with that man of hers'. Etta did not approve of Hugh either.

Rosa was not dressed for dancing, nor was she in the mood, so she went in search of Patricia whom she found sitting alone on one of the long leather-covered benches in the Press Club lounge. She was dressed in blue with a huge pink silk rose on the lapel of her jacket and looked lovely. Her face lit up when she saw Rosa, and she held out a hand as she said, 'Come and sit down. I've so much to tell you!'

'Where's Hugh?' Rosa asked looking around. Thankfully there was no sign of him and the lounge was empty.

'He's buying another round. Do sit down and listen. I decided not to go to bed with him again – not yet anyway, but I've said I'll marry him, Rosa.'

She couldn't even pretend to be pleased. After Noonan and Mary Callendar this was too much. Had the whole world gone mad?

'Oh my God, no!' she gasped and at that moment the door swung open and the man himself came through with two glasses in his hand.

He was not at all pleased to see her. 'Cassandra herself,'

he said rudely as he put the glasses down on the table. 'If you want a drink you'll have to get it yourself. I'm hard-up.'

'I don't want a drink, because I've nothing to celebrate,' she retorted.

'There's our coming nuptials,' he jeered, looking at Patricia, 'or are you anti-matrimony now that your old beau is marrying above himself?'

Rosa flushed and looked accusingly at her friend because she knew that only Patricia could have told him about her broken heart over Iain. She confided in no one else.

Standing up, she said to them both, 'Good luck for the future.' Somehow she managed to bite back the words – 'you'll need it'.

Looking guilty, Patricia jumped to her feet as well. 'I'm going to the ladies'. Come with me, Rosa,' she said hurriedly and grabbed Rosa's arm before she could get away.

When they were alone, she said, 'I'm sorry. I told him about you and Iain but I didn't think he'd throw it in your teeth like that.'

'It doesn't matter really,' Rosa replied and in a way it was the truth. Iain was the past as far as she was concerned. She was good at putting things behind her. 'What I need now is something to look forward to,' she said to Patricia.

'Come to my wedding. Be my bridesmaid,' Patricia asked. In spite of being contrite about Rosa, she couldn't hide the fact that she was flying high on delight.

'When is it?'

'As soon as possible. Next month. There's no point waiting.'

Rosa groaned. 'You're my friend, Patricia, but I couldn't bring myself to stand by holding your bouquet and watch you marry that man. Have you thought this out? Do you know what you're doing?'

Patricia didn't take offence. Turning away from the mirror that she'd been staring into, she faced Rosa and absolute decision shone from her. 'Yes, I've thought about it. I know he's got faults. I know none of my friends like him but I *love* him, I really love him . . . I know that if I go to bed with him again, he'd probably drop me afterwards, but I want him so much. I don't know why but I do. I'm sorry you feel the way you do about him but . . . Anyway, if it doesn't work out I can always get a divorce.' She laughed in a high, brittle way and Rosa suddenly saw how she would be when she was older. She seemed more like Dorothy Parker than ever.

Some lines of Parker's ran through Rosa's head and she wondered if she dare quote them to her friend . . . 'By the time you swear you're his, shivering and sighing, and he vows his passion is infinite, undying – Lady, make a note of this, one of you is lying.'

She kept them to herself however and pleaded instead, 'Oh Patricia, don't do it.'

'He's asked me and I'm marrying him, Rosa, and that's that. It might be a mistake but I'm going to do it. Please understand,' said Patricia firmly.

What a start to another year, thought Rosa as she drove back to her digs. I'm in a mess because I've got myself involved in the murder of someone I know; my best friend insists on committing a terrible mistake; and the man I love is marrying someone else. Maybe I should go out on Monday and buy a one-way ticket to Australia. Judging by Alan and Stella, it doesn't seem to be the sort of place where people spend a lot of time worrying about hang-ups or emotional nuances.

Twenty-Four

It was Saturday again and Rosa wakened with a mood of despair hanging over her, which was only partially dispelled by the arrival of an airmail letter from Cyprus. The island was beautiful, the sun was shining and the sea blue, wrote Roddy, and, holding it, she stared with a jaundiced eye through the window at the universal greyness of Northumberland Street in January.

He missed her, he said and she thought, *How can he when I'm never anything but horrible to him?*

Maybe he was another emotional masochist like Patricia. It would serve her right if he met an exotic Cypriot woman and forgot all about her. That idea made her even more depressed. Was it possible that she was missing him too?

The office was in its Saturday mode with the sports writers and subs all busy and the rest of them more or less twiddling their thumbs. Thankfully Patricia was on her day off again, and there need be no awkward exchanges between them. She was probably at home, making her wedding dress. There was no one to lighten Rosa's mood by accompanying her to lunch at the Chinese restaurant. The alternative of canteen soup and sandwiches didn't appeal, so she wandered up the High Street to the Pop Inn, where, on quiet days like Saturdays, they did a good cheese omelette. Not exactly sweet and sour pork but better than a canteen bacon roll.

Near the City Chambers, she spotted Mallen and Boyle coming across the street from the police station and heading down the street towards her. They were both wearing heavy overcoats and felt hats because the temperature had dropped again and there was a whisper of more snow in the wind.

When they drew abreast of each other, Mallen stopped, touched his hat brim and gave her his sarcastic smile. 'Hello, Miss Makepeace. Where are you off to? What bit of mischief are you about to meddle in today?'

Boyle did not stop until he had walked on a few paces, turned his back on them, pretending not to listen, and stared off down the street towards the Tron. He seemed to exude scorn. There were bruises round his eyes and the sight of them gave Rosa pleasure because she knew how he came by them, and he didn't know that she knew! Nasty of her, she accepted, but she couldn't help it.

She glared at Mallen and said stiffly, 'I'm not in the habit of making mischief.'

He shrugged. 'Aren't you? We had a young lady in the office this morning wanting to give a statement on behalf of Mr Noonan and she told the officer who interviewed her that you persuaded her to do it.'

Rosa's heart lifted. She felt like skipping and dancing. So Mrs Callendar had come up trumps. And so quickly. Good for her. It was important not to let Mallen see how pleased she was, so all she said was, 'I'm sure you'll be pleased for justice to prevail. You wouldn't want to convict the wrong man, would you?'

Boyle was still facing in the other direction a few feet away, but, like a dog, he seemed to be bristling, giving off rays of suppressed rage. She was sure he knew about her intention of writing about his treatment of prisoners in the cells.

'What I'd like to know is how you tracked down Mrs Callendar and if you have any more useful information up that little sleeve of yours. You seem to be able to pull things out at will like a rabbit out of a hat,' said Mallen.

She almost laughed at the analogy, which he certainly would not mean to be funny, but managed to look serious as she said flippantly, 'Even if I had more ideas, I'd not tell you, would I? I want to keep you on your toes so you'll go on buying the *Dispatch.*'

Perhaps that was too cheeky because suddenly he was back in his heavy law-enforcer mode. 'It's not a good idea to keep important information to yourself, you know. I think I've told you before that you might know more than you realize or is even good for you,' he warned her.

A gust of icy wind came sweeping down from the castle and whipped round her legs, making her shudder. She remembered Duncan Skinner, who probably knew more than was good for him too.

She hunched her shoulders to quell involuntary shivering and said, 'I'm not hiding important information if that's what you think. If I knew who killed Marie, I'd certainly tell the police.'

'I'm glad to hear it,' said Mallen and tipped his hat to her as he turned to walk away. Boyle fell into step beside him like a soldier on parade as they headed on down the street, their shoulders almost touching and their backs broad. She knew they were talking about her.

After she ate her omelette, she was hurrying back to the office down the High Street when she noticed a huddled figure weaving drunkenly down the pavement in front of her. It was a hatless woman and her yellow hair stuck out like stalks of straw, so brittle that it looked liable to crack into little pieces of chaff if she made a gesture towards tidiness and passed a comb through it. Suddenly she stopped and Rosa drew level with her.

'Hello, Mrs Jamieson,' she said.

Sadie's mother looked round. Her eyes were pouched and her skin mottled with the tell-tale purplish markings of a serious drinker. She was wearing the same black skirt and blouse, crumpled and dirty now, that she had on at her daughter's funeral but she was stockingless and her veined legs were stark white. A foul smell of stale alcohol and cigarette smoke came off her.

'Whit the hell do *ye* want?' she rasped.

'Nothing. I just said hello,' Rosa replied.

'Well keep yer hellos to yersel'. Whae are ye onywey?' She didn't remember Rosa.

'I came to see you with Sylvia Playfair after your daughter died,' Rosa explained.

'Oh *her*. She brought the money frae Flora. Have you ony mair?' She stuck out a filthy hand and waggled her fingers.

Though the woman was obviously hopeless, something about her woke pity in Rosa, who reached into her pocket and found a florin which she dropped into the importuning palm. Betty Jamieson eyed it and pursed her mouth in disdain at the smallness of coin.

'I'll no go far wi' that,' she said.

'You could go home. It's very cold and it's getting colder,' said Rosa looking down at the bare legs. Betty Jamieson looked wrecked and it was obvious she'd got through Flora's money and was in need of more.

'A wee nip'd keep the cold out,' wheedled Betty. Rosa was devastated to realize that she actually did not care a great deal about her daughter or anything else. The centre of her existence was the next drink. But Rosa was shelling out no more. Instead she changed the subject.

'Did the police tell you that a man was arrested on suspicion of murdering Sadie?' she asked.

'I heard,' Betty replied, eyeing Rosa cautiously.

'Do you know who it is?' Rosa persisted.

'They said it was Paddy Noonan,' Betty said flatly.

'Were you surprised?'

'Naething surprises me ony mair. I ken a' the Noonans. His mother has a tongue that could clip cloots but Paddy wasnae a bad laddie . . .' Betty sounded weary.

'Then you'll be glad to hear that it wasn't him. The police have let him out because he has an alibi,' Rosa told her.

'They said Sadie was seen on the street with him,' said Betty.

'But his alibi was for the second girl, Marie Lang. The same man killed them both. Have you any idea who else might have met your Sadie on Old Year's day?' Rosa asked.

Betty snapped, 'How would I know? Sadie never said she was goin' to meet onybody when she was wi' me.' It slipped out without her thinking and Rosa seized on it.

'So Sadie came to see you on the day she disappeared. You said that she didn't.' Rosa remembered the scepticism of the red-haired girl in Danube Street about the veracity of Betty's evidence.

'I forgot, I was fu'.' Obviously she was lying.

'You forgot? Try to remember now. When did she come?' Rosa reached in her pocket and pulled out a pound note.

'The police said I wasn't to talk to the press, but she came after denner time . . .' When the pubs closed in the afternoon, she meant, because dinner to Betty was eaten at midday.

'Why did she come?'

'To see me of course. She brought me a couple of quid for the New Year, and she showed off a new braw scarf she'd bought from Jenners.'

Poor wee Sadie, Rosa thought. Her death seemed even more tragic when she heard about that pathetic little lie.

'Who told you not to talk to the press?' Rosa asked.

'Peter Mallen. He came in and telt me about Noonan being picked up, asked me if I thought it was possible and all that,' said Betty with her eyes fixed on the pound note in Rosa's hand.

'Do you know him well?'

'I ken them a' and he's no' the worst,' was the reply.

'What did you tell him?'

'The same as I telt you. That Paddy Noonan never seemed like a bad laddie.'

When Rosa was about to hand over the money, she remembered what Tom once told her about the interviewer's technique of keeping an important question for the point of departure. People were often so relieved to see you go, he said, that they blurted out unprepared admissions or observations.

'Did Mallen tell you who saw Sadie and Noonan together? It must have been somebody who knew them both.'

She sighed. 'He said it was somebody trustworthy that saw them, another copper, he said.' So Patricia was right. Rosa gave Betty the money knowing that she'd have it drunk within an hour.

Her afternoon of meeting people was not yet over for, running down the close that led to Cockburn Street, she spotted Etta coming up with a small parcel in her hand. The bar was closed by now of course, and Etta was on her time off.

As she passed Rosa she nodded without smiling and said, 'I'm just off to see Sylvia. She's in the Infirmary?'

Rosa stopped in mid stride. 'What's the matter with her?'

'It's bad, I'm afraid. She sent a message two days ago asking me to visit her and when I went she didn't seem too bad, but today the ward sister said on the phone that she's very weak and I won't be allowed to stay long. I think they've sent for her parents . . . but I'll know more tonight. Come in and see me when we open at five.'

'I'm so sorry. It's awful. Please give her my best wishes,' Rosa said as Etta bustled away with a cursory nod.

The rest of the afternoon was passed reading the horoscopes in the paper and Rosa was quite optimistic because it said she was going on a journey and could look forward to a period of excitement in her life. She wished she could believe it but she knew how the horoscopes were written.

Anybody idling in the office without something specific to do risked being told to update the obituaries or write the horoscopes. Horoscopes were the least favourite job and people did them by scouring the archives for old ones, cutting them out and pasting them in under different zodiac headings. The temptation was to reserve the best predictions for their own birth dates.

Lawrie was the only one who enjoyed the job because he slipped in sexual innuendos like 'your affairs will reach a climax this weekend', 'take precautions' or 'be specially careful when dealing with strangers'.

Jack rarely bothered to read what the horoscope said and, over Christmas, Lawrie had decided to brighten up the lives of the readers by urging excess for every zodiac sign. His messages included: 'Abandon your usual caution', 'turn no offerings aside', 'allow the unexpected to win you over', 'stop worrying about your bank balance/doctor's advice/usual prejudices', 'you can afford to sail close to the wind this week', 'take a risk!'

He was most disappointed that the citizens of Edinburgh did not break out in a bacchanal frenzy but went about their day-to-day business with the same pinched respectability that they habitually exhibited.

'I don't know what you expect,' said Patricia when Lawrie complained that there was no appreciable change in the city or in the willingness of the young ladies at the Plaza to yield to his importunities. 'None of the readers back the horses you tip either.'

At last it was time to leave work and Etta was back behind the bar, looking sad when Rosa pushed open the door at half past five. Etta didn't ask what Rosa would drink, just grabbed a glass and pressed it under the optic of a brandy bottle perched on the back display. Then she pushed it across the bar top, saying, 'It's on me.'

Rosa lifted the glass and sniffed at it. Brandy always made her think of Dickensian Christmases with fat, jolly Mr Pickwick holding up bumpers in joyful toasts.

'It's Courvoisier,' said Etta, as if she thought the brand was being criticized.

'Thanks,' said Rosa. She took a sip, coughed a little and then asked, 'How was Sylvia?'

'That's why I'm giving you a brandy. She's not good,' was the reply.

'Oh hell! Is it her leukaemia?'

'Yes. The sister in the ward told me that she's slipping away. They can't help her any more. Apparently she's lasted about a year more than any of the doctors estimated. They all really like her up there too . . .' Etta, looking grim, reached under the counter and brought out a packet of cigarettes, offering it to Rosa after shaking out one for herself. The offer was accepted. Like brandy, cigarettes did little for Rosa, but, as usual, she didn't want to appear unsophisticated by refusing.

When Etta's flaring match set fire to the tobacco, she said, 'Sylvia was asking about you. I think she'd like to see you.'

'I'll certainly go. How – how long do they think she's got?'

'They never tell you that! She's quite *compos mentis* and able to talk but she gets very tired. I don't think you should wait too long before you go to see her though,' was Etta's reply.

'Maybe I could go now?' Rosa suggested.

'Visiting time starts at seven. She's in a private room . . . in the haemo-something department. The nurses are nice, they'll maybe let you in early, but, mind, only ten minutes. It's all she can take.'

'Is there anything I can give her?' Rosa asked, remembering the parcel Etta was carrying when they met earlier.

'Take her something to drink. It doesn't matter now,' Etta replied.

'What do you think she'd like?'

'She used to drink malt whisky or gin in here but they need mixers and she wouldn't be able to drink them straight . . .' was the doubtful reply.

'I know what! She likes champagne. I'll get a bottle of that if I can find a shop open,' Rosa exclaimed, looking at her watch, but it was getting late and the off-licences would soon be closing.

'I've a bottle in the cellar but it should be chilled,' Etta offered.

'Sell it to me. By the time I've carried it up to the Infirmary it'll be frozen,' Rosa told her.

There was not much demand for champagne in the Cockburn, and Etta sold her a cobweb-encrusted bottle for £2, which, she said, was its 1939 price.

'It won't have gone off, will it?' Rosa asked doubtfully, only to be reassured, 'Champagne gets better with age. Any place else they'd charge you a tenner for a bottle like this. It's Veuve Cliquot, you know.'

Nursing the bottle with its glamorous scarlet and gold label, Rosa hurried off into the darkness. Her car was parked at the bottom of the hill, near Market Street, and she carefully picked her way down towards it. Sleety rain was falling and glimmering on the old paving stones, making them as slippery as sheet ice and she didn't want to fall and smash her precious burden.

There was only one grumpy man on duty in the porter's lodge at the gate of the Royal Infirmary. She stopped the car and ran in to ask him, 'Where's the ward for haemotology – blood diseases?'

He told her and then warned, 'Ye cannae go in though. It's no' visiting time yet.'

'Press enquiry,' she said grandly and ran back to the car while he shouted angrily after her, 'Where's your pass then?'

Driving off, she waggled a handy piece of paper off the floor at him. It was actually an old race card for Musselburgh races but he was not to know that.

Sylvia lay in a single room at the end of a long ward on the second floor and Rosa was given a lecture by a stern sister about visiting out of hours, but she said she was from out of town and unable to come any other time so the sister relented. Sylvia was a favourite.

She was lying on her side on a high metal bed with her yellow hair tied back from her face. The sockets of her eyes were sunken and her face looked very strained with the high cheekbones sticking out starkly. She was wearing a blue nightgown with a bodice of creamy Valenciennes lace but her arms were bare and skeletally thin.

When Rosa tiptoed in, her eyes were closed but they opened when the nurse touched her hand, propped up her pillows and turned to Rosa with a whispered warning: 'Only ten minutes, remember.' Sylvia must have had other visitors because there were several bouquets of expensive flowers in her room. There was even an exotic white orchid in a pot.

'Hi, Sylvia,' said Rosa, putting her handbag on the floor and reaching down into it to haul out the champagne bottle.

She slowly raised herself against the pillow a little and Rosa asked, 'I hope you like Veuve Cliquot? Etta says it's good.'

'I love champagne, any champagne.' The reply was a whisper.

'I'll get glasses then,' Rosa said, looking around. There was one by a water flask on Sylvia's locker and she nodded towards a handbasin in the corner where a green Bakelite mug sat in a rack with her toothbrush in it.

'Trust you to bring my favourite drink. I knew you had the potential to be a very bad influence,' Sylvia said, joking and perking up a little.

'I hope so,' said Rosa and in an effort at gaiety, she pointed the champagne bottle at the ceiling, and inexpertly prised off the cork, which exploded with a loud bang sending a spray of wine across the linoleum-covered floor. Sylvia giggled as her glass was filled and put into her hand.

'Prop up my pillows a bit more,' she said and Rosa pulled at them in an attempt to make her more upright. While she was doing this a plump, red-faced nurse came in, and, without saying anything, took over and expertly propped Sylvia into a sitting position. She grinned at the sight of the bottle and warned, 'Keep it quiet, no more explosions please,' before she disappeared.

Sylvia's hands were visibly shaking when she lifted the glass to her lips but she was smiling bravely and looked almost like her old self, though much paler, almost transparent in fact. Her gallantry was heart-breaking.

'I'm glad to see you're still surviving,' she said to Rosa.

'Oh, I'm fine,' she replied, surprised at the comment.

'I hope you're taking care. They haven't got that killer yet, have they?' asked Sylvia.

'They thought they had, but it was the wrong man. A chap called Patrick Noonan was run in but it turns out he has an alibi, and I'm sure he had nothing to do with it,' Rosa told her.

She nodded. 'Yes, Etta told me about that. But seriously, you should get out of Edinburgh till they pull someone in. Your father lives near Selkirk, doesn't he? Why don't you go there?' she said, looking at her visitor over the rim of her glass.

Rosa was surprised. 'Leave Edinburgh? Why? The murders have nothing to do with me except that I knew Marie.'

'That's the point. The murderer might be afraid that you're on to him. You're not exactly keeping a low profile, are you? He's probably got his eye on you already.'

Rosa nodded, and felt disquiet as she remembered the mystery caller at Jean Noble's and Fanny's.

'There has been somebody going around asking questions about me,' she told Sylvia.

'Exactly. Are you suspicious of anybody in particular? If you are, tell someone, write it down. Don't keep back anything in the hope of a scoop.'

'I haven't a clue. Why should I have?'

She shook her head feebly. 'I don't know. It's just that you're always around when something happens . . .'

'That's only coincidental,' Rosa told her.

Sylvia leant her head back and closed her eyes. The lids looked crêpey and were marked with blue veins. She heaved a huge sigh and slipped deeper into the pillows. Some of her champagne slopped over the sheet and she brushed at it with a feeble gesture.

'Will I go away? Are you tired?' Rosa asked anxiously.

'I'm dying but don't go yet,' she said and her eyes flashed fury at what was happening to her.

'I'm so sorry,' whispered Rosa.

'So am I.' Sylvia's voice was incredibly weary.

'Where's your man?' Rosa asked.

'Which one? I have lots of visitors. Barbara comes, so does Etta and some of my men friends – my clients I suppose you could call them. They are very good. They sent those flowers. They're paying the bills too, but only two actually come, the ones without wives to worry about . . .'

Her eyes were still closed.

'But I mean Hal. The chap who's writing the book. The one who was going to take you away on the yacht.' She had only referred to him by his first name, not his surname which she did not know.

Sylvia smiled and sighed again. 'Oh, you're so gullible. Did you believe all that? Hal's not around any more, darling. He hasn't been around for ages. When I got ill, he disappeared out of my life and set up with the girl in Mayfair.'

'But you told me—' Rosa said, shocked.

'Wishful thinking,' Sylvia snapped. 'When you're sick like me you need illusions. I used to think he'd come back if I thought about it hard enough but of course he didn't. You actually believed me, did you?'

'Yes, I did. Of course I did. You made him sound so real.'

'That's because I wanted him to be there. As if I could bring him back by talking about him.' She closed her eyes again and seemed to drift away. Rosa sat silent, wishing she'd never brought the subject up and desperately searched around in her mind for something to talk about.

Sylvia opened her eyes and said, 'My parents are coming. They'll be here tonight. Did I tell you they think I'm an interior designer? That bit was true. If you meet them don't let me down.'

'Of course not.' Rosa stood up and filled Sylvia's glass again.

She held it with both hands and drank it down as if it was water, before she said in a stronger voice, 'Isn't champagne wonderful? It has such a miraculous effect. Maybe I should ask to have it pumped into my veins instead of all that blood.'

Rosa laughed and was about to pour the dregs of the bottle into Sylvia's glass when the door opened and the friendly nurse came in. 'Sorry,' she said, taking the bottle out of her hand. 'Time's up.'

Rosa didn't argue. One look at Sylvia was enough to tell her that she must leave. Picking up her bag from the floor, she leaned across and patted the bare arm. The bones felt sharp beneath the crinkled skin and she didn't know what to say, so she blurted out, 'I'll come back again. Try and rest.'

Sylvia's eyes opened and amazingly flashed again. 'Rest? Why waste the time I've left? This is a *bugger*, you know.' Her precise English accent made the word 'bugger' sound very prim.

'I know. I'm sorry,' said Rosa feebly. Her usual glib facility with words seemed to have left her.

She was turning for the door, when Sylvia said, 'Do what I told you. Go away for a bit.'

To satisfy her, Rosa nodded and said, 'Yes, all right. I'll go to see my father this weekend.'

'Good,' said Sylvia and closed her eyes.

In the corridor Rosa checked her watch and saw that she'd been in with Sylvia for exactly eleven minutes. The sister was watching through the open door of her office at the end of the ward, and she boldly stepped in to ask, 'How ill is Miss Playfair?'

The sister stared expressionless at the girl for a moment and then said, 'Are you family?'

'No, I'm a friend.'

The other woman relented. 'She's very ill, I'm afraid.'

Rosa felt tears prickle in her eyes and she said, 'I hope she won't suffer.'

'She'll probably sleep away,' was the reply.

Rosa was crying as she walked along the hospital corridor. It seemed so grossly unfair that Sylvia was dying at an age when the future should be expanding before her. She was not a bad person, she'd done nothing to deserve this.

Why were the Fates so malign? They'd snatched Marie, and little Sadie. Now they were taking Sylvia, plucking them off one by one, like blossoms from a branch. She ought to have many more years of life and grow old like Great-aunt Fanny. It was obvious that she was not resigned to dying.

It's a bugger, she'd said. What an understatement!

Rosa was angry, very angry, as she pushed her way through the hospital doors that led into a sinister, pitch-black night.

Twenty-Five

Rosa's car was sitting on its own in the middle of a shining slick of tarmac parking area behind one of the bleak hospital wings. She looked at it with a sinking heart. Her room at Mrs Ross's house was waiting; but the thought of sitting there alone, going over and over the visit to Sylvia, was very depressing. It was Saturday night and her friends would be gathering in the Cockburn drinking, laughing, competing with each other over stories they'd done this week but her mood was also too sombre to join them.

Journalists gathered together to talk shop and make a lot of noise because they were extroverts and egotists. It was necessary for them to develop thick skins and forget sensibilities or they couldn't go on working. If she tried to confide to any of her colleagues about how much Sylvia's fate had upset her, they'd either think she was too soft for the business, or else they'd advise her to capitalize on the situation and write a piece about it.

How to comfort a dying person . . . Everything was material for a piece.

As she was about to unlock the car door, she was gripped by a nameless fear. Sylvia's fevered insistence on taking care had unsettled her. Bending down, she tipped the driver's seat forward to make sure no one was hiding in the back. Then she opened the boot to find the metal lever that was used for prising off hubcaps when she had a puncture. Putting it down beside her on the front passenger seat made her feel safer.

247

She wished she had someone to talk to, someone to give her good advice. In spite of what everyone seemed to think, she was not hiding information. It seemed as if she had wandered into a potentially dangerous situation by mistake.

She had told Sylvia she would drive into the country and stay with her father. She could be there in a couple of hours or so and spend a peaceful, safe Sunday with him. She needn't stay long – Sylvia was obviously being overcautious. On Monday she'd feel rejuvenated and ready to go back to work.

That's it. I'll head for home, she thought.

First, she'd ring up Mrs Ross and tell her she was going away for the weekend. Turning quickly, she ran back into the hospital and found a public phone box. 'I won't be back tonight. I'm going down to Selkirk to see my father,' she told her landlady.

The sprawling buildings of the Infirmary looked deserted and hostile, with only a few lights shining in some of the wards, when she started the car and drove towards the main gate. There she had to wait for a gap in the passing traffic to edge into Lauriston Place. Impatience made her decide that it would be easier to turn left, head for the Art College, and then drive down into the Grassmarket.

The tall tenements there loomed over her, each of them holding terrible secrets from the past within their thick stone walls. Over the centuries, they must have witnessed many terrible things, as bad as or worse than the killing of Marie and Sadie, or the untimely death of Sylvia. The atmosphere of this misty winter night seemed to be full of awful memories.

By the time she reached the big stone well head in the middle of the road at the far end of the Grassmarket that marks the point where Victoria Street leads up to George IV Bridge, she made a sudden decision. She indicated to the left, and pulled on the steering wheel to go round the well, at the same time glancing into the driving mirror, knowing that she didn't do that often enough.

Her first look was casual, then, with a rush of adrenalin,

she looked again and what she saw made her start to shake with nerves.

On her tail, a few yards away, was a dark car with only one headlight working.

Don't be silly! It's a coincidence, she thought. *Edinburgh is full of cars driving around with only one headlight.* With shaking hands and a funny prickling in her scalp, she turned left, but, to her horror, the car behind turned off too.

It was so close that she could see it was a middle-range Austen model, an A35. There were hundreds of them around because they were very popular cars. She nearly drove on to the pavement as she craned her neck in an effort to see the driver but all she could make out was a dark shape slumped over the wheel. There was no passenger visible.

Sweat began breaking out on her face and the backs of her hands. She was terrified though she knew there was no logical reason for feeling that way – lots of cars had only one headlight, lots and lots of them, she told herself.

But this one was practically on her tail, as another one had been the night Marie died. Her inner voice was crying out, *I'm being tailed. Where will I go? What will I do?*

Her instinct was to go straight to Selkirk. *In my father's house I'll be safe because, in spite of his obsession with isolation and inventing things, he is a loving parent and a sensible person who has only ever given me very good advice*, she thought.

Their relationship was well defined – she didn't pester him about trivialities like money and her romances, but if she had a big problem, he would help. On the day her mother died, he hugged her and, through tears, promised that no matter what she wanted or needed, he would always be there for her.

She badly needed him now, so she was going home.

Instead of turning left down to the High Street at the top of Victoria Street, she turned right and headed back towards the Infirmary again. The traffic was quieter by that time and she was able to accelerate, hoping to shake off her pursuer. Because of driving all over Edinburgh in pursuit of stories, she knew the side streets well, so she was able to go along Lauriston Place and slip down past the nurses' home, taking a short cut into the Meadows.

The car behind sat doggedly on her tail. Its driver obviously knew the way around Edinburgh as well as she did. The only other person of her acquaintance with such a good knowledge of the city was Iain.

Could it be him? Where had he gone the night she left him on the pavement after going to St Giles? She'd never asked him.

She drove up Causewayside, took a sharp left turn into Newington Road, and tore down it past a large house with a big garden where the Basher and she were sent to get the details about a robbery of silver on Christmas morning. At the time she thought, *What a day to wake up and find your family silver has all been stolen!* Now she knew worse things could happen.

Heading out of the city, she put her foot down, skidding sharply round bends on the way to Dalkeith where the road to Galashiels and Selkirk headed off through the mining villages of Fushiebridge and Gorebridge.

As always, the foul smell in the air there made her gag and she wondered how people could live in such a place. Did they stop smelling it after a few years?

The road led on to the beginning of Middleton Moor, where dirty snow was still lying banked on the verges, and there she was faced with her first problem. Did she turn off into the hills and take the shortest road that crossed empty land to Innerleithen, and then went over the hills to the Gordon Arms Hotel at the head of St Mary's Loch?

It was her father's preferred way to Edinburgh because it cut out at least seven miles because his cottage was only two miles from the Gordon Arms Inn, but it was a desolate and empty road, even during daylight. There was little traffic and only a few houses where one could stop, most of them very isolated.

If the car that was still sticking doggedly to her tail tried to run her off the road somewhere in those desolate empty hills, there would be no witnesses, and she would become just another statistic in the road accident tables, a rash driver who took a sharp corner badly.

Reluctantly she decided it was safer to stay on the longer but busier road where someone might see her being attacked or kidnapped.

It was raining, a sleety, drizzling kind of rain that was not really heavy enough for the windscreen wipers and made them emit a horrible screeching noise against the glass that set her teeth on edge. She wished it would either pour down, snow, or stop altogether but doggedly she drove on, heading for the village of Heriot, where there was another decision to make.

A second, short side road cut off there, not quite as lonely as the first but still not much used. For the same reason, she resolutely drove on past it. The one-light car was still only a short distance behind her.

As she passed the Heriot turn-off, she glanced at the fuel gauge and cursed when she saw that the needle was hovering on zero. She had forgotten to fill the tank. Why did she always neglect to buy petrol until it was absolutely necessary?

On the left, at the unfortunately named Hangingshaw Corner – what had gone on there to give it that name? – stood one petrol pump. There were no lights in the booth but Rosa drove on to the cracked concrete forecourt, frantically sounding her horn.

She decided that not only would she buy three gallons of petrol, but would also say, 'Phone the police. I'm being tailed by a murderer.'

Nothing happened except that the car with the single headlight shot past and headed on down the road at considerable speed. She stared after it. All she had been able to see was that the driver was a man wearing a felt hat. As she watched its disappearing tail lights, she wondered if she had imagined the whole thing. Was it really tailing her or was she being stupid?

She sounded her horn again, louder this time, and an old man with an umbrella came out of the deserted-looking house to the left of the pump, walking as if he had all the time in the world. Leaning down at her open window, he said, 'Ye needna make all that din. We're closed.'

She spread her hands in entreaty. 'Please sell me some petrol. I've run out and I've still about thirty miles to go.'

'We close at half past five,' said the old man implacably.

She looked at her watch. It was half past seven. 'Please. If you don't let me have some I'll have to park here in front of your house all night – and I'll make a noise,' she said desperately.

The prospect of a noisy squatter on his doorstep seemed to worry him, so he said, 'All right, but dinna come back another time when we're closed. Wait here till I get the key.'

After what seemed like an eternity, he reappeared, carrying a huge key, growled at her window and asked how many gallons she wanted.

It would have to be worth his while, she supposed, so she said, 'Five gallons please,' thanking the gods that she had this week's expenses envelope, originally containing three pounds ten shillings, in her coat pocket. The champagne had cost her two pounds and petrol was about two shillings a gallon – her ten bob note would cover it, and leave her with a pound.

Grudgingly he started cranking up the antique machinery of his pump, a process that took him a very long time. As she sat listening to the liquid squishing into her tank, she began to feel calmer. She was halfway home and the memory of two tail lights disappearing into the distance was reassuring. The car she so feared had not come back looking for her. It must be miles away by now.

'The till's locked. I hope you dinna need any change,' said the curmudgeon of the pump when he finished doling out her petrol and she reassured him – even if she'd needed change from a pound she would have let him off with it. The release of fear and tension made her feel almost light-headed and she began to enjoy the trip – the comforting, safe Borders were calling to her, beckoning her in. Soon she would be safe at home.

She drove more slowly now, relaxing in her seat and watching the play of the headlights on the twists and turns of the road as it dropped down into the valley of the Gala Water. The Borders were a secret and mysterious part of the world where time seemed to stand still.

All the cottages at the side of the road were unchanged from the days when Rosa was a child – hazel trees and beech hedgerows still overhung the tarmac strip of road, and occasionally animal eyes glittered when her light caught them.

After about fifteen minutes the rain stopped and a watery-looking moon peeped out from behind a bank of cloud. A dog fox slunk across the road in front of her with his brush sticking out bravely and his little eyes glinting with evil. She playfully tooted her horn at him but he was one of those defiant foxes who wouldn't deign to break into a run. Impressed, she slowed down to let him cross.

At Stow, there was a red telephone box on a corner and, when she saw its light shining out, she debated stopping to phone her father and warn him she was on her way. But her panic had disappeared and what she aimed for now was to surprise him.

On Saturday nights he usually listened to the Palm Court orchestra on the radio and if she reached home soon, she could sit by his log fire and share the pleasure of the warmth and the music with him.

Driving past the church that reared proudly up above the roadside in Stow, she idly looked in the driving mirror again and – *wham!* – all her tranquillity disappeared in a flash.

The car with one headlight was behind her again, not fifty yards away.

Where had it come from? She had not passed another vehicle since Hangingshaw, so it must have been hiding in a lay-by or waiting behind the phone box where the road led off to Stow's Cross Keys Hotel. It was really chasing her after all. What should she do? Where could she go?

The part of the road she was on was not good for racing because it was a series of long, deceiving bends, but she put her foot down nonetheless and her tyres squealed in protest. When she almost overturned on a corner, caution forced her to moderate her speed. To go off the road there would mean a plunge into the bed of the river Gala.

But how could she reach her father's house without this relentless pursuer intercepting her? His car was more powerful than hers, so cunning was required. Rosa was very familiar with the road, knowing all the little side roads where she might be able to lie low while her pursuer flew past. Hopefully, the driver behind her was a stranger to the district, so she had that advantage.

Her first big decision was which road to take to Selkirk. Should she stay on the main road which ran through Galashiels and was usually fairly busy at this time of night because it was not yet half past eight? The chances were if her pursuer stopped or attacked her, someone would see and come to her rescue.

But she knew of another route that branched off to the west two miles before Galashiels and then went six miles over the hills to Clovenfords. A stranger would not know about it and it was hard to find because the turn-off was situated on a very twisting part of the road. If she was lucky enough to reach that particular corner when out of sight of her pursuer, she could probably dodge down it and make a clean getaway.

Her little car had never taken corners so fast. It barrelled round them on two wheels, but the car behind kept up the pace too in a sort of cruel cat-and-mouse game. She wondered why the other car, an A35, did not easily overtake her if that was what he wanted, and he was a good driver too because the distance between them never seemed to get any less no matter how hard she tried to shake him off.

Her escape road was coming near. Driving under a canopy of overhanging trees, she sat forward and gripped the wheel tightly as she tried to spot the Clovenfords turn-off coming up on her right. Putting her foot down she tore round the last bend on the wrong side of the road, praying nothing was coming in the other direction. For only a few seconds, the other car was lost from view, but that was just long enough for her to dash over to the right without indicating, and head down the narrow road into the tree-sheltered valley.

Take care, take care, she told herself, *if you crash now and kill yourself, you'll have done his dirty work for him.*

In the dip ahead of her, the road went under a low railway bridge, and, a bit farther on, a right-angle bend led past the castellated gatehouse to a mansion called Bowland. She had forgotten this way was so twisty but perhaps that was a good thing because the other car would be slowed down too. In a few seconds she would be round the corner and completely out of sight of anyone on the main road.

She let out a gasp of air at last. Wow! She'd done it! She'd lost him. There were no lights coming down the straight behind her. He had fallen for her trick and gone on to Galashiels.

It would be good to keep up her breakneck speed but caution forced her to slow down for this road was very narrow and there were a couple of ancient stone bridges set at right angles across the river which forced her to change gear and go very slowly in order to negotiate them. It was better to take a bit more time rather than end up smashed against a stone wall or upside down in a ditch.

On the right-hand side of the river she saw the lights of lovely Yair House and wondered what the people in it would do if she drove up to their magnificent front door and asked for help.

It wasn't necessary to do that now though, thank God. She'd shaken him off. The long road behind her was completely empty.

Suddenly she felt weak with hunger and remembered there was a bar of Cadbury's milk chocolate in the glove compartment, so she groped over to get it out, unpeeled the silver paper wrapper and took a huge bite. The sugar perked her up because she'd had nothing to eat since the Pop Inn omelette. Hunger pangs seized her and she hoped that Eckie had been poaching and given her father some pheasants. One of his pheasant and apple casseroles would go down very well.

The road was still empty and deserted as she crossed the hill and started to drop down into Clovenfords. Exhilarated, she began singing Harry Lauder's song 'Keep Right On Till the End of the Road' when she drove into the middle of the village and saw the familiar white-painted statue of Sir Walter Scott at the door of the hotel. Opposite it, the road to Selkirk turned round the wall of a line of greenhouses where big succulent black grapes grew on an ancient vine.

Nearly home: only six miles to Selkirk, then another ten to Catslackburn where her father's cottage stood.

What an address – *Catslackburn Cottage, Yarrow.* She loved it, and before she left home she had entered all sorts of competitions just so she could fill her name and address on the entry forms. She imagined people in London reading her entry and saying, 'Where on earth is this from?'

No one had ever been able to tell her what *Catslackburn* meant. 'It's aye been called that. What a lassie you are to spier!' was Eckie's invariable reply when asked about the origin of the name.

'Keep Right On Till the End of the Road,' she carolled happily.

The lights of the manufacturing town of Selkirk shone out

in a long line on the left-hand side of the road as she drove along the west bank of the Ettrick river, past the imposing farmsteading of Philipburn. The rain had stopped completely, and the clouds had cleared leaving a void of deep purple, dotted with stars. The temperature dropped, promising frost later, and a huge silver moon like a giant's medal hung in the sky casting so much light that it would have been possible to drive without headlights.

On a similar night, just before Rosa left home to go to university, she and her father had taken a drive to St Mary's Loch and watched the reflection of the hills and trees reproduced like a photograph on the flat, silver surface of the water. It was magical, like being in a dream.

If an arm 'clothed all in white, mystic, wonderful' appeared out of the water bearing aloft Arthur's sword Excalibur, she wouldn't have been surprised and she'd never forgotten that weird night.

Still singing, she reached the junction of two main roads – the one she was on coming from Clovenfords, and the other, bigger road from Galashiels that went through Selkirk town. There were a couple of cars parked on the grass verge near a cottage and she didn't worry about them till, with a sickening lurch of the heart, she realized that as she passed, one suddenly switched in its lights – *or light* – and started up.

It was an A35, it was him again. He'd got to Selkirk before her and was lying waiting, knowing she must pass there . . . He must have driven at a terrific rate in that car of his – and worse, he must know exactly where she was going.

With a clench of the stomach she remembered the mystery man who questioned Fanny about her father's address. He'd been building up his Rosa Makepeace dossier. God knows how long he'd been watching her.

If Fanny said that Rosa's father lived at a place called Catslackburn – 'such a ridiculous name,' she always added

– all he needed was an Ordnance Survey map because there was nowhere else with a name like that.

Rosa panicked, wondering *What do I do now? Where can I go?* She could drive as fast as possible in the hope of shaking him off, but that was not a particularly good idea because the road from now on was without many escape routes. Or she could pretend she had not seen him and keep on going as slowly and steadily as she had done for the past few miles. He might think she hadn't noticed him.

She took her foot off the accelerator and kept the needle on 30 miles per hour, giving her pursuer plenty of opportunities to overtake her but he stayed at the back, fifty yards behind, and they went sedately on as if in caravan. One after the other, they passed the turn-off to the Duke of Buccleuch's estate at Bowhill and then reached the hamlet of Yarrowford.

The pursuer's grim determination not to lose sight of her was almost palpable – she could feel his implacable eyes at her back and they terrified her. Now she knew what it was like to be hunted. Before Yarrow church the road negotiated a sharp series of turns to the right and then the left, and, as she approached the churchyard, she hurriedly devised a plan of action.

She knew that by the graveyard there was an unmarked cart track that led off into the fields and then to her father's cottage. It was so rough they never drove over it but tonight she was not in a position to worry about damaging her springs.

The church was coming up, she could see it. There was the corner where the track began. Without slackening her speed, as soon as she was round the corner, she switched off her headlights, swung off the road and plunged into the track. If the gate had been closed she would have crashed right through it because she was travelling fast, but, for a miracle, someone had been working in the field and left it open as they often did. From her darkened car she saw the pursuer flash past round the corner and go straight on.

He'd soon discover she was not ahead however. She had only bought a little time.

Her father's cottage was half a mile along the track and, bucketing along, she dropped down over the last hill, to see its lights shining out in welcome.

'Thank God, thank God,' she said aloud. She'd made it home. The gate leading into their yard was also open, so she tore through, parked the car on the cobbles and ran for safety towards the house, leaving her car door open and its lights still burning.

The ground near the house was muddy with melting snow and her father's dog Jess, who was shut up in the outhouse, gave a sharp little yap of recognition. She sensed it was Rosa and she never barked at people she knew.

Strange, father never shut Jess up until he went to bed himself or unless he was going out, thought Rosa. Then she turned and looked at the open garage. Its door stood wide open and his car was not there. He was out. Her stomach clenched in fright.

Where was he? He hardly ever left home at night in winter unless it was to play chess with Eckie but he didn't need the car to go there. Sometimes though, if there was a good film playing, he'd go to the cinema in Galashiels or Selkirk. That must be where he was.

Why tonight though? Why, when she needed him so badly?

Thank God he had left the cottage door unlocked – which was not unusual. It was rarely locked. She rushed in, closing and barring the door behind her. The clock on the mantelpiece told her it was nine twenty-five. She'd been driving for over two hours. If father was at the cinema, he'd be back soon. He didn't like to be late.

The room was warm because he had gone out and left the fire burning, without even putting a guard in front of it. That was odd because he was usually very careful about fires, so he must have been in a hurry.

Rosa crossed the room to where a desk stood in the

window, piled high as usual with sheets of paper and intricate drawings. There was a grassy bank behind the window and beyond it, a faint light flickered. That was from Eckie's cottage fifty yards away.

He lived there like a hermit, surrounded by blackthorn bushes and tucked into a V-shaped hollow between two hills. His cottage was invisible from the track or the lane. Only its light at night showed it was there, and unless you knew about it, you would never find it.

Seeing Eckie's light made her feel safer and she searched about looking for the telephone, which, as usual, was lost in the chaos of the room. But even if she did find it, who to phone? Eckie had no telephone, and the nearest farmhouse was about a mile away towards the Gordon Arms.

There was no real reason for ringing the police either. What would she say? *I think I was followed home* . . . It sounded pretty feeble. Besides it would take the police ages to get to the cottage from Selkirk.

It was best to find the phone though. She'd feel better if she had some contact with the outside world.

Following the long wire, she tracked the receiver down behind the sofa where it was lying off its cradle as if it had been thrown down or dropped. She hauled it up and held the receiver to her ear. It was working all right and she was about to ring Mrs Ross to tell her she had arrived safely, when the beeping noise stopped and the line abruptly went dead.

It had been disconnected.

Frantically she shook it, pressed the cradle up and down, shook it again, but it was dead. Someone had cut the cable.

She started talking aloud, conducting a frantic dialogue with herself – *Don't be silly. I'm not being silly. Someone is out there. He's found me. Who is it?*

She hadn't heard a car drive up. Could the phone have gone dead because of a fault or an unfortunate coincidence? Perhaps it wasn't cut. She was wondering if she was brave enough to open the door and look out when Jess started baying and throwing herself furiously at the door of the shed.

A stranger was in the yard. In a panic Rosa ran around the room piling up furniture against the front door. Outside, everything was eerily quiet except for the baying dog.

She stood in the middle of the room with a poker in her hand waiting, but nothing happened. The silence was intense because Jess had stopped barking. She jumped when a piece of burnt wood fell out of the fire and landed on the hearth.

Somewhere a mouse scrabbled in the wainscot. She turned slowly around looking into every corner before fixing her eyes again on the door. Still nothing happened. Her breath was rasping in her chest. Jess started barking again but all she could hear in the house was the sound of mice and the soft settling of ashes in the fireplace.

It seemed an eternity till she heard a noise outside. Someone was trying to get in the front door.

'Go away!' she shouted.

Silence. The rattling stopped. Rosa's nerves were stretched to snapping point and hopefully she lifted the phone again but it was still dead.

Once again there was a thud at the door. 'Go away! Who are you?' she shouted again.

Silence. Did she really hear heavy breathing or was it her imagination?

'Who are you?' she called again, but whoever it was didn't answer.

She wished she could attract Eckie's attention. But how? His window looked across at the cottage but it was unlikely he'd be gazing out at this time of night. He usually went to bed quite early anyway.

Then she had an idea. Father kept old newspapers in a big basket by the fireside. He never seemed to throw any of them out. She grabbed an armful and piled them onto the red ashes. They went up in a whooshing blaze, sending whirling bits of charred paper round the room and making the chimney pot crack alarmingly.

She piled on more, hoping that somebody would see the flames and sound an alarm, or send for the fire brigade perhaps.

She was bending down packing more paper into the hearth when there was a terrible noise of breaking glass behind her and the window over the desk literally caved in. A man, brandishing the tyre jack she'd left on her car seat, leapt off the grass bank and came through the glass feet first.

The window wasn't difficult to break because the wood was old and rotting but the shock he gave Rosa was spectacular. She fled towards the door screaming, her voice ringing out in the terrible silence. That started Jess barking once more.

Grappling with the stiff door bolts, she kept her eyes fixed on the figure clambering through the gap where the window had been. He was like something from a nightmare because his head and body were wrapped in a huge black overcoat, and he was wearing a black balaclava. His hands were gloved and he was carrying a man's white dress scarf.

The bolt was either jammed or Rosa's hands had lost their power. She could not get the front door open, so she backed against it, staring at the intruder.

'Who are you, who are you?' she shouted.

He looked very big and bulky as he jumped down from the top of the desk, shaking himself, scattering bits of wood and glass all around. He walked towards her, still carrying the jack. She cringed, screaming, with the poker held out in both hands.

When he was within reach, she was going to hit him full in the face with it.

The most terrifying thing about him was his implacable silence. He didn't utter a word as he advanced slowly towards her. She stopped screaming and slid along the wall so she was standing at a right angle to the broken window and facing the door into the kitchen. If she could dodge under his arm, she'd make her getaway through it.

'Don't come any nearer or I'll hit you,' she told him.

But she knew it was a useless threat. He knew it too and kept on coming. Now his back was to the kitchen door. He dropped the jack and took the end of the scarf in his other hand, holding it in front of him at shoulder height. He was going to strangle her.

Desperately she swung the poker – and missed. He was very near now. His eyes were shining through the holes of the mask. She struck again. This time she connected with the covered face and something crunched beneath the blow. She hoped it was his nose.

'Bitch!' he shouted, the first word he'd uttered. He leapt at her, grabbing the poker's tip. She tried to twist it out of his hands and failed. As she wrenched it round, she felt a bone in her left wrist break. She'd always had fragile bones and broke her arm twice just by tripping over when she was small.

Adrenalin was running high though and she felt no pain whatever. She tried to pull the poker out of his grip with her good hand but he had a tight hold of it. Then he got a grip of her, grappling round her shoulders. She leaned into his chest in an attempt to stop him putting the scarf round her neck and in doing so, she grabbed at his mask and it came off, revealing his face.

When she saw him, her terror increased because she knew there would be no mercy for her from this man.

His face was contorted with hate and fury. His eyes were bloodshot and the lips drawn back, showing his teeth. For the first time in their acquaintance he was looking straight into her eyes.

It was Boyle, the Burgh Court sergeant.

Twenty-Six

B *oyle!*

It wasn't Alan or Sandy, Hamilton-Prentice, Iain or any of the possible suspects. It was Sergeant Boyle – a policeman. She had never considered him a suspect but now, wise too late, she knew she should have. He patronized brothels; he knew Marie; he was brutal and he could not look directly at a woman.

They swayed to and fro across the floor, with her fending him off as he tried to wind the scarf round her neck

'You bitch, you're a bitch, a bitch,' he kept on muttering with terrifying fixity, but that was all he said.

'Go away, go away!' she shouted as she struggled to keep his hands away from her but her strength was fading and her wrist was hurting. He was too strong, too determined for her. *I'm going to end up as another victim*, she thought.

In desperation, she knocked over a little table and a pile of books crashed to the floor, tripping him, but he jumped back to his feet and closed in, dragging her towards him by the collar of her coat which she had not had time to take off.

She heard her own screaming, a terrible, ragged sound, and fell back into a wooden chair, which toppled over with a crash. That gave him the chance to loop the white scarf round her neck and she felt him pulling it tight.

Choking, she tore frantically at his hands. In the distance Jess was barking and there was so much noise that neither of them heard the kitchen door opening.

Rosa was facing in its direction and with almost her last

264

sight of anything, she saw Eckie, in stocking feet, emerge from the darkness outside with a double-barrelled shotgun in his hands. He paused, raised it very deliberately, and fired into the ceiling. The report was deafening. Plaster showered down on to their heads and Boyle let go of her so that he could whip round to stare at the intruder.

Eckie calmly nodded at him as if they were old acquaintances who had met in the street.

'Come on now, let the lassie alane or I'll blaw yer bloody heid aff,' he said calmly.

But Boyle was not to be intimidated. Probably encouraged by Eckie's appearance of antiquity and grey hair, he jumped towards him, but he'd chosen the wrong man. Eckie levelled the gun and calmly shot him in the lower leg. Blood and bits of flesh flew everywhere. Boyle fell to the floor, grasping the wound, screaming and cursing spectacularly – Jack would have been proud of him.

'I warned ye. Lie still or ye'll get more,' said Eckie, lowering the gun. Even to Boyle, it was obvious that he meant what he said.

Sobbing and gasping, Rosa sat on the floor massaging her throat with her good hand and cried to her saviour, 'Oh thank God you came, Eckie. He was trying to kill me . . .'

Eckie walked across the floor and stared down at Boyle who was lying groaning and clutching his leg. The trouser leg was torn and ragged revealing a gaping red wound from which blood was flowing. Eckie bent down; lifted the discarded white scarf from the floor, and tied it just under Boyle's groin in a tourniquet.

'Stop yellin'. Ye'll live,' he told the injured man and then said to Rosa, 'Phone for the police and a doctor.'

'The phone's not working. He cut it off, I think,' she managed to say.

'Then get in your car and go to the Bains to use their phone . . .' Eckie ordered. Mr Bain was the neighbouring farmer who lived near the main road.

'But I can't leave you. What if he attacks you?' she protested.

Eckie shrugged. 'Dinna bother aboot me. I'll be all right. If he tries to get up off that floor I'll shoot him in the heid. It doesnae matter to me if I kill him. By the time they get me in court I'll be deed mysel'. I'm eighty-six so I've naething to lose.'

When Boyle heard this, the fight seemed to go out of him. He stopped struggling and lay still with his injured leg sticking out. Blood was flowing out of it and soaking the rug. Eckie looked at it and said, 'Ye'd better hurry and get him an ambulance or I might no' hae tae bother shootin' him.'

Rosa was not convinced that Boyle would accept defeat easily. 'Before I go let's lock him in Jess's shed,' she suggested.

Eckie prodded his captive with the gun and said, 'You heard the lassie. Get up.'

'Can't,' groaned Boyle.

'Get up,' said Eckie again.

Boyle rolled over and propped himself in his hands before hauling himself up on to his good leg and leaned against the cupboard. Rosa hoped Eckie wasn't going to tell her to help Boyle because she wouldn't be able to put a hand on him.

She looked around for something to give him as a crutch and found a floor brush. He took it and supported himself on it, groaning loudly. Eckie, levelling the gun, watched impassively.

'Where's my father?' Rosa asked Eckie who said, 'He got a phone call telling him you had an accident in Edinbury and he was aff like if the deil was on his tail.'

'When?' she wanted to know.

'About an hour or so ago. He ran ower to tell me he was goin' so when I heard the dug howlin' and saw the fire in the lum I kent something was wrong.' He spoke as calmly as if this sort of thing happened every day of the week.

Rosa looked at Boyle who was still leaning against the

cupboard and said accusingly, 'You phoned him, didn't you? You had to get him out of the house.' He probably made the phone call while he waited for her in Stow, she realized.

Father would have taken his favourite short road to Edinburgh by Middleton Moor which meant he was driving up there while she was coming down through Clovenfords.

From the way Boyle was leaning on the brush, she guessed he was considering using it as a weapon. Even when wounded, he was still powerful and dangerous and if he got hold of Eckie's gun, he would be lethal.

'Let's get him into the shed and then I'll go to phone the ambulance and the police,' she said to Eckie, who gestured with his gun towards the door and prodded Boyle in that direction. He limped pathetically across the open yard where there was nothing to hold on to but she still hated the idea of touching him. Finally they reached the shed.

When the bolt was thrown back Jess, delighted to be free, charged out and tried to lick Rosa's face. Eckie forced Boyle in among the straw, and, before he locked the door, he ordered Jess back in too. 'Watch him, lass,' he said and she drew back her teeth in a snarl.

Eckie had trained Jess. She did everything he told her. If Boyle tried to get away or attack Eckie, she'd tear his throat out.

'Now go and get help,' the old man told Rosa. Her car was still sitting with its lights on and doors open. Though it was only about fifteen minutes since she was in it, it seemed a hundred years ago since she was last behind the wheel. It was only when she tried to shift the gear lever that she remembered her left wrist was broken, but she was so grateful at being alive that she didn't mind the pain.

The kindly Mr and Mrs Bain were astonished by her story but, when they recovered from the shock, they were obviously thrilled by such a dramatic interruption to their Saturday night. It was obvious that they were looking forward to telling and retelling this adventure over and over again.

Everyone in the district would hear about it within hours.

Their two sons were down at the Gordon Arms having a drink, so Mr Bain phoned the police and the ambulance service, before he set off in the farm Land Rover to relieve Eckie.

Mrs Bain, who worked as a district nurse before she married, looked at Rosa's wrist and pronounced it to be a simple break or maybe even just a sprain. She gave the patient a large brandy, bandaged the wrist and put it in a sling fashioned from a strip of old sheet, making Rosa feel like a casualty from the Crimean War being looked after by Florence Nightingale.

'I want to go back to the cottage and help Eckie,' Rosa said when the bandaging was finished.

But Mrs Bain shook her head. 'You'll stay here by the fire and calm down. You've had a terrible shock,' she said, but staying put was impossible for Rosa. She was highly excited and would not stop being involved now.

'I have to go back,' she said firmly, so Mrs Bain said, 'All right, but only if I drive your car. You should rest that arm.'

Back at the cottage they found that a slightly bewildered policeman had arrived from Selkirk. He'd been alerted by a phone call from Edinburgh Police asking him to look in at Catslackburn in case someone was in trouble there, but he found Eckie and Mr Bain perfectly in control of the situation, sitting side by side watching the shed door from the front seats of Boyle's car, which was parked in the yard.

They advised him not to go into the shed until reinforcements arrived, and he was happy to do as they suggested.

'I thought it was some sort of hoax call at first,' he said. 'What I can't understand is how Edinburgh knew something was going on down here and we didn't.'

Eckie was still nursing the gun and his own black and white sheep dog, Floss, came slinking over and was lying by the car door resting its chin on its paws. Jess could be heard growling inside the shed. There was not a sound from Boyle.

'Is he still in there?' Rosa asked anxiously.

'Oh aye. The dug'll no' let him move. He's there till the rest of the police come,' said Eckie calmly. He seemed to be enjoying himself.

Mrs Bain put a hand on Rosa's arm. 'You must go into the house. You're as white as a ghost.'

Rosa agreed because at that moment she felt as if she was about to faint. It took all her strength to walk through the front door and sit down on the sofa. Mrs Bain went with her, put on the kettle and made tea. As she was drinking it, she started coming back down to earth and realized how badly her arm was aching and how her whole body was shaking with nerves. Suddenly she began to weep, huge gulping sobs and shudders that convulsed her, because only then did she appreciate how close she had been to death.

Mrs Bain held her and let her weep. 'Do you know that man in the shed?' she asked eventually.

Through her sobs, Rosa said, 'Hardly at all. He's a policeman from Edinburgh. I can't understand it. I've never done anything to him. Why should he want to kill me?'

'Hush, hush, stop thinking about it,' kind Mrs Bain was saying when they heard more cars coming into the yard. Doors banged, voices shouted, and the cottage door burst open as Rosa's father erupted into the room.

Rushing over to where she was hunched up like an amoeba in the sofa, he knelt beside her and took her hands. 'Oh, thank God you're safe. Thank God, thank God. I got a police message to say you'd had an accident in Edinburgh and were in the E.R.I. but when I got there, they said they'd never heard of you.'

'Boyle, who's in the shed, did that. Eckie shot him. He rang you up to get you out of the house,' she sobbed and put her face against his shoulder. Immediately she felt safe again.

'Who's Boyle?' he asked, looking round, and Mrs Bain started to tell him the story but was interrupted by the entrance of another uniformed policeman and the Edinburgh policeman Peter Mallen.

The sight of him terrified Rosa. She clutched her father and cried out, 'What's he doing here? Don't let him come near me!' Because of her shock about Boyle, she distrusted anyone associated with him.

Mallen stopped and held up both hands in a gesture of pacification. 'Now, now, Miss Makepeace, calm down. Everything's all right. I won't hurt you. I'm sorry you had to go through this but your father came to the station to ask if you'd had an accident and when he told his story, I knew something bad was going on.'

Still gulping with hysterics, she managed to gasp, 'How did you know I was here?'

'Your landlady told us.' *What a good thing I phoned Mrs Ross*, she thought.

'Your sergeant Boyle's in the shed,' she sobbed. 'He tried to kill me.'

Mallen's face was grim. He turned to Rosa's father as he said, 'It's my fault. I should have listened to my instincts. But – you know how it is when you've been friends with a man a long time. I didn't think it was possible. The other chaps are getting him out now. I'll have to go and see what's happening.'

After he left, Rosa and her father sat side by side and he told her, 'The police brought me back down with them. I showed them my shortcut here but I don't think I've ever made the journey so fast – what a driver that Mallen is! I was sick with worry in case we were too late . . . I couldn't have borne it if you'd been hurt, Rosa.'

She knew he couldn't bring himself to say *killed*. It was her turn to comfort him now. 'It's a good thing I'm such a slow driver then, Dad, isn't it?' she almost joked.

Then she asked, 'Did Mallen know it was Boyle who phoned you to get you out of the house?'

'I'm not sure. I told him that the man who called said he was from the High Street police – that's why I went to the station after the Infirmary. He asked about his voice

and I described it as well as I could. I said he had an
Edinburgh accent and a deep voice with a sort of guttural
note in it – like this: "Your daughter's had an accident, Mr
Makepeace . . ."'

'Clever you, Dad,' she said. Boyle did have a rough note
in his voice that she had not really noticed until her father
imitated him. Dad was a good mimic.

'Sergeant Mallen was fetched and he seemed shaken when
I told him my story. It was as if a penny dropped with him.
We were on the road in minutes, but he never told me who
he suspected. I think he was hoping he was wrong,' said
Rosa's father.

'I was shaken too when I found out it was Boyle. But now
I realize that the pieces fit perfectly. He's always had such
an air of repressed violence, maybe not with his friends but
certainly with me and Patricia and with those poor souls in
the lock-ups. I think he hates most people, and especially
women. Have they taken him away yet, Dad?'

Her father went over to the half-open door and looked out.
'There's an ambulance out there now and they're getting him
into it. They're half carrying him. Eckie seems to have made
a good job of stopping him in his tracks.'

Rosa got up and stood behind her father. An ashen-faced
Boyle was being helped out of the shed while Eckie held a
snarling Jess by her collar. If the state of the white scarf was
any guide, he must have lost a lot of blood. Mallen was help-
ing to support him and she heard him say gently, 'Come on
now, Jim. Come quietly, old man . . .' almost as if he was
sorry for him.

When the ambulance and one of the police cars drove
away, Mallen came back into the cottage. He looked
exhausted, and Rosa's father went over to the wall cupboard
and found a bottle of brandy. 'You need a drink,' he said,
pouring out a glass.

Mallen took it gratefully but said, 'I shouldn't drink on
duty but this has been one hell of a night.'

Then he looked at Rosa, who was in the corner of the sofa and said, 'You've been very brave, Miss Makepeace. Did he chase you all the way from Edinburgh? It's a good thing you didn't stop on the road or he might have killed you there. He's a bit mad, I'm afraid.'

'A bit! He's raving,' she said because her nerve was slowly returning. 'I knew I had to keep on going because I thought my Dad would be here. It was awful when I found the house empty. I hadn't time to go for Eckie before he burst in.' She indicated the broken window through which a night wind was blowing. None of them had really noticed it before because they were huddled round the fire.

'He's not denying anything. I asked him what he was going to do and he said he was going to dump your body in St Mary's Loch. He thought he'd be back in Edinburgh before anybody found you.'

Eckie appeared through the door at this point and said, 'No' if I could help it.'

Mallen nodded. 'He didn't know there were any neighbours nearby. You certainly put a stop to his plans. That shot went clean through his calf and broke his shin bone. We won't be charging you with assault, but I suppose you've got a gun licence, have you?'

Eckie laughed. 'Oh aye. The local bobby'll vouch for me. I often gie him the odd poached pheasant or a bit o' salmon.'

'I don't think they should charge you even if you killed him, Eckie,' said Rosa. 'You saved my life.'

'When did you realize you were being chased?' Mallen asked her.

'In Edinburgh actually. I was visiting a friend in the Infirmary and his car tagged on to me when I was leaving. I thought it was my imagination at first but he followed me as far as Heriot, then he passed and I was sure I'd made a mistake. It was only on the outskirts of Selkirk that he caught up with me again and I knew that whoever was on my tail was the killer,' she replied.

'How did you know?'

She looked at him levelly. 'Because his car had only one headlight. I told you about that and you said it wasn't important.'

Mallen nodded. 'I know. I thought about it though. Then a couple of nights later I saw that Jim's car had only one light. I deliberately didn't mention it to him. I was getting suspicious then, I suppose, but I didn't want to be. But things were falling into place.'

'So he hadn't noticed himself?' asked Rosa. 'In that case it's a good thing I didn't write anything about the car with one light or he might have repaired it and I wouldn't have known I was being followed.'

'Keeping things to yourself again, Miss Makepeace. This time I approve,' said Mallen with a glimmer of a smile.

'What else made you suspicious of him?' Rosa's father asked Mallen.

'He was acquainted with both of the murdered girls. He knew Sadie's mother because he'd had her in the cells often enough for being drunk and disorderly. Sadie used to go and get her out in the morning. Marie Lang lived next door to him. He once told me he fancied her but I knew her too and saw how she flinched away from him when he went near her. I think he made an unwelcome pass at her once. Maybe by pure accident he saw her waiting on the N.B. steps on her own that night, and offered her a lift. He'd act very decent to make her get into his car – he could do that when he wanted. Then he wouldn't be able to control himself. He was a very lonely, frustrated man. Going with hookers in Leith didn't satisfy him.'

'I was told his character changed after his wife was killed in a car accident,' said Rosa.

Mallen shook his head. 'He was a bit odd before. She used to complain to her friends that he knocked her about sometimes but she never made a charge against him. He was always handy with his fists, even on the rugby field. When

I started thinking about him, things fell into place.'

'Did he kill Skinner?' Rosa asked.

Mallen shrugged. 'I don't know. Skinner had all that money, so it looked as if somebody paid him to keep quiet and he would have seen the man who picked up Marie. He knew Jim because they both drank in the Blue Blanket. Jim could get his hands on a hundred quid without any trouble because he never spent much. He didn't like standing his hand – that's why he went to that rotten pub – and said he was saving his money so he could buy a house in Spain when he retired.'

'He won't be going to Spain now,' said Rosa's father and Mallen nodded as he said, 'No, poor sod. He was talking away about killing the girls as we were putting him into the ambulance. We have his admission, so he'll plead guilty.'

Rosa was still wondering about the doorman. 'But what about Skinner? Did he throw him over the bridge?'

'God knows. He's strong enough. He probably got him drunk and did it,' said Mallen. 'We'll find out in time, I expect. It was the Noonan business that added to my suspicions about him though. He came to me and said he'd seen Noonan in the High Street with Sadie the day she died. He had it in for Noonan. They'd been fighting, I think, but it did turn out Noonan had met the girl. Then he got an alibi, so that one fell apart.'

He looked at Rosa and went on: 'That's when you were added to his list of big enemies and he decided to get rid of you. He heard from somebody that you were planning to write about brutality to prisoners and after that you arranged Noonan's alibi. He read every word you wrote. It was too much for him.'

'But surely the authorities knew about the way he behaved to people in the cells,' said Rosa.

Mallen looked shifty. 'That goes on sometimes. A lot of them deserve it . . .'

'I suppose knowing that Boyle was waiting for you if you

were arrested might have been a deterrent for some people,' said Rosa sarcastically and Mallen said nothing.

It was well past two in the morning before Eckie and Mallen left and Rosa was able to get to bed.

At half past ten next morning her father woke her with tea and took her to Peel Hospital on the other side of Selkirk, where her wrist was encased in a bracelet and mitt of plaster. It was not a serious break, she was told, but she shouldn't try typing for a while. Back in the cottage there was a steady stream of local press and visitors, all burning with curiosity to hear about the drama.

In the afternoon Mallen phoned to say that Boyle had given a full admission to the murders of Sadie and Marie, and also said he intended to kill Rosa but denied murdering Skinner. The doorman's death would go down in the records as suicide after all. Boyle was under medical supervision and it was almost certain that he would be certified and taken to the prison for the criminally insane at Carstairs.

Only then did Rosa collapse. In a storm of weeping, she fell into her bed and her worried father sent for a doctor who prescribed sedatives and absolute quiet until she recovered from the trauma of almost becoming another of a madman's victims.

Twenty-Seven

Two days later, when the telephone was reconnected, Rosa's father rang the *Dispatch* and she overheard him telling the story of her brush with death to Jack, whose voice came back over the line loud enough for her to hear what he was saying.

'My God, I knew she had the reporter's touch but she's overdone it this time. Which wrist did she break?' Jack asked.

'Her left one.'

'And she's right-handed, isn't she? That's good. Tell her to write out five hundred words by long hand and phone it over to us. It'll go on the front page. It's a great story – *Dispatch Reporter Attacked by Berserk Killer*. Tell her to go all out – say what she was thinking while he tried to strangle her, that sort of thing. It'll make her name,' enthused Jack.

Alex Makepeace was horrified and, with a look of disapproval, he told her, 'That boss of yours wants you to write an article about what happened to you!'

'I know. I heard him. He's right. It's a great story. I'll do it now,' she replied, looking around for some paper to write on.

Her father sighed. 'What's happened to you, Rosa? I never thought you'd turn out like this.'

'You sound like Great-aunt Fanny,' she told him with a laugh because she was beginning to feel better and knew that writing about the nightmare experience would be cathartic. Putting it down on paper could help clear her mind of the lingering horror that she still found difficult to think about without a clench of nausea.

She was right. When it was finished, she began to feel almost normal. After it was phoned over – to a chastened Eileen – Jack sent the Basher down to take a photograph of Rosa and Eckie. They posed for him in the cottage sitting room with her plastered arm prominently displayed, and though Alex had tidied the room up for the Basher's visit, he wanted it to look more chaotic, as if the fight with Boyle had only just taken place. Reluctantly, Alex upturned chairs and threw books and papers on to the floor again, grumbling that he shouldn't have bothered to tidy up in the first place.

The hole Eckie blasted in the ceiling with his first shot was still unrepaired and that pleased the Basher who threw bits of plaster here and there before he took his pictures.

When the *Dispatch* hit the street and the police announced that Boyle had confessed to the murders of Marie and Sadie, Catslackburn was besieged by reporters from other news-papers and radio stations. It was exhausting and salutary for Rosa to be on the other end of a news hunt, answering the same questions over and over again, fighting to stay pleas-ant and co-operative.

Surprisingly Eckie was a better interviewee than she was and he enjoyed the publicity. He ordered all the daily news-papers from the Yarrowford shop, and started a scrapbook, spending hours pasting his cuttings into it. It took his mind off Milton.

On the fourth day of Rosa's sick leave, Patricia rang up for a chat. She said that Jack's stock with the newspaper management had been re-established because the *Dispatch* was outselling all its rivals, and because the people influ-encing management had relaxed. 'They're not worried about all their little skeletons coming out of the cupboard any more, now that somebody has been arrested for the murders,' she said.

'So Jack won't be leaving?' Rosa said with relief.

'No, not at the moment but I've given in my notice. I go at the end of the week,' said Patricia.

Rosa's heart sank. 'You can't! How will I survive without you? Are you leaving because you're getting married?'

The *Scotsman* newspaper group operated a no married women rule. Anyone who married lost her job – even copy-taking girls. It was rumoured that Harriet Holliday had been married to a photographer on the *News* for years but carried out an elaborate charade of pretending to live in sin. Quite the reverse of the usual practice when sinners pretended to be living pure lives.

Patricia's voice became careful as she said, 'No, I'm not getting married, not yet. I've been offered a place as a sub on *Woman* in London and I've decided to take it. I start next week.'

'But what about Hugh?' Rosa asked.

'We've put it off for a bit. I've said I'll go to London for six months at least. After that I'll know if I still want to marry him. I'm as mad about him as ever though, so you'll probably be seeing me again soon.'

'I'll miss you but I hope you don't come back, for your own sake,' said Rosa fervently. 'The Chinky will miss us. Nobody else in the office likes Chinese food,' she added in an effort at flippancy.

Patricia laughed, then her voice went solemn again and she said, 'There's something else I must tell you.' Rosa could tell she'd been wondering how to break this next bit of news.

'What?' she asked anxiously.

'Your old boyfriend Iain married Brenda Hamilton-Prentice in the Queen Street registry office yesterday.'

Rosa waited for the pain to hit her but amazingly it didn't. She was completely unaffected. She couldn't care less. From the significant silence on the other end of the line, she knew that Patricia was waiting to hear her reaction to the news however.

'Is that all? I thought something awful had happened. She's

welcome to him,' Rosa said and laughed, feeling wonderful
that the laugh was genuine. She hadn't thought about Iain for
days and her infatuation with him had vanished completely.

Relieved, Patricia laughed too and said, 'That's good. Now
you can console yourself with Mike.'

'No, no, Mike is yours. Don't let's fight over him,' Rosa
told her jocularly.

'Talking about fighting,' Patricia went on gleefully, 'there
was a terrible row in the office about Stella. She's been
running four or five men at once and they all fell out when
she decided to go back to Australia with Alan. His last book
of poetry has won some big prize out there and he's a
celebrity, so the pair of them are going home.'

Both girls giggled and Rosa said, 'But Stella never reads
anything except Mills and Boon. How will they get along?'

'With *sex*, darling,' said Patricia.

As Rosa listened to her friend, her longing to be back in
the office was overwhelming, she missed it so much. She
was even homesick for her room at Mrs Ross's.

By the end of a week her plaster was grubby and as covered
with signatures as Jacques Tati's, though not with the same
sort of people. There were many more names she wanted to
add to it however and eventually she prevailed on her father
to drive her to Edinburgh by saying, 'I must go back. I'm
worried in case I lose my job.'

He gave in at last, and Eckie followed them to the city in
Rosa's little Morris Minor, an arrangement that worried her
slightly because she didn't think he had a driving licence.
He took the same cavalier attitude to that as he took to gun
licences. All she could do was hope he wasn't picked up by
the police on the way.

They reached Northumberland Street without incident
however and Mrs Ross enfolded Rosa to her vast bosom with
apparent pleasure. 'Let me look at you. My word, what a
terrible thing to happen. I read the piece in the paper and
nearly died of fright about that awful man trying to kill you.

I took the liberty of copying the address off the back of one of the doctor's airmail letters that came a few days ago and wrote to tell him about it. I hope you don't mind.'

Rosa was appalled. As soon as Roddy received her letter he'd be on the phone, if not on a plane, and she didn't want that complication at the moment. In fact, she had deliberately avoided sending the tale to him.

'I hope you didn't alarm him,' she said.

Mrs Ross shook her head. 'Oh no, I said you were safe and very brave.'

But bravery had nothing to do with it. Jack was right. She was cursed with a facility for being around when things happened. It was like the Chinese curse 'May you live in interesting times'.

It was strange going back into the office. She felt like someone who had been very ill and was trying to walk again. She dreaded having to tell her story over and over again – but she needn't have worried. News does not stay hot for very long in newspaper offices.

When she walked into the newsroom, the other reporters looked up casually, and said, 'Oh, hello,' before getting back to their work. Her adventure was old news. What was hot today was a train crash on the Edinburgh to Glasgow line.

Before he even visited the site of the accident, Mike, looking frantic, was churning out sentence after sentence of purple prose about bleeding survivors staggering out of upturned coaches, and was obviously disappointed when the ambulance service reported that nobody had been killed.

At half past five, as if nothing had happened to her, Rosa went with Mike, Tony, Patrick and Lawrie to the Cockburn for a drink. When she saw them coming in, Etta emerged from behind the bar and crossed to their table – something she never normally did. The Cockburn was a self-service bar.

Laying a hand on Rosa's shoulder, she said, 'Good to see you back. You had a close shave. That Boyle was a bastard. I thought you'd want to know about Sylvia . . .'

Rosa nodded eagerly. Sylvia was someone else she had put to the back of her mind except for making a couple of phone calls to the hospital to pass on her good wishes. The nurses who took the call both said Sylvia was 'as well as could be expected' and refused to be more expansive.

'How is she?' Rosa asked.

'She died yesterday,' Etta said bluntly.

Rosa was devastated. She remembered Sylvia with her bright golden hair cascading down on to the black fur of her coat, her giddily high heels and her brittle way of talking. It was not possible that she had been snuffed out like a candle. Tears gathered in her eyes, and seeing them, Etta patted her shoulder. 'It was peaceful,' she said.

'I wish I could have said goodbye to her,' Rosa said brokenly.

'She heard about your adventure and left a message for you. She said you've to go into Greensmith Downes and collect a dress that she bought for you. You'll know which one. And you must go because it's paid for. She wanted you to go dancing in it one day.'

Rosa put both hands over her face and started sobbing. It was not only Sylvia she was crying for – it was Marie, and Sadie, even Skinner. The last of the repressed shock fuelled her tears till they flowed like a river, astonishing and embarrassing her friends.

'For God's sake, Makepeace, blow your nose,' said Mike, passing her a red and white handkerchief. Trust him to carry gypsy hankies.

'And you'd better have a whisky,' said Lawrie. 'If Jack hears about you blubbing, he'll think his star reporter's gone soft, and you wouldn't like that, would you?'